# Eloise Undercover

## SARAH BAKER

Catnip
PUBLISHING LTD

*For Freddie*

CATNIP BOOKS
Published by Catnip Publishing Ltd
320 City Road
London
EC1V 2NZ

This edition first published 2017

1 3 5 7 9 10 8 6 4 2

Text copyright © Sarah Baker, 2017
Cover illustration copyright © Jessica Courtney-Tickle, 2017
The moral rights of the author and illustrator have been asserted.

Cover design by Will Steele

A CIP catalogue record for this book is available from the British Library.

ISBN 978-1-91061-1135

Printed and bound by CPI Group (UK) Ltd., Croydon, CR0 4YY

www.catnippublishing.co.uk

# Chapter One

## May 1940, France

At first there was just talk in the village. My Amma said it was gossip and I wasn't to listen, but someone at school said his father had seen enemy soldiers in Monteaux – the very next town.

Then, on one completely normal day – the sky an endless blue, the crickets chirping and the sun half baking us already – Maddie, Albert and I were practising spying. We were perched at the top of the slumped old oak tree that sat at the side of the road leading from Monteaux to Amboise when we saw something ourselves.

'He won't suspect us. We have the element of surprise. It's an excellent plan,' Albert said, baguette crumbs falling from the corner of his mouth.

Maddie tutted, took the binoculars from him and wiped the lenses with the edge of her sleeve. 'It's only excellent,' she said, peering through them, 'if you forget that we're three children and he's the size of *two* men.'

I squinted at the tall, thin blob of green as he walked towards us. His face was a smudge, but we could hear the *clip, clip* of his boots on the road as he got closer.

'And,' Maddie continued, 'he probably has a gun, and all we have is this tree, a pair of binoculars and some sticks. We'd hardly frighten a field mouse.'

Albert snapped off a small but sturdy branch and held it out to Maddie. She ignored it and he turned to me.

'Eloise, tell her what Monsieur X said about surprises and using what you have to hand.'

'Let's look,' I said, pulling out Monsieur X's latest adventure from under my arm. But as I let go of the branch I was holding, it swung back into my face. I gave a yelp as my feet slipped and, scrabbling for a foothold, the book fell. It tumbled through the branches and landed with a slap on the road.

Albert grabbed my jumper, just in time to stop me tumbling after it. My left leg scraped against the trunk but my nails dug into the bark and, gasping against the stinging pain, I let him and Maddie pull me up.

'Eloise,' Maddie hissed, 'are you alright?'

I was about to say that I was fine when we heard the *clip, clip* of boots crunch to a stop.

We looked at each other, then peered down through the branches. The soldier was right beneath us. We watched as he bent down and picked up my book. Maddie sucked in a breath. My knuckles whitened around the branch. Suddenly this wasn't a game. It was real. The soldier might do anything. His rifle looked new. His eyes were keen. We'd heard the Germans were searching for spies, for Resistance fighters plotting against them – for anyone who seemed suspicious. We were hiding in a tree with binoculars. We were definitely suspicious.

The soldier looked up.

'Now!' Albert yelled and without thinking I shimmied down the trunk – branches, leaves and twigs scraping my skin – but I didn't feel a thing. Everything was going three times faster than normal.

Albert swung off the lowest branch and landed on the road. Maddie half slipped, half fell, but managed to end up in a patch of wildflowers. Me? Somehow I landed right on the soldier, knocking my book out of his hand.

I rolled off and grabbed for it, but he got there first.

His eyes travelled over the front cover, which showed a large, spooky-looking old house. The soldier lifted one corner of his lip, which might have been his way of smiling but wasn't at all reassuring, and my stomach was tying itself in knots because this close I could see he really was as tall as two men, and almost as wide. He was wearing the green uniform all the enemy soldiers wore, with the hat like a small, upside-down, paper boat balancing on his bald head. His face was round and he had jowls that wobbled when he sneered, which he did now as he stared at us. I noticed three brown teeth and a few more that were yellow.

'Give it back,' Albert said. 'It's our book.'

The soldier looked at Albert in amusement, but quickly swung his head towards Maddie as she crept out of the verge, brushing grass off her long hair.

She froze as if he'd glued her to the spot. He looked at her like she was a rabbit ripe for the cooking pot. As if he hated her. But how could he? He didn't know her. He didn't know any of us.

'Hey, you,' said Albert, 'leave her alone.'

The soldier reached for his rifle.

Albert gasped.

The soldier gripped his gun, as if he was weighing it, his eyes darting back to Maddie.

'I didn't mean to jump on you,' I said, holding my hand out for the book. 'It was a mistake.'

The soldier slid his eyes onto me. I dropped my hand.

'I'm really very clumsy,' I said, thinking fast. 'Always falling out of trees.' He didn't speak so perhaps he didn't understand what I was saying. Maybe the soldiers only spoke German. I had to distract him, make him think we were just playing a game so I nodded at my book. 'It is a very good story, monsieur,' I said. 'One of my favourites.'

I forced a smile to my face. The soldier lowered his rifle and my heart stopped pounding quite so wildly, but I noticed he kept a firm, grubby hold on the book. *My* book. I was about to say something I would probably really regret when I heard a low grumble, like an old man clearing his throat. There was more *clip, clipping* on the road – much more.

'Look!' I pointed behind him.

The soldier turned to see. Behind him, coming from the old road that led into the town, were soldiers. Lots of enemy soldiers.

'Go!' I hissed to Maddie and Albert, then I reached out and plucked the book right out of the soldier's hand. He gave a shout of surprise, but I was already pushing my way into the hedge, grabbing Maddie's outstretched hand. Albert gripped my other hand then together we raced into the tall grass beyond.

Behind us we heard trucks cough their way closer, followed by the *stamp, stamp* of a hundred boots. There was shouting, and a sudden *rat-a-tat-tat*. We ducked down quick. We heard more shouting followed by more gunfire. Why were they shooting at us? We hadn't done anything wrong. I clutched my book to my chest and with a glance at each other, we ran as low as we could across one field and into the next, our hearts racing as fast as our feet. We had to be out of sight by now, but we didn't slow down until we were through the old orchard and heading up the long drive to Albert's house, Maison de Noyer.

Albert's family had lived in the big house for ever. It was huge, with three floors of shuttered windows and a big, wooden front door that looked like it had been stolen from a castle. When I visited it was often to the kitchen first, where the cook would sometimes let us dip fresh bread in jam. Seeing the house standing tall and proud against the blue sky, with its bright red flowers overflowing the tubs on either side of the front door, made me feel safe. Even if the shutters were missing a few slats and the stone was weathered and looked like peeling, old skin, everything would be alright here.

Albert pulled us towards the back of the house and into the kitchen. We tumbled in, half tripping over each other in our eagerness to get inside, making Albert's cook look up from the large stove where she was stirring a pot of something that had two scaly legs and a plucked wing sticking out of it.

'Sorry,' Albert said to her, pulling us around the large table, under the twinkling copper pans and out into the hallway.

We stood in front of the tapestry I liked the best, the one with the woman in the hooped skirt and the boy with the blond curls who looked a little bit like Albert, if you squinted. That's where his mother found us. Laughing so hard our bellies hurt, a strange, giggling relief that hid just how terribly afraid we'd been.

Madame Brodeur's perfectly-rouged lips pursed as she sent Maddie home to her mother, and she patted her perfectly-coiffed hair as she told me she'd be having a word with my father. But I could cope with Father being cross because we'd escaped not just one enemy soldier, but a whole battalion of them! *And* I'd got my book back. Walking home I couldn't stop grinning. It was straight out of a Monsieur X adventure. I knew Amma would have words with me as well, harsher words, but it was worth that too. Even after what happened later. In fact, especially because of what happened later.

# Chapter Two

## May 1944

'You're going to be late, *mon chou*.'

I smiled. Amma was always calling me that, but it still didn't make me look up.

'Five pages more, Amma. Monsieur X has just found another clue.'

A loud thump hit the table and a puff of flour wafted across my pages from the lump of dough Amma was kneading. I waved it away with my book, but the spell had been broken.

'Alright, alright, I'm going.'

I slurped my half cup of milk, cold now, popped the book into my satchel and then slung it over my shoulder. I pushed my chair in, careful not to scrape it across the stone floor because it would set Amma's teeth on edge. I lifted the heavy latch on the back door, then let it go and turned back, grinning, to throw my arms around her. They sank into the dip of Amma's warm middle where her striped apron was pulled tight and tied twice behind her back. She stopped pounding the heels of her hands along the large slab of dough and shifted her feet. She smelt of fresh bread, spiced pastries and clothes dried to a crisp in front of the fire. When she sighed I felt her shoulders drop, just a little.

'You had better get going. Your friends will be waiting for you,' she said.

'Will Father be here when I get home?' I asked, leaning around to see her face.

Amma didn't answer and I knew not to push. She'd been taking care of me since I was a baby, after my mother died and Father had needed help. She picked up the dough, shaping it into a rough circle before throwing it back onto the table. Wisps of flour floated around the kitchen like tiny clouds.

I watched them puff towards the radio on the small wooden shelf above the sink. It had been switched off for years. Amma said Radio Paris wasn't worth listening to any more for all the truth it told since the enemy soldiers arrived. First one or two soldiers, then whole battalions, spreading through the town and countryside like a rash. But it would be over soon, everyone said so. The Allies would come and push the German forces out of France. Then Father could get his old job back and wouldn't have to travel so much.

Of course it wasn't the first time he'd stayed away longer than expected. He'd been a professor at the university in Tours, but after the war started they'd sent the boys to fight and there'd been no one left to teach, he said. So he'd started helping old lady Garamonde with her broken hen coop and then delivered the local newspaper on his bicycle. That hadn't paid much and Amma said we must tighten our belts. Then, out of the blue, he got a job as a salesman, but it took him away from us most weeks.

'The work comes when it comes, *ma rose*,' he'd said just before he left that first time, then smiled and pulled me closer. I'd thrown my arms around his neck and buried my head in his thick jersey. 'I'll be back before you know it,' he'd whispered.

Father had left at five that morning and was back two days later. I wrote it in my diary. The second time he left at midnight. I hadn't been allowed to stay up, but I did anyway.

'Hmmm,' he'd said, finding me. 'My little rose appears to have fallen asleep.'

I'd jerked awake, almost toppling out of the attic window, where I'd wedged myself, and onto the pantry roof. But my father had me. He was sitting next to me, arms tucked around me, holding me safe.

'No need to worry. I will be back, as always.'

And he was.

Oh, sometimes he was late, but only by a day or two at most. Until now. We'd expected him home a week ago. I wanted to wait at home for him, to make sure I was there the moment he came back. But Amma would have none of it. Apparently school was more important.

I pressed my face into her back, then swiped two fresh croissants off the cooling rack next to the range.

'I saw that, you rascal,' she murmured.

'Bye, Amma,' I yelled, skipping out of the back door. I leapt onto my bicycle, sending three chickens skittering across the yard, and pedalled to the lane where Maddie and Albert would be waiting for me.

Albert always acted as if he didn't know I was coming, looking in the opposite direction or cleaning his nails with a stick, but my bicycle brakes still squeaked because Father hadn't got round to showing me how to fix them yet, so I knew it was a game. Today I decided I would pretend to cycle into him by accident. That would teach him to ignore me, and give Maddie and me a good laugh.

The air was sweet; it was as warm a June as any. Crickets buzzed and three turquoise butterflies fluttered around a clump of pink clover as I cycled to the end of the lane. When it was beautiful like this, you could pretend there wasn't a war. Mostly.

I pulled to a stop, looking at my watch, then back up the lane. There was no one here.

I waited a few minutes, making a tight figure of eight from one side of the road to the other, but they still didn't come. Maybe Amma was right – maybe I was later than I realised. Except we always waited for each other. Always.

'One for all, and all for one,' Maddie had said just the other week, flicking her hair as she rode towards Albert and me, late again.

Albert had screwed his face up. 'Even in detention?'

'Especially in detention,' she laughed, before speeding past us both. We'd pedalled hard to catch up before reaching the school building, but we'd still had to write out twenty pages of a King Louis XVIII quote about punctuality, in as small writing as possible. It was torture, but we did it together.

I looked around again. No. Something was wrong.

I started cycling towards school and got to the corner of Rue Plumereau and Rue Colbert, only a street away, when I saw her. Maddie was alone and she was walking.

She looked up at the squeal of my brakes, then dropped her eyes straight back to the ground, but not before I'd noticed how red they were and how her skin looked washed out, as if she hadn't slept.

I spun my satchel round, took out the still warm croissants and held both out to her. She stuffed them into her mouth, one after the other, while I brushed flakes of pastry from my school skirt.

'Do we have to go?' she asked in a small voice.

I buckled my satchel and frowned. Maddie usually loved school.

'Maddie, where's your bike? Why didn't you wait for me? And where's Albert?'

She swallowed and looked up at the sky. 'Grandmother said it's an auspicious day for a walk.' She ran her hands through her long brown hair, tucking it behind both ears.

I crossed my arms. 'Auspicious?'

She gave a small smile and some of the colour came back to her cheeks. 'Oh yes.'

'What's lucky about today?'

She grabbed my arm. 'Let's go to the forest. Just you and me.'

It was tempting. I remembered the times we'd run through those trees, me, Maddie and her little brother, then chatted with her grandmother about the plants we'd found. I liked helping her quiet, pretty mother too. She'd showed me how to mend shirts and would sometimes squeeze my hand and smile at me for no reason, which made me feel warm from the top of my head to my toes and think how lucky Maddie was to have her. I even liked all the noisy, visiting aunts and longed for the days I could spend at their home, collecting wildflowers, foraging for food, playing statues and chase. I loved the big pots of stew at the end of a hot sunny day that we'd all share outside on the grass, and the singing at night, the whirling dancers as Maddie's uncle with the eyepatch and the earring played the violin, the aunts telling stories hundreds of years old.

But I thought of what Amma had said when she'd caught me sneaking back late the last time. People were always watching, she said. She'd raised her voice and my words had wobbled as I explained I was only with Maddie and her family, that I was safe with them. A strange look had passed Amma's face then – she looked sad, but angry at the same time. She'd said it was important not to stand out these days. I didn't understand how anyone would care about me spending time with my very best friend, but Amma wouldn't say any more.

I shook my head at Maddie. We couldn't risk skipping school.

'Come on,' I said and, after a pause, Maddie hopped onto the back of my bike, wrapped her hands around my middle and we cycled off towards school.

We were almost there when something knocked the back wheel and I felt it skid. I kept pedalling, but that's when the first stone hit us.

# Chapter Three

'Oof!'

I squeezed the brakes and the back wheel swerved as Maddie fell off. I flung bicycle away from me and looked around for her, trying to figure out what had happened. She lay on the road a few metres behind me, clutching her head. I was rushing to her when I heard something rustle.

From behind a low wall, Antoine, the tallest and widest boy in our class stepped out. He was the butcher's son, but we knew him as the boy with the spiky red hair who picked his nose and flicked it at the girls when the teacher wasn't looking. There was another boy behind him, head down and feet shifting. When he finally glanced at us over Antoine's shoulder, I gasped.

'Albert?'

As they clambered over the wall and walked towards

us I noticed Albert's shirt was untucked and hanging over his blue shorts, one sock pulled up and one rolled down. His tufted brown hair stuck out at all angles like he'd been asleep in the hedge, and his grey-blue eyes wouldn't settle on anything. I thought I heard him mumble, 'Go!' but I couldn't tell if he meant we should leave or if he was cheering Antoine on. His brows furrowed as I ran to Maddie. Why was he looking at her like that? Had they argued? We sometimes quarrelled, usually about who played Monsieur X, but this seemed so much bigger. And what was he doing hanging around Antoine?

'Go back to where you came from, Gypsy scum!' Antoine said, leering down at us.

My jaw dropped. Antoine was often mean, but the hate in his eyes and words was new. The enemy hated people like Maddie, I'd learnt that the day the soldier singled her out, but I never thought anyone who knew us, who knew Maddie, would ever think like that. I was so shocked I couldn't find any words to shout back.

Maddie answered him instead by rolling onto her side. Blood dripped from a cut just above her eye, but she still got to her knees.

I looked back at the boys, and saw Albert was now clutching a large, rough stone. His eyes darted from Antoine to Maddie.

'No!' I cried, but it was too late.

Albert threw the stone. Everything went quiet. Even the sky held its breath. Then I watched Maddie fall onto her back. Antoine stood over her and, with a quick look to check Albert was still close by, drew his foot back.

'Get lost, Antoine!' I yelled, throwing myself in front of Maddie, but the next thing I knew I caught a kick around the side of my head that made my ears ring.

Only now did Maddie scream. I pushed Antoine away and he fell backwards.

Behind him Albert jeered. 'She's the one who should get lost.' He stared at Maddie. 'You're not welcome.'

I shook my head to try to shake off the spinning, sick feeling. Did Albert really say that?

Antoine had got to his feet, ignoring me and staring at Maddie. She held one hand over her eye, blood seeping through her fingers and down the white sleeve of her blouse.

'We don't want your kind here,' he said. 'Do you understand?'

He scooped up a handful of gravel and threw it at her. 'Get lost, Gypsy girl!'

He picked up more and offered a handful to Albert who shouted, 'Yes, go away – and don't come back!'

I stared at the tiny stones slipping through his fingers, then back at his face. He was red and sweating.

I tried to think of what Monsieur X would do. He

always said to take some thinking time when facing danger, but my head hurt and was full of angry feelings that made me want to pick up as many stones as I could and throw them right back. I couldn't make sense of anything. Antoine was a bully, but why was Albert being like this? He was our friend.

'Albert?' I tried. 'It's Maddie,' I said. 'It's me.'

Albert glanced nervously at Antoine, then looked back at me before straightening his shoulders. He spat his next words out. 'Get lost. Both of you. No Gypsies, no friends of Gypsies. Not at the house, not at the school, not anywhere.'

'One of our cows disappeared and I bet she knows where it is,' Antoine said, elbowing Albert. 'And Monsieur Comptois says four sheep died after her grandmother crossed their fields.'

I shook my head furiously. 'That's all rubbish and you know it.'

'You saying we're liars?'

I felt Albert's spittle in my eye.

'Yes!' Maddie said.

I saw Albert's hand lift and I stepped forward. He raised his fistful of stones higher, his eyes wide, his breathing hard and fast.

'Go on, then,' I shouted, bracing my legs and curling my hands into fists.

In the seconds of silence the school bell rang from the end of the road.

*Dung, dung, dung. Dung, dung, dung.*

Albert and I stared at each other. Then Antoine clapped him on the shoulder.

'Come on,' Antoine said, 'we'll be late.'

Albert nodded. He lowered his arm and opened his hand, letting the little stones *pitter-patter* to the road. Antoine called him a true patriot.

Behind me Maddie started to cry.

'Pigs!' I yelled. 'I'll get you.'

I leapt after them just as Maddie reached a hand for my ankle. She pulled me back so hard I tripped and fell down, scraping my hands and one cheek. Antoine and Albert laughed and hooted before hurrying off.

'Run, you cowards!' I shouted after them, shaking my fist, but they only laughed harder.

'And you,' I said, turning to Maddie, pulling my leg out of her grasp, 'why did you stop me?'

'They're not worth it,' she said, wiping her nose on her sleeve. The bleeding had stopped, but was congealed around the cut on her forehead and one sleeve of her blouse was splattered red. I brushed tiny bits of stone and twig out of my hair, touched the cheek I'd grazed to check I wasn't bleeding, and sighed, remembering what Amma had said. We would definitely stand out.

'You've got salt,' she told me.

I frowned, rubbing my knees, wincing. They had rosy red patches and stung like mad.

'Salt?'

'That's what my grandmother calls it. It means being brave.'

'Oh,' I said and grinned. 'Antoine's always been a bully, but you wait till I tell Amma about Albert! She'll tell Madame Brodeur and he'll get the hiding of his life for what he said to you.'

Maddie shook her head. 'It won't make any difference,' she said.

She looked up at me. A bruise had begun to flower across one side of her face. She pushed her hair behind her ears. It was long, thick and silky. I'd always wished mine was like that, but my pale yellow hair was too wispy and no matter what I did, would always flop over my eyes. If Maddie was a doll, I was a scarecrow. I combed it off my forehead with my fingers.

'It's not the first time he's said something like that to me,' she admitted, 'he's been doing it for a few weeks, though he only said things when you weren't around.'

I stood up, stilled. 'What? Albert? But –'

'We'll be late for school,' she said.

I shook my head. There were too many confused thoughts in it. 'School? After all that?'

She nodded.

I crossed my arms. 'I thought you wanted to play truant. I thought it was an *auspicious* day.'

Maddie stood and grabbed my hand. 'I won't let them get to me, Eloise. Grandmother says we have to be better than them, even if they call us names and steal our bicycles. So let's go to school and show them they can't break us.'

She smiled then and that's how I remember her. I don't think about the bruises or the blood or the fact that our best friend turned on us and hurt us inside and out. I just remember that warm, defiant smile, because that was the last day I ever saw my best friend, Maddie.

# Chapter Four

'Chores.'

I nodded, picked up the next pair of shoes in the pile and the chamois leather cloth.

'It's important to –' Amma began.

'Keep up standards,' I finished for her. I knew all Amma's sayings by heart.

She pressed the iron onto the sheet stretched across the kitchen table until it hissed.

'Just because there's a war on doesn't mean we give up,' Amma said. 'We hold our heads high. They may have taken our town, but they will not break us.'

I glanced at the silent radio.

Steam puffed from the iron. 'We made it through the last war, and we'll make it through this one.' She took a deep breath. 'Whatever it takes.'

I rubbed Father's Sunday shoes till I could see my face

in them. He might not be wearing them today, but I'd make sure they were ready when he needed them again.

'Amma . . .'

'Your father will be back when he can, you know this.' She looked up from her ironing. 'Work is hard to come by, *mon chou*. He must take it where he can, and sometimes it may delay his return home.'

I spat onto the tip of the shoe and rubbed the cloth into the worn grooves.

'Father would let me go to see Maddie,' I said in a small voice.

The iron hissed.

Amma was frowning, but she didn't say a word. She looked at me as if she was trying to add up a particularly difficult mathematics problem.

'We could visit their cottage,' I said, 'together. Maybe she's ill. They might need our help.'

Amma shook her head, and I concentrated on polishing the shoe, but I wasn't letting this go. It had been six days since I'd seen Maddie. Six days since I'd cycled to our spot and waited for her until I'd been late. Six whole days since Albert had thrown that stone and six days since we'd run into class, a whole ten minutes late. It was only when I'd sat down, got my breath and turned around that I realised Maddie wasn't behind me.

I asked our form teacher, Madame Poullard, if Maddie

was with the nurse, but she stared at something above my head instead of answering. I checked for Maddie at lunch and waited after class till I knew Amma would start to worry. I thought she must have gone home after all. The next day I cycled to our spot and waited for her until I was really late. I asked Madame Poullard where Maddie was before we assembled for registration and sang *La Marseillaise*. She stretched her neck out like a chicken, which usually made me laugh because her surname sounded a lot like *poularde*, and I could picture her clucking like one of our hens – but she waved me away. On the third day I asked about Maddie she put me in detention and called round to speak to Amma after school. I was sent to my room while they argued downstairs. When she'd gone, Amma told me Madame Poullard was a short-sighted idiot, which I was most definitely not to repeat. Then she'd told me, gently, that Maddie wasn't allowed to attend school any more. My words caught in my throat. Why? What had Maddie done? We'd both been late. I asked if I could cycle over to Maddie's house, but Amma shook her head, which meant definitely not. I hadn't given up asking every day since, though.

'Is Albert at school?'

Amma's voice was different, as if she was being careful with her words, testing them out.

I watched her fold a sheet, then press the iron into the corners.

I shook my head. I didn't want to talk about Albert. I'd told her what he'd done, but instead of marching round to the big house to speak to his mother, Amma had shut her eyes, then told me off for getting into a fight. It seemed everyone was acting strangely these days.

The thing was, he hadn't been back to school either. But, unlike Maddie, his mother and father had still been seen around the town.

So much seemed to be changing. But I had a plan to get answers.

That night I lay on my cot in the attic reading *Monsieur X and the Mystery of the Hidden Caves* until dark. I listened for Amma's heavy shoes to *clop* up the stairs and her bedroom door to shut, then I pulled the top half of the window down and swung out onto the little roof above the pantry. From there I dangled over the edge till my feet found the drainpipe and I could shimmy down to the water barrel and jump onto the grass.

I crept round the back of the house, passing my bicycle with a sigh. I couldn't take it with me; the brakes would give me away. Instead, I tiptoed round to the front of the house and along to the end of the lane. Keeping close to the hedge, I hurried up the road towards the big house.

The moon was high and bright and my plimsolls didn't make a sound. All I could hear was my breath, which caught in my mouth each time an owl hooted or something scurried past my feet. Sweat prickled down my back. With the moon so bright, I'd be easy to spot. There was a curfew now, and ever since our run-in with the soldier long ago, I knew they wouldn't hesitate to shoot. But I had to check if Maddie was back and, despite what he'd done, I wanted to know what had happened to Albert. I needed answers. That's what I told myself all the way to the tree that marked where the road led off towards Maison de Noyer.

I stared at the big house. The shuttered windows on the ground and first floor were pulled tight, except for the one on the left that hung from its corner as if it was about to fall any minute. Everything was so still, as if they'd all left, though the building didn't feel abandoned. I shivered. In fact, it felt like I was being watched.

Maddie and her family lived across the yard, behind Maison de Noyer's kitchen door. Their home was a small barn building like ours, with a large kitchen, two bedrooms upstairs, and a third hidden in the eaves. We both had a pantry and a bathroom, and Maddie had the attic space, just like me in my barn, though ours was made of stone bricks and Maddie's was made of wood.

I took a deep breath and cut across the field before I

could change my mind. The flat trail we'd made through the tall grass by running so many times from the road to Maddie's house was waiting, the hundreds of spindly trees standing silent in the distance. I'd not even got halfway when I saw there was a light on in Maddie's house.

She was home! I ran faster.

Suddenly arms came out of nowhere and grabbed me.

I screamed, and a rough hand pressed against my mouth. I squealed and kicked and squirmed, but whoever it was held me tight, pinning me to the ground.

'Quiet, girl!'

I shook my head as panic swept over me.

'Do you want to get us both killed?' asked the voice.

I tried to bite his hand, but an arm tightened round my waist, squeezing all my breath out.

'Watch!' the voice commanded, and the arms loosened a little, so that I could push myself up on my elbows.

I looked over at the house, and stilled.

Maddie's front door opened. An arc of yellow light swung out into the dark and two soldiers stepped out. One lit a cigarette, the smoke curling in the air. I stiffened and held my breath, but they hadn't seen us. The soldiers closed the door, turned and walked up to Maison de Noyer.

The arms holding me let me go. I scrambled to my feet and stepped away, gasping and spitting out the taste of dung and straw and rotten apples. I turned to see Farmer

Raymon. He was thinner than when I last saw him, and dirtier too. His jacket hung off his shoulders and his cap looked as if it was about to fall off. Deep lines crisscrossed his forehead and his moustache drooped to one side. His pin-prick eyes peered into mine, as if gauging whether I'd understood what was happening.

I shook my head again then turned and ran towards Maddie's home.

One window glowed yellow. The curtains had been left open. I peered round. At first it looked as if Maddie and her family were still there – I saw her uncle's violin, the baskets we used for foraging – but then I noticed the mess: piles of crockery heaped up in the sink, the little wicker horse trampled to bits on the floor and a pair of dirty grey boots on the kitchen table.

'You shouldn't be here.'

Farmer Raymon had followed and was glaring at me from the shadows. I suddenly noticed the rifle in his hand. My heart was beating so loud I could hear it.

'They're gone now, girl.'

His other hand tightened like a claw on my shoulder and I realised he didn't mean the soldiers. He meant Maddie.

'And good riddance,' he said, 'their sort shouldn't be here. I'm glad they're gone. You tell people that.'

He shook me. Tears sprung to my eyes.

'You hear me? You tell people I wanted them gone!'

I nodded fast. He stared at me, then his voice softened. 'Go.'

He released my shoulder. I took one step back, then another and another.

'Go now and I won't tell your Amma you were here!'

I turned and ran.

It was a few evenings later when I discovered he hadn't kept his promise.

'Monsieur Raymon tells me Maddie's family . . . have gone,' she said, looking at me out of the corner of her eye. So Amma knew I'd been over there. I waited for her to scold me, but she didn't say another word.

I felt my cheeks burn and stared at the inside of the pan I was scrubbing. 'Gone.' That's what everyone said when they didn't know what had happened. People were 'gone' all the time. First it was a friend of a friend and then suddenly it was your best friend. Father had put his head into his hands when I'd asked him where everyone was going. When he'd looked at Amma, she had cut in quickly and said most people were trying to 'get out' before it was too late. Her words had made me feel cold. I wanted to ask more, ask her where they were getting out to, and what happened if they didn't get out in time, but she'd spoken again before I could, and told me once more that this was why anyone who stayed had to make sure they didn't stand out.

But not having real answers made my head ache and my heart hurt. Had Maddie got out before it was too late, or had she been taken away by soldiers because she stood out?

'What if . . .?'

I couldn't finish. I thought of the soldier, of the shots his battalion had fired into the field at us when all we'd done was take back what was ours and run away.

I put the pan down and faced Amma.

'Father would know what to do,' I said.

Suddenly there was a knock at the door.

I leapt up – Father was back at last! But when I opened the door it wasn't him, it was an older boy I'd never seen before. He was tall with dark brown hair growing in messy curls and the beginnings of a brown beard cut close to his chin. He was tanned, as if he was outside all the time, and his trousers were wide, streaked with what looked and smelt like oil and held in with a thick leather belt, as if he'd bought them a size too big. He wore a large, navy woollen jumper over the top that looked scratchy. He frowned at me, then saw Amma and nodded at her. I moved aside, but as he opened his mouth to speak, I saw that Amma had gone white and was shaking her head.

'It's important, Tante,' he said, his voice low as he thrust a small brown basket towards her.

The basket was covered with faded but clean blue and white checked linen. I imagined fresh sloes or juicy blueberries hiding underneath and reached for it, but Amma suddenly shouted.

'Leave us!'

I jumped, snatching my hand back.

'It is not the time for gifts, monsieur,' she said.

I stared open mouthed. Amma never shouted, and he'd called her 'Tante' like she was family, but she called him 'monsieur', all formal.

'Not now,' she said in a strained voice.

She looked at me, but I was totally confused.

Amma baked bread and pastries for everyone in the village and in return they gave us milk or cheese and sometimes fruit, and once, a bar of chocolate all the way from Germany along with a brand-new Monsieur X book – *Monsieur X and the Mystery of the Invisible Thief*. The war wouldn't touch us here, Amma had always said, but that was early on, and it had touched everyone and everything now. The soldiers were everywhere, Maddie had disappeared and Albert had turned nasty. Plus I hadn't had a new Monsieur X book in a long time.

The boy looked from Amma to me and back again, but he didn't leave.

'I'm not sure you understand,' he said, holding the basket out towards her.

'Leave us, *mon chou*,' she said.

There was a growling in Amma's voice, but there was something else in the kitchen as well now, something thick in the air, invisible, but pressing on us all. The way the boy and Amma kept looking at me felt like something important was going on, and I had to know what it was, so I didn't move an inch.

He lowered the basket onto the table and Amma let out a breath that sounded as if the air had been let out of her. She sank into her chair.

'I am sorry,' he said.

'What's happened?' I asked.

He glanced at Amma, who put her head in her hands and nodded.

He turned to me. 'I am sorry, little one,' he said again, 'but I have news of your father.'

He paused and I heard the *tink, tink, tink* of the tap dripping into the sink. Then he spoke.

'I'm afraid he has . . . gone.'

# Chapter Five

I watched Amma, her head still in her hands, then I looked at the boy.

'Eloise,' I said.

'Pardon?'

I straightened my back.

'My name is Eloise,' I said. 'Eloise Sophie Boudin. Not, "little one".'

The boy's brow furrowed, as if he was confused, then he nodded gravely.

'Of course,' he said. 'I am François.'

'Do you work for him?'

His eyes darted to Amma.

'My father's sales work takes him all over France,' I said. 'So if you have news of him, you must work with him.'

The older boy stared at Amma as if he could force her

to lift her head with his eyes. He coughed twice.

'Monsieur,' I said sharply, 'when did you last see him?'

Finally Amma raised her head, but she didn't tell me off for my questions. Instead she looked at François as if she wanted answers too.

He swallowed and gestured to a chair. Amma nodded and he sat down, turning to me. 'I work with your father, sometimes, yes.'

The air in the kitchen changed from something heavy into something prickly, like when you'd been running along the rug in the school library, bumped into someone and got a shock all the way up your arm.

'But I don't know where he is.' He looked away.

'You're lying,' I said.

'Eloise!'

I looked at Amma. 'But he is! I can tell.'

François narrowed his eyes and cocked his head at me. 'How can you tell if I am lying?'

'I read it in a book.'

'She reads a lot of books,' mumbled Amma.

I counted my reasons on one hand. 'One, you won't look me in the eye. Two, you touched your nose when you told me you didn't know where my father was. And three, you are swallowing a lot, monsieur.'

There was a pause, then he barked out a laugh.

'You have a true sleuth here, Tante!'

A small smile found its way to Amma's mouth. 'She plans to be a detective, this one.'

François smiled, then just as quickly his face became serious again. He held up his hands. 'Well,' he said, 'it is good to be reminded to keep my wits about me in these difficult times.' He glanced at Amma, who stood.

'Thank you for coming,' she said.

François stood too and made for the door.

'Wait!'

They turned to me.

'He hasn't *actually* told us anything!' I faced him. 'Where's my father? When is he coming back? It's just a stupid job selling telephone directories. Why would he go missing? No one even wants telephone directories.'

I stopped and looked at the basket on the table. The gears in my head that helped me work out who committed what crime before Monsieur X did began to click.

No one wanted to pay for telephone directories.

*Click.*

My father had got a job selling them.

*Click.*

My father had disappeared.

The gears stopped clicking. The answer was just out of my reach. I ground my teeth in frustration.

'Goodbye, monsieur,' Amma said, as she shut the door behind François.

'Wait! I have more questions.'

'Not now, *mon chou*.'

'But –'

Amma sighed and picked up the basket. Her movements seemed heavy, as if it weighed four times what it should. 'I have bread to bake.'

'But –'

'To bed!'

I jumped at the force in her voice.

'And be grateful I don't scold you for your rudeness to François.'

I turned and huffed out of the room, stomping my way up the stairs to the little attic. I wondered if all grandmothers were as hard on you, or was Amma like this because she was all I had? I stared at the door and thought about slamming it, but I'd tested her enough and, anyway, the hinges were loose. Father hadn't had time to tighten them the last time he'd been home.

*Father.*

It took me all of five seconds to decide.

I listened out for Amma but, hearing nothing, I made a lump with my bears at each end of the bed with a pillow in the middle to make it look like I was sleeping. Then I slipped out of my window, climbed over the edge of the pantry roof, and shimmied down the drainpipe till my feet hit the barrel. I jumped onto the grass, then crept round the back of the kitchen as quickly as I could after François. I was going to follow him and find out exactly what he wasn't telling me.

The light was on in the kitchen but, as I watched, Amma's shadow flitted in front of the window as she closed the shutters for curfew. I could hear her talking, but her words were muffled. It was the same thing over and over again, as if she was reading something out loud and wanted to get it right. I was tempted to stay and listen, then I remembered my mission. François. I ducked down, crab-crawling beneath the windows, then scampered as fast as I could to the end of the lane.

I looked left and right, but François seemed to have disappeared into the fading light. I took a deep breath, closed my eyes and thought about what happened in my favourite Monsieur X story, *The Mystery of the Invisible Thief*. What would Monsieur X do? He'd examine the facts.

I ran through them quickly. I didn't know François so he couldn't be from our town because everyone knew everyone else here. He couldn't have come from the left as that led up to the big house, then into the hills and Farmer Raymon's land. I closed my eyes and shuddered, remembering when he'd caught me looking for Maddie.

Then I snapped them open again. Monsieur X said indecision helped no one. So I turned right, heading for the town. François had to be walking through it to Monteaux.

I'd counted forty paces when someone stepped out of the bushes right in front of me.

I squealed, then gasped, covering my mouth with both hands as the shape resolved very definitely into François' scratchy jumper, wide trousers and cap.

'Eloise?' he whispered. 'What are you doing?'

I took my hands off my mouth and put them on my hips. 'I still have questions for you, monsieur.'

François blew out a breath. 'You shouldn't be out here,' he said. He looked behind me. 'Not on your own.' He crouched down so his eyes met mine. 'Look –'

'I'm not going until you tell me what you know,' I said.

He shook his head.

A dog barked somewhere behind me.

François shot up.

'It's just a dog,' I said, not understanding why his eyes had gone so wide.

François didn't seem to hear me at first, then he turned and held my gaze, weighing something up.

'I can't take you home now . . . not if they're so close . . . How brave are you, Eloise?'

I straightened my shoulders and pushed my fringe out of my eyes. 'As brave as any detective.'

His eyes softened and he shut them for a moment.

The dog barked again and it did sound closer now, and as if there was more than one. In fact, it sounded like a whole pack. My heart started to beat fast. It must be a guard patrol. But what were they doing out here already when curfew had only just begun?

François stiffened. 'Come now,' he said, 'quickly!'

I frowned. 'Where?'

He held out his hand. 'To get your answers, Eloise.'

I put my hand in his and we ran.

# Chapter Six

We ran for what seemed like for ever, with sharp barks and yips making it sound as if the dogs were getting closer and closer. I'd seen the enormous guard dogs around town before. I pictured their thick tongues lolling out, their hot steamy breath at my heels. François must have felt the same as he quickly swept me up onto his back and ran even faster. The little stones on the road crunched beneath his feet, reminding me of Maddie, the last day I ever saw her, the day Albert attacked and left us both bruised and bloody. I missed Maddie so much. I clung onto François' scratchy jumper. If they caught us, would the soldiers and their dogs make us 'gone' too?

'Where are we going?' I whispered.

'Shhh,' he said.

'How far is it?'

'Don't speak. Just hold on!'

We made it into the village, but found it as empty as a ghost town. Our footsteps echoed swiftly along the main street. All the houses were dark, their shutters pulled tight. I never thought it really mattered when Maddie and Albert and I used to creep out after curfew and meet halfway between my house and the big house – at least, until Amma made it clear it was serious – but here, in the village, curfew was law. The mayor had made a speech about it on a blinding hot afternoon. We'd all had to stand in the square and listen as he read from a piece of paper about how you would get arrested if you were caught out and about after seven.

'Shot, more like,' a large man in an apron standing behind us had said quietly, and Amma had moved me away, but I already knew first-hand they didn't need much of a reason to start shooting.

Remembering the soldier, I clutched François a little tighter and willed him to run faster.

Suddenly François ducked around the side of the church andstiffened. I held on with my back pressed to the cold stone, and listened. I couldn't hear a thing. Then, somewhere to the left, I heard the dogs again. They'd stopped and were sniffing for something. We were out only just after curfew, but this didn't feel like an ordinary patrol. At seven o'clock, they'd start their rounds in town before moving outwards. This patrol had already been on the outskirts when curfew started.

François squeezed my hands, and I knew then this was about more than the curfew. He was scared. Were they after *him*?

I held my breath and squeezed back. I counted to twenty, then another five, and just as I was about to burst from the tension we heard barking again – further away this time.

I let out a long breath and François' shoulders relaxed. He shifted among the gathering shadows, edging round the church walls till he'd reached the square. Then he stopped and looked left and right.

'Can you see anything, Eloise? Anyone at all?'

I shook my head then realised he couldn't see me, but he must have felt me move. He dashed across the lane behind the church, down a small, winding passageway and up to a thin, old wooden door with a rusty knocker. The house looked as if it was leaning into its neighbour, and that was the only reason it was still standing.

'It's me,' he said, then knocked four times. *Di-da-di-da*.

There was a pause, then the door cracked open a sliver. François slipped through with me still on his back and the door was shut tight and bolted behind us within seconds.

Silence.

There was the rasp of a striking match and a small

lamp in the far corner of the room began to glow.

Two people stood before us and both were staring at me.

François unhooked my arms and I slid to the floor. I ducked round so I was standing next to him.

A man with a grizzly grey beard but dark brown hair on top sat in the middle of the room at a table. It had a wad of newspapers shoved under one leg to keep it even. He sighed and gathered up the piles of notes he had in his hands.

'What have you done, Franc?'

'He's brought us a new one, haven't you?' said a tall, thin girl of about sixteen or seventeen, who stood behind him. She had straight, light brown hair cut close to her head like a choirboy's and dark green trousers with a jumper and shirt tucked in. She was shaking out a match with one hand. She winked at me. I liked her straight away.

'A child, Franc,' said a crackling voice. 'What were you thinking?'

Hidden in the corner, near the lamp, was a man sitting in an old armchair that was losing its stuffing. The man looked a bit like that too. He had almost-black hair, which he'd slicked back with some sort of oil, and a large nose. He whipped out his tongue to lick the papers of the wrinkled cigarette he was making.

'And she's seen our faces,' Grizzly Grey Beard added, his lip curling. I stepped closer to François.

'Out with it then,' the girl said, crossing her arms.

I stared at her trousers, longing for a pair of my own. She was the only girl I'd ever seen wearing them, which must've given the old gossips in the *tabac* plenty to talk about as they bought their newspapers and stamps.

François coughed. 'This is Eloise,' he said.

I smoothed down my school skirt.

'This is a mistake,' the man in the armchair muttered, just as Grizzly Grey Beard stood up, his chair scraping across the stone floor.

'Did you even deliver the goods?'

François ignored him and gave me a tired smile.

The man in the armchair sucked his cigarette and wheezed. Grizzly Grey Beard took a step towards us, but the girl put her hands on his shoulders and eased him back into his chair. She nodded to François.

He cleared his throat.

'The package has been delivered,' he said, 'and it doesn't matter that Eloise has seen our faces.'

He looked at each of them in turn, defying their stern faces with his calm one.

'It's Eloise's father who's gone missing.'

The two men in chairs looked at each other. The girl looked at me.

'That's all very well, Franc,' she said, 'but –'

'I want to know where he is,' I interrupted.

She smiled, sadly. 'So do we.'

I looked around the room, at the banknotes on the table, at the drawings on the papers laid out next to them. Grizzly Grey Beard saw me looking and turned them over, but all I'd seen were lines, like diagrams of buildings. Wait . . . Blueprints!

Something shifted. The gears in my head began to stir.

I thought about what François had just said, about a package being delivered. I thought about my father working as a salesman, selling telephone directories that no one wanted. Now he'd gone missing.

. . . and *click*!

'You're with the Resistance,' I said, my mouth dropping open. 'And so's Father!'

Grizzly Grey Beard stood up again and this time the girl didn't stop him. François looked at me and nodded.

There was a squeak of armchair followed by a cough. 'So what are you going to do about it?'

I turned to the greasy-haired man who'd spoken. He was rolling his second cigarette. I rubbed my nose and straightened my back.

'I'm going to join you, monsieur.'

# Chapter Seven

I could hardly believe it. The Resistance here, in our very own town, fighting back for France against the German soldiers that had taken over our country. Maddie, Albert and I had heard tales at school and in the *tabac*, and the café too. The Germans said the Resistance were dangerous people who put the safety of all France at risk, but the stories of how they rescued prisoners, blew up bridges to disrupt army transports, destroyed weapons factories and stopped German supplies getting to their troops in Paris were legendary. And my father was one of them? Of course I wanted to join them!

The man in the armchair cackled. 'Join us? A child?' His laugh turned into another cough. He hunched over, one knobbled hand gripping his chair.

Grizzly Grey Beard began sorting through the blueprints. The girl said nothing.

'It's not as crazy as it seems,' François said, shrugging.

'What's crazy is you letting a child in here,' Grizzly Grey Beard said without looking up.

'I'm not a child!'

He turned. 'No? How old are you?'

'I am twelve, monsieur.' I swallowed and stood up straight. 'But I have skills.'

The man in the armchair laughed. 'Skills?' he said. 'Will you fight the Germans with skipping? Astonish them with your times tables?' He took a long suck on his cigarette then stood, his joints creaking, and joined Grizzly Beard at the table. The two men began a hushed conversation.

I looked at François. Surely he wouldn't dismiss me. 'Please let me help, François.'

I turned to the girl, thinking fast. 'I can carry packages. No one would suspect me.'

I turned to the two grumpy men. 'If you think it's ridiculous that I'd be part of the Resistance, perhaps the enemy would too.'

I looked back at François, remembered him arriving at our back door.

'And not to be rude, monsieur, but you do look a little strange carrying a picnic basket.' I rubbed my nose. 'But I wouldn't. I could make your deliveries.'

Grizzly Grey Beard's chair screeched. He and Armchair Man stopped talking.

'I know my way around the town,' I carried on, 'and I'm studying to be a detective. I can use invisible ink and I know Morse code.' I felt a knot in my stomach. 'I want to find my father and I'll do whatever it takes.'

'We've all lost someone,' the girl said, 'but it doesn't mean you should put yourself in danger.'

I thought of Maddie and Father. Too many bad things were happening. Shouldn't I do whatever I could?

'I'm not afraid,' I said, sure that if I said the words, I'd believe them. 'Let me help.'

The girl looked at François. He looked around at each of the group.

'It's true,' he said. 'The soldiers won't suspect a schoolgirl of helping us.'

'It's a risk,' Grizzly Grey Beard said.

'But we do need a convincing courier,' the girl said.

There was a pause.

I felt all sorts of words bubbling up to the surface and had to hold my hands behind my back to stop myself shouting them out. I was perfect for the job, perfect. Ever since I'd started reading the Monsieur X books I'd longed to be a detective. I'd been practising all the skills he said were necessary, and now I had a chance to prove myself. But it wasn't just that. Father was missing, Maddie too – and they weren't the only ones. People had been disappearing since the day the soldiers arrived. A lot of men and older boys had gone off to war, but there was nothing for us children to do. We had to go to school and go to church and help at home and pretend that everything was normal, when it wasn't. Now there was a real chance for me to find Father and Maddie and to help, to do something to make it all stop. I'd be part of it. They just had to agree.

The four of them looked at each other as if they were communicating without speaking. Armchair Man spoke first.

'Invisible ink? Creeping around the streets? This is not a game.'

'I know that, monsieur,' I said, nodding fast.

Did that mean I was in?

François blew out a breath, and stepped up to the table, beckoning me to join him.

There was a harsh rap at the door.

All five of us turned.

Three more raps followed, then we heard the sound of dogs snorting and sniffing.

The temperature in the room dropped. No one moved, then suddenly everyone moved as if they were speeded up.

Grizzly Grey Beard gathered all the papers and shoved them into the fire before laying out a chess set on the cleared table. The smoking man shuffled the banknotes and put them down the front of his stained shirt. When he caught me looking he grinned and I saw he was missing most of his teeth.

'Eloise?' François whispered, but not to me.

'I'll take her,' the girl said.

She beckoned to me, grabbing one of the woven baskets in the kitchen as we slipped through into an outhouse and beyond that into a garage. François followed.

'Go with Nan,' he told me. 'She'll get you home safe.'

'But . . . am I joining you?'

He smiled. 'I will be in touch, but till then I have to hide . . .' He tapped the side of his nose with his finger, and slipped out the garage door.

Nan handed me the basket. 'Ready?'

I nodded but was thinking of the dogs. I could hear them snuffling and growling and whining, just waiting to attack.

We heard the front door creak open and then slam back against the wall.

Nan and I slipped outside.

It was starting to get dark, and cold, but the stars weren't out yet. Goosebumps prickled along my arms.

Nan pulled me round to the left, keeping close to the other houses along the narrow passageway. Each one we passed stayed dark, shutters bolted against the curfew and anything that happened outside. We heard shouts from the house we'd just abandoned, the sound of a table being turned over and bottles smashing, and we began to run. I felt half sick and half dizzy from breathing so fast. The thought of being found breaking curfew and the dogs chasing us like we were rabbits went round and round in my head.

'Halt!'

A soldier stepped out from the shadow of the *tabac* at the end of the street. I squealed. Nan pulled on my hand and I tried to turn my guilty squeal into a cough.

'Where do you think you are going?' said the soldier.

I looked up at Nan.

'Not her,' he said, shining a light into my eyes. 'You answer.'

I turned to him. I was blinking fast and remembered how in *Monsieur X and the Mystery of the Haunted House* that meant someone was making up a story, so I took a breath and met his glare.

'I am sorry, monsieur, it is all my fault.'

I let go of Nan's hand and took the basket from her.

'I came to collect these for my Amma and forgot the time.' I looked up at Nan. 'She was kind enough to walk me back home. I was so worried Amma would be cross.' I made a face then whispered, 'I do not want another hiding.'

The soldier looked down at the basket, then up at me.

I hoped the darkness would hide my knocking knees. He looked over to Nan. He was thinking too much about my story. I had to do more.

'Of course, you'd be welcome to have some, monsieur,' I said, thrusting the basket towards him.

He stepped forward and I was surprised at how young he was, like one of the boys at school. He even had spots, a rash of red pimples across his forehead and chin.

I felt my heart start to beat fast. I didn't know what was in the basket. It could be anything – banknotes, blueprints or worse. I felt around under the cover and my hands grabbed something hard and round. I grinned as I pulled out an apple. It had a brown spot, but it was firm. I held it towards him.

'She won't notice one missing, monsieur. Please, take it.'

The boy licked his lips and with one quick look around he snatched the apple and bit into it. 'Go,' he said, pointing his rifle along the road ahead.

I reached for Nan's hand and we ran.

'You'll do fine, Eloise,' she said in between breaths as we passed through the square. It was too dark to see, but it sounded like she was smiling. 'You'll do just fine.'

I grinned so hard you could probably see it in the dark. I'd done it. I'd joined the Resistance!

# Chapter Eight

Nan and I ran hand in hand the whole way home. And all I could think about was that I was part of the Resistance. I hugged that thought to me like a soft, warm blanket. I would deliver their messages, find Father and Maddie and all her family, and we'd all work together to get the Germans out of town – out of the whole of France! I wondered if I could get Amma to make me a pair of trousers like Nan's and if she'd let me cut my hair short too.

Amma!

The thought stopped me dead on the road, and I let go of Nan's hand.

Nan turned. 'Eloise?'

I was supposed to be in bed. Amma would be more than furious if I suddenly knocked at the front door. I hadn't been joking when I'd told the soldier I was worried about a hiding.

The moon peered out from behind a cloud. I stared at the dark sloe berries hanging heavy behind their leaves along the side of the road. I glanced at Nan.

'We should keep this a secret,' I said, 'from Amma.'

She narrowed her eyes.

I cocked my head to one side. 'In *The Mystery of the Strange Messages*, Monsieur X says that sometimes it's safer the less someone knows. So we should probably keep Amma safe, shouldn't we?'

Nan bit her lip and stared at me for what seemed like a long time before she spoke.

'Come on,' was all she said.

Did that mean she agreed?

But at that moment we heard the front door creak. Someone stepped out and shouted into the dark.

'Who is it? Show yourselves – now!'

Amma!

Nan reached for me, but I thrust the basket at her instead, slipped under her arm and straight into the hawthorns that sat in a loose guard around the house.

'I have a gun!'

I stopped, my head and shoulders snagged halfway through. Wait. Amma had a gun? Why did Amma have a gun? I heard Nan say something. I couldn't make out the words, but it sounded like they were talking calmly, whispering even, as if they were friends. Perhaps Nan was buying me time . . . I wriggled through to the back garden and hopped over the vegetable beds to get to the back of the house and the barrel.

Only it wasn't there any more. Had Amma found me gone and moved the barrel so I'd have to own up?

My heart sank.

I looked up at my bedroom window. There was no way I could reach the bottom of the pipe without the barrel. The brick was old. I touched it and bits brushed off like powder. Father said our house had been an old barn before, one of several that served the big house. He'd been patching it up ever since I could remember.

A light came on in the kitchen, peeping between two shutters that didn't quite close properly.

I looked around me, but there was nothing for it. I'd have to try or suffer the consequences – I'd probably never be allowed out again, which would mean no helping the Resistance!

I dug my foot into a hole by the pantry windowsill, then reached up to the ridge above the window. With one hand gripping the stone, I stood on tiptoe and stretched my fingertips towards the drainpipe, but I couldn't quite reach. I'd need to jump.

I leapt up, and my fingers gripped the pipe. It wasn't easy, but I heaved myself higher till I could feel the guttering at the edge of the pantry roof. I swung my legs up towards it, but my hand slipped and I dangled off the drainpipe for a horrible moment before managing to grab at the gutter and cling on. It cracked like a shot echoing through the night. I swung my legs again, and this time scrabbled up and over. I lay flat on my stomach, panting and shaking. My hands throbbed and my knees stung. I'd cut my grazes open again.

Then I heard a door bang. Was Amma back in the house?

I pulled the shutters open, tugged up my window, and tumbled inside.

Clogs banged up the stairs.

In a flurry of movement, I closed the shutters, shut the window, threw the bears out of my bed, plumped up my pillow and leapt under the covers.

A second later Amma flung open my bedroom door.

I pretended to sleep, trying to pace my breath and threw in a fake dream grumble as I rolled over to face away from her, pulling my plimsolled feet under the blankets.

There was a pause.

'Hmmmmmpfff.'

The door closed.

I heard her feet creak back down the stairs, then silence. I turned onto my back and pushed my fringe out of my eyes. Then I bolted upright. What about Nan?

Where was she? And what about the Resistance? How would they get in touch? When would I see them next? I crept to the end of my bed and listened at the window.

Nothing.

I opened the shutters a little, pulled up the window.

'Naaaaaan?' I called, as loudly as I dared.

Still nothing.

Nan was gone.

I didn't hear from Nan for weeks. Or François. Or any of them.

At first it was really exciting to be back at school – my secret burning inside and no one else knowing a thing about it. I imagined writing my own Monsieur X story, *Monsieur X and the Resistance Girl*, but when I didn't see or hear anything more from them, I began to wonder if it had really happened.

When days became weeks, I thought perhaps they'd been teasing me.

My excitement turned to anger and then to worry.

There was still no sign of Father, nor of Maddie or Albert. At school Antoine had been crowing about Maddie disappearing, saying it was good riddance to bad rubbish and he hoped she'd rot in prison, but he was quiet now that Albert was missing too, and after Rene told him the soldiers had emptied the local prisons.

Rene's father was a policeman, or he used to be. Rene hadn't said anything else, even when Antoine threatened him; he said even his father didn't know where all the prisoners had been taken.

Our whole class stared at the two empty desks as if they'd give us answers; we knew the teachers wouldn't tell us anything now that Monsieur Truchon was gone too. We had a new mathematics teacher who was much stricter and didn't explain things half as well. He'd thrown a board duster at one of the boys in class when the boy told him we didn't have tests a Fridays and then asked where Monsieur Truchon was.

I couldn't help wondering if the people around us even knew where the missing were going anyway. People who asked questions tended to disappear as well.

The German soldiers had multiplied too – just like Monsieur Truchon had said they would, to strike back against the Allied invasion at Normandy. As I went to and from school, I passed by them with their brown shirts, trousers and heavy boots, stamping on street corners, standing guard around the town square.

Amma hadn't believed me when I told her there were more soldiers. She'd said I must be mistaken. She hadn't seen them because she was busier baking than ever before and hardly had time to go into town now.

But her being busy meant she wasn't keeping such a

strict eye on me, so I sometimes took a bit longer to come home.

I'd stop to listen at the *tabac* for a few reasons. One, I might hear something about Maddie or Albert. Two, because after I'd told her about all the extra soldiers, Amma had told me to keep my ear out for any news. Three, it was good detective practice.

I hadn't learnt anything yet, but Monsieur X said a good detective never gives up, and tomorrow could be different. One day after school, I leant my bicycle against the wall and bent down, pretending to tie my shoes, even though they had buckles. It was just like Monsieur X in *The Mystery of the Secret Room* when he was listening in on the burglars. The *tabac* door was open and I peered in, but all I heard was local gossip about the soldiers filling up the hotel bar, and the station master getting cross because the soldiers had commandeered all the trains and he was having to work longer hours.

Then they lowered their voices. I strained to hear and leant in a bit further. Then I caught a name that made my heart stop. Maison de Noyer. Albert's house. I was about to go in when I felt a cold shadow across my back. I turned to find a soldier towering over me. He was different. He wasn't wearing the same uniform as the others – his was dark, like a suit, with medals on it hanging from coloured bands. His thick black hair fell forward and he wore rings, which winked in the sunlight.

I stood aside quickly. He watched me a moment, then turned his head towards the inside of the *tabac*, where it had gone completely silent. He stepped inside. As his shadow passed me I shivered.

Then a man's voice outside shouted, piercing the quiet. 'You there!'

I jumped.

Behind me a car had pulled up to the pavement, purring like a large cat. It was black and so polished it shone. It had curves along the front and side and sat looking coiled, as if it was ready to spring. Inside was a brown-uniformed soldier in the driver's seat staring forward. In the back was a woman wearing a hat. I took a step closer. The woman turned her head towards me. She had the palest skin and the brightest red lipstick, which showed off a beauty spot just below her nose. I caught my breath. She was the most glamorous person I'd ever seen.

'Clear off.'

I turned to find Monsieur Bouchard, the owner of the café next door, staring at me.

I looked left and right, then back at the *tabac*. I wasn't doing anything wrong, was I? Well, except listening. And looking. I took hold of my bicycle.

'There's no parking here,' Monsieur Bouchard said. 'The pavement is for our tables.'

I realised then he wasn't talking to me after all. I followed his gaze to the car. He was shouting at the driver who'd parked the black car right where the *tabac* and café laid out their chairs and tables, though hardly anyone ate out these days. A *boule* set had been half crunched under the front wheel.

The driver either didn't hear him, or ignored him.

'You,' the café owner said, knocking on the window.

The moment he touched the car, two other soldiers came out of nowhere. Within seconds they'd taken the café owner's arms. He shouted and struggled and still no sound came from the *tabac* or anywhere else. I looked along the street. No one came out of the shops. The sun beat down on my head. I tightened my fingers round the handlebars of my bicycle. The soldier in the car hadn't turned round and the woman who'd looked at me now stared straight ahead. It was as if Monsieur Bouchard was invisible.

'Let me go! Let me go!' he shouted.

The soldiers dragged him along the pavement and I watched as they rounded the corner. Where were they taking him? Was he going to prison or was he going to disappear too? For shouting? For touching the car?

'Good afternoon.'

I jumped.

The man in the dark suit was standing in the doorway.

I stared up at him and gulped. Would they take me too? For watching? For listening? What would Amma say if I never came home again? Where would I disappear to? My heart began to beat so fast I could feel it in my throat. The tall man narrowed his eyes. My hands felt slippery on the handlebars. Then he coughed and looked at my bicycle, and I realised I was blocking his way. I pushed it along, letting it lead me away. The street ahead was empty; the click of my wheels sounded loud. I heard the car door open and shut, and an engine growl softly. I didn't turn back until I reached the end of the street. The car had gone. I let out a breath, relief flooding through me, and headed home.

But when I got there, I stopped dead.

The same curvy car that I'd seen in the village was pulling away from the front of our house.

I started to shake.

Amma! Had they left me and taken Amma away instead?

I dropped my bicycle and ran.

# Chapter Nine

I raced through the back door, but there was Amma in the kitchen, baking.

It was a little darker than usual because all the doors and windows were closed and she'd pulled the shutters across early, but otherwise everything seemed normal. I saw she had a spot of flour on her right cheek and I reached to brush it off, but she batted me away.

'Sit down.'

She wiped her hands on her apron, walked into the pantry, and brought out a thin, grey, lidded pail and placed it on the table. I slung my satchel over the back of a chair, grabbed a glass and poured myself some of the cool, fresh milk, my eyes on Amma all the while. The spot of flour had gone.

I was used to her silences. She'd answer in her own time, or not, but things were different now. I had to know why the car had been here. Remembering the last Monsieur X book I'd read, I decided to try to surprise it out of her. I smiled.

'You know, Amma, I wish we had a dog like in *Monsieur X and the Lost Treasure*.'

Amma didn't answer. I watched her hands work the dough. She was making another batch of her famous little loaves.

'He could be a guard dog for us.'

Amma tore the large piece of dough into twelve smaller pieces.

'He would keep away unwanted visitors.'

She rolled the twelve pieces in her hands, shaping them, one by one until they became twelve plump circles.

'At least until Father comes back.'

I reached a hand to the closest one.

'I know I would feel a lot safer if –'

'You would be a lot safer, Eloise, if you did not venture out of the house at times you were not supposed to.'

I snatched my hand back and gulped.

'And if you kept out of people's way.'

I rubbed my nose. What did Amma know? Had Nan said something? Was that why they hadn't been in touch? Because Amma had told them to leave me alone? Or did she mean the man in the suit? Had he been here to tell her I'd been in his way? Or did she mean I should keep out of her way right this minute?

'And I've moved the barrel somewhere it can't be used for sneaking in or out,' she added in an undertone.

I sipped my milk and watched her, but Amma concentrated on gathering the dough circles into a large tin so they'd bake together. She was making her sharing bread. Bread for friendship, she always said.

I itched to ask her what she and Nan had talked about. I wanted to tell her about the café owner too and ask where they'd taken him, where they were taking everyone. If the prison was empty as Rene had said, then where was everyone? And if Father was there, could we visit him? I wanted to ask her why the curved car had stopped at our house and if the man was angry with me because I'd seen them take Monsieur Bouchard away or because I'd been listening at the *tabac* or looking at the car, or all three. I'd tried asking her and I'd tried tricking her, but she was giving nothing away. I felt itchy with frustration. Why wouldn't Amma tell me anything? I'd have to try something else.

She sprinkled flour over the top of the rolls then using her blade, deftly sliced three diagonal cuts across each.

'No dog?' I said.

Amma shook her head. 'No dog, *mon chou*. It is getting hard enough to feed ourselves.'

I frowned. 'But everyone needs bread.'

She put the tin into the oven, placed a bowl of water underneath to add steam as it baked so the bread would be crusty on top, then shut the door. 'Not everyone can still afford it.'

I shook my head. 'But you're baking night and day. Someone clearly wants a lot.'

She turned to me. 'I cannot get round to everyone I would like now that I have to bake for the big house. Madame Brodeur has Albert searching for as many extra tins and trays as they can spare us.'

I grinned. 'So Albert is there!'

I let out a breath I hadn't known I was holding and stood up. I felt taller and full of energy, like when you run so fast down a hill you think you might trip any second, but you don't.

'If Albert's there after all, then maybe Maddie's family is too and –'

Amma clasped the edge of the large mixing bowl on the table. Her eyes wouldn't meet mine.

My shoulders drooped. All the excitement drained from me. 'What is it?' I said.

'*Mon chou*, sit down.'

I shook my head. Her sudden seriousness made me think I didn't want answers after all.

'Please, little one.'

'I won't fight Albert,' I said. 'I'll make up, I promise.'

Amma sighed and reached for the flour. 'I am baking for the big house, but not for Albert's family.' She added a pinch of salt to the bowl. 'Maison de Noyer is now the Kommandant's home. The man commanding all the soldiers here.'

I stared at Amma.

The tall soldier in the dark suit. *He* had to be the Kommandant! He'd had that big fancy car waiting for him outside the *tabac* and he'd been wearing all those medals and rings. Something about him had made him seem like he was in charge. It had to be him.

My jaw dropped as I put the pieces together.

The Kommandant had been here to order Amma to bake for him. I felt my cheeks redden and tried to swallow the lump in my throat.

'Amma, I heard something,' I said, 'in the *tabac*, they were talking about the big house . . .'

Amma thumped the bowl onto the table. 'Don't you listen to gossip,' she growled. 'If Madame Brodeur . . .' She shook herself, then started again. 'If Albert's mother stays to wash and cook for the Kommandant and his soldiers then that is her decision. People must do as they see fit. Things have changed. And others shouldn't be too quick to judge what people's actions do or do not mean.'

A prickle ran up my back. So Madame Brodeur was cooking for the soldiers? No wonder the gossip was ugly.

But if Amma was baking for the Kommandant . . . What would people say about her?

'People need bread,' Amma said, watching me. 'And we need to eat.'

My stomach twisted. Helping the Germans in any way just seemed so wrong, even if we needed the money now Father was gone . . . I opened my mouth to argue – I didn't want people to gossip about Amma; I'd rather we went hungry – but Amma cut in.

'Things have changed. Rations only go so far and you need to help out a little more now your father's gone.'

I bristled. 'Not for ever,' I said, 'he's coming back. They're all coming back.' I swallowed. 'And I do help. Soon I'm going to –'

I kicked my legs against the chair to stop myself from giving anything away.

'Soon nothing,' she said, pointing to a basket on the other side of the table. It was filled with six half-baguettes. 'You can start with this.'

My eyes widened.

'You want me to take it to Maison de Noyer?'

She shook her head.

'No, you silly goose. That is for Madame Levee.'

I sighed with relief at not having to go near the soldiers . . . but I felt a little pinch of disappointment too. I was longing to go up to the big house. If Albert's mother was working for the Kommandant, maybe Albert was too, and that was why he wasn't at school. I wanted to find out.

'Be careful,' Amma said as I picked up the little basket.

Thinking about the Kommandant reminded me about Monsieur Bouchard being taken away, and for a second I was going to tell Amma what had happened, then I wondered, if I did, would she would still let me make the delivery? I kept my mouth shut.

'Off with you now.'

I took the basket outside, settled it onto the front of my bicycle, then set off along the lane.

It was a still and hot afternoon. The crickets slowly rubbed their wings together, wildflowers drooped heavy with the heat along the edges of the road and there was a sweetness in the air that made you think everything was alright, even though it wasn't. Everything was wrong. Father and Maddie were missing. Soldiers were taking café owners away just for asking them to move their car. It felt like our town was an apple that had gone rotten. On the outside it still looked green and juicy, but inside it had turned to mush. I cycled through the haze, bees humming alongside me, trying to pretend it was just a normal summer's day, but when I reached the village, I couldn't even pretend any more. Two soldiers changed everything that afternoon.

# Chapter Ten

I was cycling across the town square when the soldiers came out of nowhere and stepped right in front of me. I screeched my brakes, the back of my bicycle fishtailing in the dust. The soldier on my left grabbed the handlebars while the one on my right used his rifle to lift up the edge of the soft cream linen Amma had tucked round the bread.

'What have we here?'

I swallowed. My heart thump, thump, thumped. I knew they could take anyone away without any reason. I was doing nothing wrong, but would that matter? I took a deep breath.

'Just bread for delivery, monsieur.'

The one on the left laughed. 'We shall see,' he said.

The one on the right shouldered his rifle and reached into the basket. My heart sank. This was our livelihood.

Why did they think they could take anything they wanted?

Suddenly something made my neck prickle. I looked up. François was walking straight towards me.

I stared at him, not realizing I'd pulled the basket away from the soldiers.

The soldier on the right swung his gun round towards me and clicked it.

That pulled my gaze from François. I tried to swallow, but my throat was dry. François was almost parallel now, his eyes on the road ahead, but I could tell he was still taking in what was going on. And he was doing his best not to look worried about passing so close to the soldiers. I remembered what he'd said the last time I saw him – that he had to hide. So why didn't he keep his distance? I took a breath. I needed to keep the soldiers' attention on me so they wouldn't notice him.

'Oh, monsieur,' I said to them, 'it is just bread for Madame Levee.'

When they didn't say anything, I started gabbling, looking anywhere but at the gun and François.

'It's my last order for today and I'm glad because my feet ache and I have homework to do and I promised to clean out the chicken coop.'

I sighed and pushed my fringe out of my eyes.

'I can't be late, monsieur. My Amma will –'

But the soldier held up his hand for me to stop speaking and ripped the linen cloth off the basket. He stared greedily at the bread underneath.

I felt François' shadow pass by on my left. I itched to look, but the last thing I wanted was to make the soldiers look too. I darted my eyes up quickly. He met my gaze then looked away. I forced myself to face the soldier with the gun again.

'Oh monsieur, please,' I said, starting to move away, still holding the basket, still trying to keep their eyes on me. 'I cannot be late.'

'Stop!'

I froze, then felt all the bones in my body start to shake.

But it wasn't me they were talking to. The soldiers were pointing their rifles at François' back. Had they recognised him? Were they after him? If so a schoolgirl with a bread basket wasn't going to distract them now.

He carried on walking, slowly, carefully, as if he hadn't heard them.

'You there!'

Both rifles clicked. I covered my mouth to stop myself shouting for him to run, run, run, when all of a sudden the soldier on the left screamed.

A small white dog with brown tufts on its head shaped like a hat had grabbed the soldier's ankle and was wrangling it like a toy.

The soldier kicked out his boot, then hit the dog with the end of his gun.

There was a thump. The dog yelped, but didn't let go.

'Bise, come!'

From across the square, Pauli, a boy from my class, called to the dog.

'Bad boy. Come now, Bise, come.'

He tried to click his fingers, but his hands were shaking too much to make the noise. He crept forward, half bent like an old man and crooned again.

'Bise, Bise.'

All of a sudden a shot rang out.

It echoed round the buildings like a firework and was followed by a deathly silence.

Three old men stood outside the *tabac*. The grocer dropped a brown apple and let it roll into the gutter. Everyone stopped what they were doing to stare.

Then a wail cracked open the quiet.

'Bise!'

Pauli ran towards us, but the grocer caught his shirt and pulled him back. I stared at the pile of white and brown tufts now speckled with red.

Then the soldier kicked the dead dog away from him and wiped his boot in the dust. The other soldier swung his rifle up towards Pauli, who was hysterical, flailing his arms and crying for his Bise.

'Just a stupid boy who couldn't control his dog,' the grocer was saying as the soldiers moved towards the boy. 'There was no harm intended, and he's lost his dog now. Punishment enough, don't you say?'

He caught my eye and inclined his head as if telling me to scram.

I grabbed the linen from the ground, threw it over the basket of bread, and pedalled out of the square as fast as I could.


I cycled all the way to the other side of town to Madame Levee's house. It was the third terraced house on a small lane that sat in a dip made between two rows of tall trees shaped like green lollipops – they were so high they made a puddle of cool shade for each house – and ended in a little overgrown park.

I propped my bike against the wall, grabbed my basket and knocked on her door.

No one answered.

I knocked again and noticed my hand was shaking.

'Madame Levee?'

I looked around me but all the houses were shuttered against the afternoon sun. They squatted low and dark and green beneath the trees.

I felt prickly again, like eyes were watching from behind each shuttered window. There was a flicker of light from the house on the left, as if someone had peered out, but when I looked again the doors and windows were shut tight. I must have imagined it. I swallowed and lifted my hand to knock at the door one last time. It opened onto a dark hallway.

'Madame Levee?' I called.

'Get inside, child.'

It was a man's voice in the shadows. I took a step back, but I was yanked into the house. The door slammed shut behind me. It took a few seconds for my eyes to adjust to the dark. When they did, I gasped.

'You!'

Standing in front of me was Grizzly Grey Beard.

'Where's Madame Levee?'

Grizzly Grey Beard tutted and walked off. I stood idling in the corridor, clasping the basket of bread close, unsure what to do next.

'Hello, Eloise,' said a familiar voice.

François stepped out of the gloom in his raggedy sweater and ran a hand through his hair.

'François! You're safe!'

I took a few steps towards him before stopping, remembering I was a part of the Resistance and shouldn't behave like a kid.

Behind him Nan popped her head round the door. I forgot about being a kid then and ran to give her a hug.

'You're alright,' I said. 'I was worried after I didn't hear from any of you.'

She gently pushed me back. 'A lot has happened, Eloise,' she said.

I turned to François. 'And where's Madame Levee?'

'Come,' he said, ushering me into the small parlour. It was even darker in there – cool, but stuffy, with the thick smell of a place no one has been living in for a while.

'She left,' Nan said, a hand to my shoulder.

'She has family she can stay with,' François said. Then, shaking his head, 'There are parts of France that are safer than here for people like Madame Levee.' He looked me straight in the eye. 'Do you understand what I'm saying, Eloise?'

I thought about Antoine shouting at Maddie, blaming everything that went wrong on her grandmother.

'Like it not being safe here for the Gypsies?' I asked.

François nodded. 'Madame Levee is Jewish,' he said.

'Like me,' Nan added.

Grizzly Grey Beard made a noise that sounded like he had something stuck in his throat.

'She should know,' Nan said. 'I trust her.'

'But you're not leaving?' I asked her.

Nan shook her head. 'My parents are dead and I've work to do,' she said, lifting her chin.

I nodded. 'So who asked Amma for bread? She told

me it was for Madame Levee.'

François grinned. 'Excellent question, detective. I told you she'd be an asset,' he said, looking over me at Grizzly Grey Beard, who only grunted.

François looked back at me. 'That was me.'

I squinted at him.

'Welcome to the Resistance, Eloise. You've completed your first mission.'

# Chapter Eleven

I shook my head. 'What mission?'

Nan reached for the basket of bread. She counted them. 'Six,' she said.

Then she handed them to Grizzly Grey Beard who broke one open and pulled out a piece of paper.

I could hardly believe my eyes. Each half-baguette had a slip of paper hidden inside! Grizzly Grey Beard unfolded the slips and pressed them out. He gathered all six together, pushing them around the coffee table till they made sense to him. I could see there was something written on each slip, but couldn't make out what. It looked like some sort of code. I edged closer.

'We thought it would be best if you didn't know you were carrying something for us,' Nan said, 'at first.'

I thought about the soldiers. How greedily they'd looked at the bread.

'But what if the soldiers had discovered the notes inside?'

François shrugged. 'But they didn't,' he said. 'You kept your wits and fed them a story they could believe. And you escaped as soon as you had the opportunity.'

I frowned. It felt like they'd played a trick on me. I remembered the soldier's gun pointed straight at me. Still felt the fear creeping through my bones.

François took both my hands in his. 'I was there,' he said, 'ready to cause a diversion if anything went wrong.' He smiled. 'There was no way to know you'd be stopped,' he said, 'but you did well, Eloise. You didn't panic. Now we know we can rely on you.'

I felt a tingle in my palms that stretched all the way to my shoulders and to the back of my neck. I felt half happy, half fidgety.

'Do you think you could do it again, but knowing you're carrying something important?'

I nodded, even though something about all this was bothering me. I just couldn't put my finger on it yet.

François grinned. 'Good.' He straightened and stretched, rubbing the small of his back. 'Go and have something to eat – Nan will show you where. We have some planning to do.'

I didn't want to eat, I wanted to help with the planning, but Nan laid a hand on my shoulder and steered me towards the kitchen. She held out some bits of the bread that had been hiding messages.

'You might find something in the cupboards too,' she said. 'Madame Levee had to leave quickly, so . . .'

She shrugged.

I turned to the nearest cupboard and opened it, but the shelves were bare. I tried the one above and the one to its right, but these were just as empty. I thought of Maddie and her family. They'd gone too, but when I'd peered in through their window, there'd been lots of plates of half-eaten food sitting on the table. I shut the cupboard and leant my head against it, suddenly realizing that the food had probably belonged to the soldiers who lived there now. Had Maddie and her family escaped like Madame Levee, or had they been taken? I turned to face Nan.

'Will she be safe?' I asked. 'Madame Levee?'

She gave me a small smile. 'As much as anyone can be,' she said.

'But what about you?' I asked.

'Let's just say I'm swapping safety for something else,' she replied. 'Now don't let that bread go to waste,' she added, then left.

I began to search the rest of the kitchen and, right at the back of the cupboard under the sink, I found a jar of blackcurrant jam so sticky I had to wash it under the tap then have three goes at twisting the top before it would open. There was a little film of mould on top, but once I scraped that off, the jam underneath was thick and gloopy and smelt delicious.

I dipped the pieces of bread straight into the jar then stuffed them into my mouth. After the scares of the morning, I was ravenous. As I looked around the kitchen, I noticed the small round tablecloth didn't quite reach the edges of the table. It was faded, a white and brown pattern with holes in on purpose – the kind of thing Amma used to make before she got too busy. The whole kitchen was very small, almost a cupboard, with everything packed away neatly inside. It reminded me of a kitchen I'd seen inside a boat once, and as Nan left me at the table, I found myself remembering Father taking me there.

We were going on an adventure with a friend, Father had said as he woke me in the dark. There was a puzzle to unravel. 'And if you're going to be a detective, you must learn to act like one.'

I yawned.

'It had better be a good puzzle this early in the morning,' I'd grumbled, but I couldn't hide my grin.

We wouldn't use our bicycles, Father said, so we walked, but the challenge was that we mustn't be seen by anyone.

'It's a game, *ma rose*. Get us to the river without anyone

seeing us, and there's a prize for you.'

So I did.

It was exciting, imagining we were sneaking around. I took us through the back of the garden into the forest. The land belonged to the big house, but my father said nothing, so I led us on, crossing through the tall pines, the needles crunching beneath our feet.

'Shhhhh,' I told him, grinning. 'You're too noisy. They'll catch us!'

But my father only gave me a thin smile.

We walked right through the forest to the meadow beyond that ran along the road towards town. I kept us near to the trees and then continued round the boundary of the Maison de Noyer estate. Father kept looking left and right and checking behind him. I wore a big smile, thrilled he was playing the game properly.

Eventually we came to an outbuilding and the beginnings of a dirt track. Father said it led to a small tributary of the Loire River on the very outskirts of town. I wasn't listening; I wanted to solve the puzzle so I raced ahead, but Father pulled me back.

He took my hands. 'Remember this, Eloise.'

I frowned. He was squeezing my hands so hard they hurt a little.

'If you need to, you could come here, follow this route. Do you understand?'

I didn't, but I nodded all the same because he seemed to be waiting for it.

He closed his eyes and let out a sigh. Then he let go of my hands.

All the fun of the game slipped away with his words. Suddenly I'd felt cold and wide awake.

'Good,' he said, pasting a smile back on, one that didn't quite reach his eyes.

Then he led me to the boat.

It looked like a cross between an old fishing boat and a tug, with a wide white bottom, three small portholes and a stained wood cabin at the top with glass windows. It was moored against the bank, nudging it gently. My father helped me up onto the swaying deck, then unlocked two little wooden doors, which we peeled back to reveal a cabin with a galley kitchen.

Inside everything was compact and fitted into white painted boxes. One little door opened to reveal two small gas rings and another held an empty icebox. There were two taps over a tiny sink, and some grain and four loaves of hard bread hidden under the seats.

We waited there for two hours. The boat had creaked and the water lapped at the side, gently rocking us, but I felt the opposite of sleepy. Father had said we couldn't light a candle and the food wasn't for us, it was for his friend. But his friend never arrived, though we played three games of chase the ace and six of crazy eights with a deck of cards that he said was my prize for getting us there safely. After I won the last game, Father sighed and said we had to go.

'Your friend isn't coming after all?'

He shook his head.

'Perhaps he got the wrong day?'

My father ruffled my hair. 'Perhaps.'

My stomach rumbled. I thought of the tins of food behind the tiny cupboard doors, the bread under my seat and looked at my father.

'Come,' he said. 'We don't need that. Amma will have plenty for us.'

He didn't look behind us so much on the way home.

The game was over.


As I sat at her table, I admired Madame Levee's simple but cared-for home. She must have felt upset leaving it. I hoped she'd found safety somewhere else, and wished that Father and Maddie had found their way there too, wherever it was. But I couldn't quite believe that. It wasn't just the things Antoine said at school about Maddie going to prison or worse, the day he'd said shooting was too good for her. It was something in the looks the adults gave each other, over your head, when people like him said these things, as if they thought you were blind. They were sad looks, empty looks; their eyes saying that the rumours were true – that there really were terrifying places for people the soldiers didn't like. Prisons that no one would ever come back from, even if the war ended.

All at once everything that had happened rushed back. Finding the messages in the bread, the soldiers almost rumbling me, Bise the dog shot and lying bleeding at my feet. What if Maddie was lying somewhere shot and bleeding? What if Father was . . .

The bread in my mouth turned to dust. I stood and ran the tap above the sink, then thrust my head under the lukewarm trickle and lapped at the water till the taste went away.

I thought of the last time I saw Father. He was leaving for work. The skin under his eyes had looked bruised in the early morning light; his chin had been bristly against my cheek. He'd forgotten to shave and he was supposed to be going to work. I hadn't noticed at the time and I only remembered it now. Some detective I was going to be.

Murmuring interrupted my thoughts. Nan had left the kitchen door open, but not the parlour door, so I could hear their voices if not the actual words.

I turned off the tap.

They weren't going to leave me out, not again. I

couldn't sit around in a kitchen eating bread and jam while soldiers took everyone away. I had to do something. What if they took Amma next?

I stood up.

I might not be as old as them or as experienced, but I'd proved I could help. I had salt, after all, like Maddie had said. Now I needed to convince the Resistance that they could trust me, then they'd let me do more. Delivering messages was all very well, but I had to find Father – whatever it took.

I eased my way round the table so the floor wouldn't creak, and tiptoed across the hall right up to the parlour door. The voices became clearer. I heard Nan say something about some documents and heard a long rustling, as if a map or a newspaper had been spread out. Then it went quiet.

Would they still trust me if they knew I was eavesdropping? I'd have to take the chance they wouldn't find out. I pressed my ear to the door.

The next voice was François – I heard it so clearly he must have been standing just on the other side.

'They've got twenty of us,' he said, 'maybe more, but we need the list to find out exactly what their plans for the prisoners are.'

Nan's low voice muttered something I couldn't quite catch.

'If we're not careful,' Grizzly said, 'we'll *all* end up on a train to Struthof.'

More mutters.

'Yes,' François replied, 'we think that's where they plan to take Robert.'

I swallowed as a shiver snaked down my spine, freezing my feet to the floor. I pressed so hard against the parlour door I thought I might melt through it.

Robert.

My father.

# Chapter Twelve

Here was the truth at last! Father had been caught. Father was a prisoner! And yet I felt a whoosh of relief – letting go of something I think I'd been holding ever since François had come to our house, as if some part of me had thought Father might have been lost for ever. But if Father was a prisoner, then he was still alive!

I stared at the grain in the wooden door, tracing the rings with my finger as I strained to hear more.

'The deportation lists and schedules will be with the Kommandant at Maison de Noyer,' François was saying. I heard him sigh. 'From what we found out from the station master, they're taking the prisoners into Germany.' There was a pause. 'You know the rumours,' he said. 'If we don't get them before they leave . . . they're as good as dead.'

I gasped. All the relief I'd felt vanished, replaced by

François' words, echoing round and round my head.

Dead . . . Dead . . . Dead . . .

There was more rustling.

'It's too dangerous,' Grizzly Grey Beard said, 'we can't risk being seen at the house. We're the only Resistance left here! It would draw too much attention, jeopardise everything we're working towards.'

The murmurs continued, but I couldn't believe what I'd heard. Father was alive, but he might not be for long – and they weren't going to help him!

My throat felt tight, my hands were shaking. I pulled them into fists. I was ready to storm into the room, ready to tell them they couldn't leave him to die. But would they listen? Or would they just yell at me for listening in, say they couldn't trust me any more?

I looked away, blinking back tears of frustration. My gaze lifted to the square of glass above the front door. The sun was a little less fierce now early evening was drawing in. I thought about exactly what I'd heard.

There was a list that said what was happening to the prisoners.

The list was at Maison de Noyer.

The evening shadow crept across the floor like it was scooping me up with it.

If I somehow found the list, I could find Father and then they wouldn't have any reason not to rescue him.

I took a silent step towards the front door, then another.

I knew Maison de Noyer. Not really well, but I'd been in the kitchen plenty of times, and Maddie and I had slunk around outside the *salon* once while Amma and Albert's mother had drunk tea from proper china cups and whispered.

A plan began to take shape in my head.

I'd use the bread. Amma said she was going to be delivering to the big house. I'd take the delivery and ask for Albert. When they let me inside to find him, I'd search for the list. Simple. Though the thought of the man in the black suit with the shiny medals and rings made me shiver. He'd be there . . .

And I hadn't known I'd been on a mission earlier, when the soldier stopped me. I would know this time. I'd have a cover story, but would I be able to pretend I was really just delivering bread? Would they guess I was up to something else?

I shook myself. I'd have to try. No one else was going to do anything. It was up to me now.

I squeezed my eyes tight. Just the thought of seeing Father again made me feel better, gave me courage. And maybe Maddie's family was on that list too. When I opened my eyes, my plan was set. I was just about to open the front door when the parlour door creaked behind me.

'Eloise?'

It was François.

I spun round, thrusting my hands behind my back even though there was nothing in them.

His brow was creased and the skin under his eyes looked bruised and grey. 'I have a small parcel that needs dropping off, but I think it's best I stay inside for now,' he said. 'The soldiers will be looking for me and the others are needed here. Can you do it?'

I nodded, but didn't move.

Nan appeared beside him, and passed me a square tin. It was a little bigger than my hand, rusting at the edges with a faded picture of some leaves that looked as if they'd been half rubbed out. I wondered what was inside it – blueprints, money, plans for sabotage or instructions for a radio operator?

'Don't open it,' François said. He smiled and rubbed his eyes. 'Best you don't know what's inside.'

I nodded, but I felt itchy about it. It was as if they weren't trusting me again.

'If you don't know anything, Eloise, then you can't tell them anything,' said Nan.

I nodded. They were looking out for me, that was all, and that's what Father would do.

'Leave it at the church,' François continued. 'Under the third pew on the left, as close to the aisle as possible.

If there's a small kneeler, place it under that. If not, you'll have to find something else to hide it under.'

'What will you do if someone sees you there?' Grizzly Grey Beard stood behind François.

I thought about what Monsieur X would do and straightened my shoulders.

'I'll pray,' I said. 'Or pretend to pray until they go away.'

François looked at Grizzly Grey Beard, who nodded.

'I'll get it done,' I said.

François smiled, but my nerves wouldn't let me match it.

I took a step towards the door, then paused. Should I tell him what I'd heard, what I was planning?

Monsieur X did say that it was often safer the less someone knew, and François had just said it was better if I didn't know anything about the tin if I was caught. So, by not telling them anything, I was just being clever. I was acting like a proper member of the Resistance. And it was absolutely not because I knew they would forbid it . . . I took a deep breath and walked outside. I'd do it. I'd complete their mission, and then my own.

# Chapter Thirteen

My bicycle leant against the house where I'd left it. I placed the tin in the basket and covered it with the linen cloth before remembering the soldier had used his gun to lift the edges and look inside. With a quick glance left and right I shoved the tin up the back of my shirt, tucking the edges in. Then I pulled my socks up and brushed my sleeves as well, as if I was tidying myself up and hadn't just hidden something important.

The front door had shut behind me and Madame Levee's house looked locked up and empty. So did the rest of the houses, with their shutters closed tight. With the sun setting and the tall trees drooping, the entire street looked abandoned. I shivered.

Then I grabbed the handlebars, swung myself onto my bicycle and pedalled as fast as I could back towards town.

I stopped at the corner of the square.

The church sat on the opposite side. A small tower and a pointed steeple rose above two large, curved wooden doors, flanked by a pair of small stained-glass windows criss-crossed with lead. One showed a rose and the other showed a loaf of sharing bread – Amma's speciality.

Amma had taken me to church every Sunday until the war came, and then she said there was too much baking to be done to take a morning off. But it was more than that. There was something in the way her nose wrinkled when she said Père's name. As if the words themselves had a bad smell.

Monsieur Bouchard must not have come back yet as the tables and chairs were still stacked against the window of the café. The door was ajar but the inside was dark. I looked away. The *tabac* was closed too. The whole square was silent, as if curfew had started a few hours early. The centre of town felt as abandoned as Madame Levee's street. The more soldiers arrived, the emptier it got, as if they were hollowing us out.

I thrust my shoulders back and forced myself to walk calmly across the square, but I felt too loud. My shoes tip-tapped across the cobbles. My bicycle chain whirred and the wheels clicked. I could hear my breath.

I focused on the church, bumping over the cobbles and steering round the fountain. I remembered the *pish-plink* sound it used to make when the water ran and how

Maddie had dared me to dip my toes in after school one day. I smiled. It had been ice cold and I'd screamed and laughed at the same time, then run my hand through it, spraying her with water. She'd shrieked and tried to get me back, but the water was up to my knees and I kicked and splashed till she was as soaked as I was. Most of the adults around had ignored us or smiled even, but Père Tremblay had come out of his church, hands on hips, his forehead in a v-shape that made his nose even more pointed than it usually was, and told us we were desecrating a memorial with our childish ways.

We'd giggled all the way home, making fun of his quavering voice, our wet clothes sticking to us, the sun shining.

The fountain was dry and empty now, but for a few leaves and some grass growing through a crack around the right foot of the statue. I gripped the handlebars and hoped with all my heart that Maddie was safe.

All of a sudden I noticed Père Tremblay. He was shutting the door of the church and pushing the bolt across.

No!

I felt the tin against my back. François had said it was important. It had to be placed under the pew today.

Père Tremblay had finished bolting the door and was walking away.

I ran, pulling my bicycle along with me.

'Wait!'

He turned, and then I saw that he wasn't alone. Someone else had joined him. Someone who'd been hidden in the alcove of the church. It was a man. The man in the dark suit.

I stopped dead, but it was too late. They'd seen me.

The Kommandant, the man who now lived at Maison de Noyer, stepped out of the shadows as Père Tremblay turned around. I pushed my fringe out of my eyes and tried hard not to touch the small of my back where the tin was hiding.

Père Tremblay beckoned me over.

I pushed my bicycle over the cobbles as slowly as possible, grabbing precious seconds to think up an excuse, something that would make sense and get me into the church this minute. But it was difficult when all I could concentrate on was the man in the suit. He stood beside the parson, smoking a large cigar, grey smoke hovering around them like an ugly cloud.

'Eloise, isn't it?' said Père Tremblay, narrowing his beady eyes – like shrivelled blackcurrants, Maddie had said once.

I nodded.

'We haven't seen you at church for some time.'

I tried not to stare at the Kommandant, though I could feel him watching me.

Père Tremblay seemed to be waiting for me to say something, but I was busy racking my brains. Then, I had it.

'But I wanted to go now,' I said, 'if it's possible.' I rubbed my nose. 'I have missed it you see and –'

He interrupted me, snorting. 'And you suddenly feel the need to pray?'

I chewed the inside of my cheek, then deliberately looked away. 'Yes, Père. You see, my father has gone missing.' I looked back at him. 'And I would like to pray for his safe return.'

Père Tremblay's left eye began to twitch, then stopped. The cloud of smoke from the Kommandant wisped towards me, first tickling then burning my throat. My eyes began to water.

Père Tremblay's frown deepened. 'I think, child, that –'

To my surprise the Kommandant interrupted him. 'You're not going to turn down one of your flock in her hour of need, are you, Father?'

Père Tremblay's shoulders hitched and his head wobbled on his neck in a strange nod. 'No, no, of course not.' He lifted an arm to point me back towards the church then bent his head. 'But our meeting?' the parson asked, rubbing his hands together like he was washing them.

'We can discuss our . . .' The Kommandant paused, ' . . . agreement, after the child has prayed.'

I swallowed and raised my eyes to the Kommandant. 'Thank you, monsieur.'

His eyes were grey, large and glued to mine, as if they were searching for something.

I looked away first.

Père Tremblay jangled his keys as he harrumphed back to the church door. He unlocked it and lifted the bolt.

'Do you need to confess?'

I froze.

For about a hundred things, I thought, the past few days running through my head. But, with one hand on the door, I forced myself to look sincere. 'No, thank you, Père.'

He stared a moment then leant close to speak, spittle hitting my cheek. 'Then be quick, girl.'

He waved me in, already looking behind him for the Kommandant as I slipped inside.

The church was quiet and dim – the only light came from the muted blues, reds, greens and yellows of the large stained-glass picture of the disciples above the nave. The air was thick with leftover incense giving off a sweet, musty smell that reminded me of Sunday school. There was a low hum too, like the sound of a record before the music starts.

My footsteps were really, really loud.

I stopped at the third row of seats on the left, slipped

into the pew and sat down. My heart missed a beat when I saw there was no kneeler, then I spotted one a little further up. I slid along the pew, then dragged it back with my foot. I glanced over my right shoulder to check the door was shut and I was completely alone. Sitting back, I reached under my shirt and pulled out the tin, the wooden back of the pew hiding my movements. Leaning over, I placed the tin between my hands and clasped them round it as if I was praying. Then, I slipped to the floor on my knees, landing on the kneeler and in seconds hid the box underneath it. I grabbed the pew in front to lift me up and sat back. I'd done it!

Suddenly I could smell cigar smoke, stale and stinging my nostrils.

I froze.

'Such a quick prayer?'

It was the Kommandant. He was right behind me!

I could feel his eyes burning into my back. I resisted the urge to tuck my shirt in and reminded myself to breathe.

'Yes, monsieur,' I said, looking round at him. 'I only wanted to ask for my father to be returned to me.'

He sat resting one arm along the back of his pew, his head turned up to the ceiling as if he was listening to a concert only he could hear.

I didn't dare move.

He fixed me with a cold stare. I forced myself to meet it, scared he'd see my guilt if I looked away.

'Kommandant?' said a voice.

I jumped.

Behind us, near the door, Père Tremblay shifted from foot to foot.

The Kommandant put up a hand. 'So, Eloise,' he said, 'you have finished.'

I felt a shiver across my shoulder blades as he said my name, dragging it out like it was three words, not one, but I nodded.

'Then we will leave together.' He held out a hand as if to help me up.

My left hand clenched as I forced my right to take his. It was warm and dry and mine slipped into it shaking, hot and sweaty.

We stood.

I wanted more than anything to check the tin box was hidden beneath the kneeler properly, but I didn't dare. Instead I let him lead me to the back of the church where Père Tremblay glared.

'Thank you, Père,' I said.

Père Tremblay harrumphed.

The Kommandant still had hold of my hand. He wasn't exactly stopping me leaving, but he wasn't letting me go either. It was strange, as if I knew I had to wait for him to decide to let go of my hand. I stood there, trying to hide the shake in my legs and the sick feeling in my throat, which made me swallow so loudly I was sure it echoed round the church.

'What is his name?'

His voice was silky and so quiet it felt hushed, as if the church were full of people praying and we shouldn't disturb them.

I thought of François and Grizzly Grey Beard and the man who'd sat in the corner cackling and smoking in their meeting house, then I realised who he meant.

'My father?'

He didn't answer. Suddenly I didn't want this man to have Father's name.

If I told him, he'd find out Father was in the Resistance and a prisoner, if he didn't know already. Would he suspect me too? I felt a roar of panic, but when I looked at Père Tremblay's furrowed face, I knew I had no choice. He knew exactly who I was. He'd know if I lied.

'My father is Robert Baudin,' I said.

The Kommandant's expression didn't change, but he dropped my hand. Père Tremblay licked his lips. They shone wet in the dim light. His left eye kept blinking as if he'd developed a tic.

When neither of them said anything more, I took one step away, then another and another. They didn't follow.

I half ran towards the church door, and when I reached it and turned they were both walking towards the nave. I swallowed. The tin box was there, third row from the front, under a kneeler, as instructed. I sent a quick prayer up hoping it was well hidden and that they wouldn't find it, when the Kommandant said something that stopped me cold.

'Your shirt is untucked, Eloise.'

I stopped breathing.

He hadn't even turned around.

I put a hand to my back and hastily tucked in my shirt, then raced out of the church, hopped on my bicycle and rode across the square, skidding past the fountain and straight on past the café and the *tabac*. Did he know? Was that what he was telling me? That he'd seen what I'd done? Would he find the tin? Had I blown everything for the Resistance on my first proper assignment? If the Kommandant did take the tin, he'd definitely know I was with the Resistance and he'd watch me or worse, which would make stealing the list so much harder.

I pedalled faster and faster.

I wanted so much to help, but had I put us all in danger instead?

# Chapter Fourteen

The sky was fading into sunset, and soldiers patrolled the square. I stared straight ahead as I cycled, trying to outrace my thoughts. Had the Kommandant really seen me hide the tin? Or was he just suspicious of my behaviour? I swung through the streets as fast as I could, all the way up past the school and the houses already shuttered.

It was only along the road out of town that I slowed down and took a breath. I could cycle back to Madame Levee's house to tell François what had happened, but the crickets had quietened and the sky was a bruised purple. Curfew wasn't far off. I'd never make it in time. There was nothing I could do about the tin or the Kommandant now. I'd done the best I could, but as I cycled on, I began to wonder if my best was really good enough for the Resistance.

I wheeled my bicycle round the house and laid it against the kitchen wall. Then I opened the back door to find Amma in her blue housecoat shuffling from the table to the oven with a tray of small loaves as if everything was completely normal.

I stood in the doorway watching, my heart beating so fast and loud in my ears I felt sure she could hear it, but she didn't turn.

'Are you coming in, *mon chou?*'

I watched her count the rolls, her eyes darting across the tray, and a niggling piece of the puzzle began to make sense.

'Shut the door behind you or we'll have Farmer Raymon after us complaining about the light being a beacon for bombers, eh?'

I shook my head and stared at the tiny loaves on the tray she'd placed on the table to cool. Thirteen perfectly shaped mini batons, creamy with a crisp brown ridge across the top of each one.

'Everything alright, *mon chou?*'

It all clicked into place.

'How long have you been working for them, Amma?'

Amma lifted a second tray of rolls from the oven and placed them next to the first batch to cool.

She wiped her hands on her housecoat and looked at me.

'The big house needs bread. I bake bread. It's simple. I am not working for them, I am baking. Times have changed and we need to eat, however we can. I thought I explained this?'

'Not the big house.'

She nodded to the clock sitting on the far wall. It sat in its tiny glass case slowly ticking down the minutes to curfew.

I closed the back door then reached out for one of the little loaves. Amma slapped my hand away.

I'd have to ask her outright. Her silence wasn't going to stop me getting answers this time. 'These loaves,' I said, 'how long have you been putting things in the bread?'

Amma paused for a second with a third tray of rolls halfway out the oven before sweeping the bread onto a cooling rack.

'I saw,' I said. 'There were bits of paper in the bread you gave me for Madame Levee. Secret messages.'

Without looking at me, Amma putdown her empty tray, then reached for my hands. She was still wearing her oven gloves and her hands were warm around mine.

'You are mistaken, *mon chou*.'

'But I saw them!'

She looked into my eyes and spoke calmly. 'I'm afraid not. You are tired. We all are. There's been a lot of strain. Your friend has gone missing. Now your father.' She paused. 'It would be strange if you were *not* upset.'

'But, I –'

'It's those books,' she said. 'They give you ideas.'

How could she say this? I'd seen the papers with my own eyes! It was one thing not to talk about the war or what was happening to Father or why she really stopped going to church, but to actually lie to me? I pulled away from her.

'I know you miss him,' she said.

I shook my head, but that only made me feel worse. I didn't want to talk about Father now, but she was right: I did miss him. I missed him and I was scared for him and I was worried no one was going to help him. He was all I had. I'd already lost a mother. I couldn't lose him too. I felt something twist inside and as Amma reached for me again, it unravelled. Everything that had happened – the soldiers, the gun, the dead dog, François, hearing Father's name, finding out he was a prisoner, the church, the Kommandant, Amma's lies – all of it tumbled out in tears. There was only one thing that really mattered. I began to sob.

'I have to find him, Amma. I have to.'

Amma held me tight in her thick arms. I breathed in her apron and the smells of the kitchen: bread, yeast, milk and cocoa and felt myself get heavier, my eyelids drooping.

Amma lifted me, carrying me up the stairs, then laid me on the bed.

I reached for her, but she gently pushed me away. She'd taken off the oven gloves, I noticed.

'Get some sleep, *mon chou.*'

I rubbed my eyes and when I looked again, she'd gone.

I let my head drop back onto the pillow, and within seconds I was asleep.

When I woke it was dark and I was shivering. A small breeze whispered through the shutters and around the windowsill. I reached for my blankets but something felt different.

I sat up straight.

I was in Father's room.

It was a larger than mine, with two windows, one of which had never shut properly so it let in the cold and, sometimes, the rain. His second-best jacket hung over the chair and the pair of shoes I'd polished ready for his return sat under the wardrobe. Next to the bed, on the dresser, was a newspaper from three weeks ago, some matches, a five-centimes piece and two books, the top one's spine worn through so the threads showed.

Amma had brought me here last night instead of my room.

Why?

I pulled his blanket up to my cheek. It smelt of his cologne. I wanted to bury my head in the pillow and hide till he came back, but he'd been captured and he wasn't coming back unless someone found out what the Germans' plans for him were. And the Resistance weren't going to help, not if Grizzly Grey Beard had anything to do with it.

But he wasn't the only one not helping.

I remembered the messages in the loaves.

Amma was lying. She had to be.

She'd put me in here to make me think of Father. Maybe she thought worrying about him would keep me distracted. It had worked, a little, but not the way I think she'd planned. Waking here, being surrounded by all his things just made me all the more determined to do what I could to get him back myself. And I wasn't going to be distracted from that . . . or from finding out the truth about Amma.

I swung my feet over the bed and slipped off my shoes. I tiptoed across the room, conscious that my navy skirt was crumpled and my cream blouse underneath wasn't so much cream any more as grey, but there was no time to change. I opened the door, holding the handle tight so it wouldn't squeak and, hearing a snuffling noise from Amma's room next door, I slid down the stairs in my socks and ran into the kitchen.

There on the table, four baskets stood ready, covered in faded red and blue checked, linen cloths. I could smell the bread, taste the first crisp crunch at the back of my mouth, which made my stomach rumble, but I was sure there was more than that inside. And if I could prove it, Amma couldn't lie to me any more.

I lifted the linen cloth off the nearest basket. Inside thirteen rolls nestled together. I reached for the top one and took it out, bringing it to my nose to smell. Then I heard a creak behind me.

I threw the bread back into the basket, but it was too late. Amma was standing in the doorway, her hands on her hips. She was dressed in her blue housecoat. Only her hair, pressed in neat curls under a net, showed she wasn't quite ready for the day.

The clock ticked, then gave six off-key dings to sound the hour and tell us it needed winding.

Amma didn't say a word as she counted her loaves.

She looked me straight in the eye. 'I won't let you go hungry,' she said, covering them back up with the cloth. 'If you want something, you have only to ask. We did not teach you to steal.'

My cheeks grew hot. I wasn't sure what was worse, being accused of stealing or having to accuse Amma of lying. I felt as if I was shrinking under her stare.

I pushed my hair out of my eyes. This couldn't go on.

'I was checking the bread for messages.'

Amma started to speak, but I shook my head to stop

her and then all my words rushed out.

'There were messages in them. I saw. You baked them, so you must have put them inside. And you told me to take the bread to Madame Levee, but Madame Levee isn't there, so you must know who *does* live in that house now, and that means you have to be part of it. I think you only put me to bed in Father's room to distract me. But it didn't work.'

My chest was rising and falling like I'd run a mile really fast, but Amma still didn't say a word. Instead she walked into the pantry, brought out the pail, tipped some milk into a pan on the stove then lit the flame underneath.

'I know everything, Amma,' I said, crossing my arms over my chest. 'So you may as well tell me the truth.'

'Oh ho,' she said, her back to me. 'Everything, eh?'

Amma stirred the milk. Light crept in around the edges of the shutters. Outside I heard our goat bleating to tell us she was ready to be milked. Still Amma said nothing, but something felt different.

I stared at her back, at the housecoat and the stockings tucked into her clogs, the way they cut into the top of her calves and wrinkled all the way down to her ankles. I frowned.

She only had two housecoats and this was exactly the same one she'd worn the day before. Amma never wore them two days in a row.

I narrowed my eyes.

Amma hadn't been to bed.

'I thought you were asleep,' I said. 'I heard snoring.'

'Well,' Amma said, bringing the hot milk to the table, nudging a basket aside with her elbow to make space then pouring the milk into a cup, 'perhaps you don't know everything, after all.'

She put the pan back on the stove then reached to the wooden rack of jars where she kept her spices. She selected one then took a pinch of fine brown powder and dusted it onto my milk. It smelt like earth and vanilla and something musky and sweet and hot at the same time. Cinnamon. A treat.

I looked up as she handed me a spoon.

'Stir and drink and I will tell you what you want to know.'

I pulled out a chair and sat, stirring the brown speckles into my frothy milk. Amma put the fat-bottomed coffee pot on the stove and heated up some of the chicory grounds she'd kept from the day before. It smelt of damp corners, and she sighed. Amma really missed coffee.

She didn't start to speak until she'd poured out a small cup of the thin brown liquid, sipped it, grimaced, then gulped the lot. Then she put on her apron, pushed the baskets to one side, away from me, and sprinkled flour onto the table.

'These baskets are for the big house.'

I sipped my milk.

'Four every day.'

She reached for a box of matches and lit the stove. The flame whumped at the back and she shut the door.

'Thirteen loaves in each.'

She poured water into a bowl, crumbled yeast on top and stirred it with her hand.

'I get extra rations to make them.'

She looked at me.

'Which means extra food for you.'

I looked at my cup. I wasn't sure I'd ever get used to the idea of her working for the Germans.

'And it means we can afford to eat and stay living here while your father is . . .'

She paused.

'. . . away.'

I put my cup down.

'Someone has to bake for them,' she said.

I picked at a hardened piece of pastry stuck to the table.

'And I promised your father I would take care of you.'

I looked at the four baskets on the table. That made sense. But that wasn't what I wanted to know.

'But what about Madame Levee?' I asked. 'And the notes in the bread?'

Amma paused and sighed.

'I baked for her. I sent her messages of comfort.'

She turned to me.

'In these dark times we all need a friend, yes?'

I frowned.

'And if she is no longer at her home,' Amma continued, 'and someone else ate the bread, then all they would have read were my kind sentiments.'

My head rested on one hand. I thought about Grizzly Grey Beard opening the bread like he knew there was something inside, as if he was expecting it. He and Nan had counted the loaves.

'But –'

Amma's eyes locked to mine, as if she was trying to tell me more than her words would allow.

'That is all I have to say on the matter.'

She added flour to the bowl and stirred.

I finished my milk and stood. What Amma said made sense, but I'd seen the Resistance use the notes like they were instructions. I tried to think like Monsieur X. There was what Amma was telling me, and then there was the real story underneath. And I wasn't so sure she was lying to me now. Not exactly. It was as if she'd put all the ingredients for her friendship bread on the table, but hadn't told me the recipe because some things had to be kept secret. I'd have to figure it out myself. She was doing what she could. And I would do the same. After a second I put a hand on Amma's arm, and she nodded once to show she understood.

I stared at the four baskets of bread ready for the big house, then looked at the clock.

'I'd like to help, Amma,' I said, as casually as I could.

Amma had placed the bowl to one side and uncovered another that held a thick, bubbling dough that looked as if it was trying to escape over the edges. She peeled it out and began to shape it in her hands.

'It's a lot of work,' I said. 'I could collect supplies for you.'

I stepped closer to the table, ran my fingers across the top of the nearest basket.

'And I could deliver these. It's not far to the big house. I can make the delivery and be back in no time.'

She gave me a small smile. 'I know you could, *mon chou*, but things are not the same as they were.'

I shivered as I thought of the Kommandant . . . the way he'd said my name, the way he'd known I was up to something. 'I know who lives there now,' I replied in a hushed voice. 'But I can still deliver bread.'

Her head dropped to one side and her eyes narrowed as if she was thinking it over. I looked at the skin underneath her eyes, gathered like soft folds, and thought about how often she sighed these days, and how she rubbed her back all the time.

I reached for the handles of the two closest baskets.

'No.'

I turned round in surprise. 'But –'

She looked at the clock, brushed her hands on her apron and shook her head.

'I said no, *mon chou*. If there is to be any visiting the soldiers, I will be the one to do it.'

She headed off to the pantry and the little curtain fluttered behind her. I could hear her humph as she lifted a sack of flour.

I stared at the baskets. One simple delivery. Though it would be so much more if I could get into the house and find that list. But I couldn't tell Amma that, or how important this was to me, to Father. How it was worth any number of the scoldings that would surely come from defying her.

I'd made my decision.

I scooped the baskets up and raced out of the door.

'I'll be back before you know it, Amma. Don't worry,' I whispered, and at the time, I really meant it.

# Chapter Fifteen

I yawned as I cycled along the country lane. My stomach rumbled and yesterday's clothes felt itchy. I wished I'd had time to change and wash, but if I hadn't left in a hurry, Amma would have stopped me, and she'd probably never have let me out of the house again. She probably never would anyway, once I got back . . . so I had to make this count. I felt bad about disobeying her, but I had to try if there was even just the slightest chance I could find out where Father was.

The sun was up early and warmed my arms and legs. The road ran straight ahead between two banks of overgrown grass that had turned yellow with the heat. There was no breeze. Everything was as still as a painting. Today would be hot. Up ahead the sky was a faint blue with slashes of pink like silk ribbons trailing across it. The bicycle chain clicked and whirred in the quiet.

After ten minutes I passed the track that turned off to Maddie's house, feeling a pang like a stitch in my side that she wasn't there any more. I cycled on till the road made its curve round to the right and then the left to sweep up to the big house.

'*Halt!*'

My hands grabbed the brakes and my feet hopped off the pedals. The wooden gate to the house, which normally sat wide open, was shut and next to it squatted a brand-new wooden hut, just big enough for a person to stand up in.

I stumbled forward, running and pulling the handlebars upright at the same time to stop the baskets tumbling off.

A soldier stepped out and reached for his gun, but when he saw me properly he relaxed, rubbing his eyes and yawning instead.

I gulped.

'I have a delivery,' I said, my voice managing to sound more confident than I felt.

He looked at the baskets, waved me past and was already stepping back into his hut and sitting down again as I wheeled the bicycle up to the gate.

The bolt was stiff and I looked behind me for some help, but the guard had shut his door. I used both hands to pull it. The gate squeaked open as I rolled the bicycle through. I thought about leaving it open like it used to be, then remembered the guard's eager gun, changed my mind and bolted it shut.

The road felt longer, and was now full of holes – some so large I had to wheel around them – and loose chippings that crunched under my shoes. The grass either side was bleached grey and was as stiff as straw. Only the old trees were the same – black and gnarled like old fingers, upturned claws that looked as if they'd been burnt. Albert had told me they'd always been like that, but they seemed more sinister now. Sweat began to slip down my back, pooling under my arms as I forced my feet onwards.

I stopped at the end of the road to the big house. In front of eight huge trucks, grey-green with thick wheels caked in mud from where they'd churned the fields and trailed across the gravel. There were soldiers too. A couple were unloading crates from the truck closest to me. Another one sat revving his engine and shouting to a soldier who was looking inside the bonnet.

I gulped, gripped the handlebars and pushed the bicycle towards the house.

It too had changed since I'd last been here.

It still looked as if it was leaning towards me, and the shutters across the top two floors were closed tight, except the one on the far left, which hung by its corner. The bottom ones were open and pinned back, but the flower beds and the two tubs with bright red plants that stood on either side of the huge wooden front door had gone.

That wasn't the worst bit.

The double front door was shut and above it was a flag – red with a white circle and the strange black cross with feet – the same one all the soldiers wore on their arms. I felt goosebumps prickle along the back of mine.

I looked off to the left where a thin, worn path led round the back of the house and beyond, to Maddie's home.

The knot in my stomach tightened.

I pushed on towards the front door instead. The flag hung lopsided, curled under to one side and limp in the heat. I snorted, glad it wasn't straight.

I rested my bicycle against the wall then climbed the three steps to the door feeling as if every single soldier's eyes were on my back.

If this had been a few months ago, by the time I'd reached the house, Albert would be rushing out towards me, or he'd have started a game of chase and I'd have to run like mad to stay ahead. Or Maddie would be skipping round the side of the house or sitting in the tall grass. She'd pop her head up and I'd find her on a checked blanket, her feet bare. We'd share my book, lying back in the grass, taking it in turns to hold it in front of the sun, trying to solve the clues before Monsieur X did.

I sighed. I missed her. I missed them both.

I stared up at the house. Perhaps there was more than one secret to discover today.

The lock on the front door clicked open and my heart began to race. I thought of the Kommandant and ran over my plan in my head. I was only delivering bread, and asking after Albert. Completely normal, not suspicious at all. I took a breath, ready to speak, then as the door creaked wide, my words failed and I stumbled back down the three steps to the gravel. The shadow of the door followed me, spreading like a pool of icy water. I heard a cough. Who was it? Who was there?

# Chapter Sixteen

Albert stepped out.

I blinked hard. He *was* here! Despite how horrible he'd been to Maddie and me, it felt good to see him.

But he frowned and stared through me as if he was expecting someone else.

'What are you doing here?' he said.

Before I could answer, Albert lowered his voice and hissed, 'Go away.'

I took another step back.

'Don't you remember what I said?'

His head looked shorn and bald in places, as if he'd cut his hair himself. It made his ears stick out like handles. If his eyes hadn't been like saucers it would've been funny. But his face looked thin and pale against his favourite, red woollen jumper, as if he'd been ill and shut inside for weeks. He was in such a state my worries came flooding back.

He glanced behind him before turning back to me.

'You're not welcome here!'

He tried to shut the door. Why was Albert being like this? I felt the knot in my stomach twist. Had he joined the soldiers? Was he working for them? I ran up the three steps.

'Just you listen, Albert Brodeur,' I said, sticking my foot in the way and crossing my arms tight. 'I'm here on official business and it's nothing to do with you.'

His eyebrows jumped up his bare, white forehead and he stared, as if he thought I was mad.

'I've brought the bread for the house,' I said, pointing to the bicycle laden with baskets, 'from Amma.'

He peered round the half-closed door with one eye on me as if it might be a joke, but when he saw the bread his whole body relaxed.

'Alright then,' he said, nodding.

I reached for the first basket.

'Not here,' he said. 'Go round the back, to the kitchens. My mother will meet you there.'

The door slammed shut. My mouth hung open. The knot in my stomach began to pulse, and with pursed lips I wrenched the bicycle away from the wall and banged it around the side of the house.

'Round the back,' I muttered. 'Treating me like a servant.' Albert was acting as if we'd never been friends.

Then I stopped dead.

I forgot my anger because, behind the house, I couldn't see anything but soldiers. There were so many. Rows and rows of tents – a sea of triangles – and uniforms and guns everywhere I looked. This was the war everyone talked about. It was in our town and now our homes, our gardens – everywhere. This was what occupation really meant. I felt their eyes on me and hurried to the kitchen.

Albert's mother stood staring out from the kitchen door. Her hair was wild, as if it was attempting to escape from her bun. It made her look as if she had a halo. Her normally dark brown hair was streaked with grey and she wore no make-up. I'd never seen her without it. I couldn't look away. Her eyebrows had always been painted on and she'd worn a crimson colour on her lips that she said she'd found especially to match the tubs of flowers outside the front door. Now, without her powder, her face looked crumpled. Her cheeks sagged, her eyes seemed to turn downward, her mouth looked thin.

Before I could speak, she put a finger to her lips and looked over my shoulder.

'Delivery for the kitchen,' she said loudly, 'you can help unpack it if you like.'

I turned and saw two soldiers who'd been watching me turn and walk away.

She scooped up two of the baskets and nudged me to bring the rest in. We laid them on the table and she whipped off the covers, tipped out the loaves, counted them, then gathered them up, placing them into waiting trays on top of a peeling pale blue dresser.

'Always restless,' she muttered, glancing at the soldiers outside. Something cricked in her lower back and she closed her eyes for a moment and sighed, rubbing it, just like Amma. She focused on me. 'Tell Amma, thank you.'

I nodded and looked at the empty baskets. It had all been too quick, too much of a shock with everything changed, a hundred soldiers outside and Albert slamming the door in my face. I needed to think up an excuse to stay so I could look for the list Grizzly Grey Beard had talked about.

'Well,' Albert's mother said, trying again, 'I expect you're as busy as I am.'

'Would it be alright if I saw Albert?' I asked.

His mother started as if she'd been asleep. She shook herself, then her eyes went to the bread in their trays and her hands went to her cheeks.

'I must get on,' she said and began spreading out the loaves so they weren't touching each other. Then she turned on the taps and let the water fill the sink behind her.

'Could I see Albert, Madame Brodeur?'

She jumped as if she'd forgotten I was there. Her brow wrinkled and she rubbed her eyes again. She shook her head and reached for my arm.

'I'm afraid he's too busy to play,' she said with a shrug. 'He has errands to run for the Kommandant.'

A shiver ran down my spine. Had Albert joined the enemy or was he just having to help them, like his mother, like Amma?

Somewhere a small bell chimed. She stiffened, then thrust two of the four trays into the oven and slammed the door. Within seconds two different soldiers burst in. I jumped out of the way, pressed myself against the sink and turned off the taps before it overflowed. Suddenly the kitchen was a hive of activity.

One soldier barked something in German at Albert's mother and she looked as if she was ignoring them, but I saw her shoulders tighten and her mouth twist as if she'd swallowed something nasty.

She placed a silvered tray on the table. It was a rectangle with chopped off edges decorated with scrawls and feather-shaped leaves that Albert told me were from walnut trees. On the tray sat a matching teapot and sugar bowl. I knew them, they were her best; they'd been in the family for generations.

Albert's mother added a pale blue milk jug then took the nearest tray of rolls out of the oven and placed two onto a matching plate with her fingers as if she didn't feel their heat. She added a small pot with a smear of a rich, red jam and a round pat of butter with tiny droplets of water on it. Her hand lingered on the edge of the tray as the second soldier lifted it away and left. She breathed out a long sigh, but then three more soldiers came in.

They were lifting boxes and jars out of the pantry and putting them on the table. Another soldier walked through the back door with two rabbits slung over his shoulder. A fifth took my baskets off the table and placed them on top of each other in a corner. The table groaned with food. I'd never seen so much in one place, not even at the *tabac* or the café. No one had this much.

I dragged my eyes away and edged around the table towards the blue dresser. Was anyone taking any notice of me?

The door to the hallway was open. I peered into the corridor beyond. Empty.

I knew Amma would realise where I was. She'd be angry and would expect me back soon, but the list was here, the one the Resistance was looking for, the one that would say where Father was.

If Albert was working for them he might know something or he could tell me where to look . . . if I could find him before someone found me.

This might be my only chance. Monsieur X said you had to grasp every opportunity. In *The Mystery of the Vanishing Jewels* he'd used a distraction to make his escape. I grinned. I could use the soldiers as mine.

I slid towards the door, watching the soldiers' reflection in the copper saucepans hanging on the wall. Their backs were all to me. I'd slipped halfway out of the kitchen when I felt a hand on my shoulder.

# Chapter Seventeen

Albert's mother gripped me. Her hair had almost completely spilt out of its bun, her eyes were wide and she kept glancing over her shoulder like she had a tic. Behind her the soldiers unloaded even more food onto the table, laughing and jostling each other.

'Eloise! Don't go into the house,' she said.

'I wasn't,' I said, shaking my head. 'I mean, I was just looking and –'

'You mustn't be angry with Amma,' Albert's mother said then, as if she hadn't heard me.

'But I'm not,' I said, except she wasn't listening.

'We all do what we must.'

Albert's mother looked at the soldiers again.

'Our children need to eat.'

Then she turned and put a hand to my cheek. It felt dry and cracked, like a piece of tree bark.

'I'm just keeping Albert safe,' she said, tightening her hand on my shoulder. 'I had no choice.'

One of the soldiers shouted to her and Albert's mother flinched.

'None of us do,' she whispered, and scurried back to the table. There was a sharp smell of burning, but it was enough like toast to make my stomach rumble again. I ducked aside as another soldier carrying a steaming coffee pot walked out into the hall. I looked at Albert's mother. She seemed really worried about me going into the house. What was she so afraid of? I bit my lip. The door to the hallway was still open. She bent towards the oven to take out the remaining trays and I slid out of the kitchen, letting the door close softly behind me. I couldn't let her worries stop me.

It was dark in the corridor, but empty.

On my left it led away to the bedrooms Albert said were for guests, though I didn't remember him ever having any. Ahead of me lay the front of the house, and before that, the grand staircase. I watched the soldier with the tray and the coffee pot disappear up its steps.

Where would Albert be? And where was the list? It was a big house after all. Suddenly my plan seemed impossible, like looking for a needle in a whole field of haystacks.

The grandfather clock on my left chimed a quarter

past the hour. I stared at the silver pendulum swinging back and forth, then edged forwards. The clock ticked and tocked, matching my footsteps. It was taller than me. Even Albert's father had to get a chair to reach the top to wind it up. Where was he now? I wondered. Had he been arrested too?

I passed the *salon* on my right with its door shut tight, then the library on my left. That door was ajar, so the room was clearly being used for something. A sliver of light beckoned. I'd been in the library before. It was old, neglected. Some of the books were damp and covered in mould and others were dusty and hidden under sheets. We weren't supposed to touch them, Albert and I, but sometimes, with Maddie, we'd come in and search for treasure maps or make dens out of the sheets using the books for walls. I edged to the gap and whispered.

'Albert?'

Nothing.

I peered round the door, then caught my breath.

The library had been transformed.

The books stacked on the floor had been put back into their cases and locked in, the glass shining with polish. The table in the centre had been made into a desk and had a lamp on it, as well as papers, a fountain pen and a bottle of ink. There was a framed picture sitting there too and a telephone. I stepped in to look and noticed the rug under my feet. It was a deep rich red, green and cream with a brown and gold chain pattern around the edge. I frowned. It looked familiar.

Then I remembered. It was the rug from the *salon*, the one Albert's mother said was an antique. One time Maddie and I had been trying to count the whorls and Albert had been tracing the loops with a stick from the garden and she'd told us off. It was too precious to play on, she'd said.

Now it was spread under the table and I could see dips where the legs had sunk into its soft folds. A wastepaper basket lay on its side behind the table and a pen had rolled onto the rug, its head leaking what little ink was left in it onto a cream bit of wool. I felt sick. Albert's mother would be so upset.

I bent to scrape at the ink with my nails, but it was no use, the pen was stuck to the rug.

I straightened the wastepaper basket. It was full of paper and one piece caught my eye. I pulled it out and more paper came with it. It had pages and pages folded behind it. The heading had been ripped off, but the list underneath was clear. It was a list of names.

I gulped.

I ran my finger down them, checking each one, then flipped the page and did the same on the next page and the next. It wasn't in any order I could understand. There were names beginning with B next to those beginning with F next to names beginning with C. There was a letter after some of the names too. There was a J next to one and a Z next to another. I thought of Antoine calling Maddie "Gypsy scum". He'd used a German word that began with a Z . . . And François had said the Germans were looking for Jews too – J. My hands gripped the paper so hard I almost tore through it. Jews. Gypsies. All being sent away on the trains. Along with Resistance fighters . . . like Father.

I glanced at the door then took a breath, straightened the page and traced down the list with a shaking finger, but I couldn't find Father's name. I got to the end and clutched the papers. He had to be there, surely? I felt a fluttering in my chest, panicking that I'd missed it. I listened out for footsteps then, hearing nothing, I looked inside the wastepaper basket again and saw another sheaf of papers. I pulled those out and started again.

Nothing. His name wasn't there.

I thrust the papers back into the wastepaper basket. If they had been thrown away, perhaps they were old papers. Maybe there were newer ones somewhere . . . I stared around the room, my eyes flicking to the door every few seconds. There was a small bureau with books stacked on top so I checked underneath them then tried to pull out each of the little bureau doors, but they were locked.

I turned back to the desk. There was a heavy-looking book placed just in front of the telephone with the name of the house on its spine. I saw something sticking out underneath and pulled out more papers. Bits of golden lettering flaked off the book onto the desk.

These papers looked similar, but the heading on the papers was clear and the odd-looking cross was embossed at the top. I scratched it with my fingernail as if I could rub it out. I couldn't read the German underneath, but I made out the word *bahn*, which I knew meant something to do with trains from the classes we'd had at school.

I felt a tingle up and down my back.

This time the names were in alphabetical order.

I began to work my way through the list, my heart pounding wildly when I saw the words – Father's name was on the second page.

My finger stopped on the B of Baudin then pressed hard on the R of Robert as if it could make him appear.

I swallowed.

There was no letter after his surname, but I noticed a faint red stamp across the page. It was barely there, but once I'd seen it I couldn't unsee it. *Natzweiler-Struthof.*

Something about that word was familiar. I closed my eyes tight and begged my brain to remember. What was it Monsieur X said about remembering things? I tried to clear my mind to focus on just this one thing.

Then it came.

'If we're not careful,' Grizzly had said in Madame Levee's house, 'we'll all end up in Struthof.'

My eyes shot open. So it was a place the Germans sent people to! But was it where these people were now, or where they were going to on the train? And why had Grizzly sounded so afraid when he said it? I felt as if the carpet was swirling around me. The floor tipped and I put a hand on the desk to steady myself and that's when the door to the library banged open.

I looked around for a place to hide, but it was too late.

An angry German voice barked an order. Boots clicked on the wooden floor of the corridor as he shouted at someone behind him. Then there was a terrible silence. He was here.

# Chapter Eighteen

A pair of polished shoes marched into the library and stopped in front of me. I looked up, and my stomach lurched. It was the Kommandant.

His skin was pale and waxy, his expression blank.

I froze, and his eyes moved to the papers in my hand, but before I could say anything he shouted something over my head. I screwed my eyes shut and hunched over, waiting for the soldiers to come and get me. This was it. I'd be taken away and I wouldn't have time to tell François or any of them anything about what I'd found. And Amma! What if Amma never knew what had happened to me? But no one came. Instead, the door to the library clicked shut.

I opened my eyes.

No soldiers had come in, but the Kommandant was still there, still watching me.

I swallowed.

He waited.

I racked my brain to come up with an excuse for being here. Quickly, I forced myself to look apologetic and pretended to straighten the wastepaper basket.

'I am sorry, monsieur,' I said, my voice sounding high and squeaky. I coughed. 'I hoped to be finished before you started work.'

He stared, and suddenly reached his arm forward. I flinched, but all he did was smooth back his hair.

I dropped my eyes and I stood. Every movement felt awkward, like I was a baby deer trying to walk for the first time.

'Your room is clean now,' I said, giving a small curtsey, backing away.

The Kommandant watched silently. From this distance his eyes looked like black holes.

When my feet reached the rug they *tip-tapped* across the wooden floor. I walked backwards, my eyes on his. When I felt the door against my back, I bobbed a curtsy then turned to grab the handle.

'You forgot something.'

His voice was so low it was almost a whisper, but I heard it so clearly he could have been standing right next to me. I felt a chill on the back of my neck.

He was looking at my hand. I still had the papers! My hand shook!

I swallowed.

'I, I, I . . .'

Suddenly the door opened behind me, pushing me sideways. Albert walked in, looked at me, looked at the papers, then at the man in the dark suit.

'My apologies, Kommandant. A thousand apologies.'

He turned to me, his face red, two high spots of pink on his cheeks. 'Mother says you're not to clean in here, Eloise, you're to help in the kitchen.'

Albert grabbed my arm and turned to the Kommandant, his head bowed, his eyes darting up and then down again. 'She is sorry to have disturbed you. It will not happen again.'

He pulled my arm and I felt a whoosh of relief that I would get out of there after all, but the Kommandant spoke again.

'Eloise.'

It was half whisper, half question. I froze.

I stopped. Albert gave me a look then dropped my arm. I gulped, my eyes wide, my legs shaking as well as my hands. I took a breath and forced myself to turn round to face him.

The Kommandant waited, staring, then his eyes dropped to my hands.

'Will you only be throwing out those papers, and not the rest?'

I twitched, looked down at the overflowing wastebasket and shook my head.

Albert answered for me. 'No, no, no, Kommandant, she will take everything.'

He moved towards the rubbish, but the Kommandant put up a hand to stop him, then curled his fingers, beckoning me to come forward.

I glanced at Albert, but he was looking at the floor as if there was something really interesting there.

I took a deep breath then walked heel-toe, heel-toe across the rug, feeling my feet dip into its softness as if it was sucking me forwards.

When I was standing in front of him I looked at the wastepaper basket and reached for the rest of the papers. His fingers wrapped round my wrist.

I squealed.

He unfurled my hand from the list, taking it from me. Then he looked over my head to where Albert stood spooked in the doorway. 'There is no need to clean this room whatsoever,' he said. Then he turned to me, bending close to my ear.

'Did you know what was in the tin, Eloise?' he whispered.

I stepped back, looked up at him.

'I . . . I don't know what you mean, monsieur.' My words scratched against my dry throat.

His eyes were as deep and dark as the quarry pool we used to swim in before the war. I wanted to shut my eyes to stop him looking into mine and finding my secrets, but I couldn't. It was as if he'd forced them open.

He dropped my wrist.

I gasped and ran back to Albert, who was standing as though stuck, half in and half out of the doorway. I pushed him through in front of me, twisting back to pull the door shut behind us. As I did, I caught a glimpse of the Kommandant staring after us. The corners of his lips were turned up in a copy of a smile, and it was the scariest thing I'd ever seen.

I shut the door and turned to Albert. The Kommandant knew I'd put the tin in the church. He knew I was with the Resistance – I had to get out of here!

Albert was staring at the floor and panting slightly. I shook his arm, then when he didn't shift I clicked my fingers in front of his face.

'Albert?'

Nothing. I turned towards the kitchen, but heard boots echoing on the wooden floor. *Trap, trap, trap, trap.* Two soldiers were coming in from the back of the house. Had the Kommandant summoned them to take me away?

I pulled on Albert's arm. 'Albert, soldiers! I need to hide! Where can I go?'

Behind us the floorboards in the library began to creak. The Kommandant was coming too. If he knew about the tin, he must know I was working for the Resistance. If he'd looked at the papers, he'd know I'd been trying to steal them. People had disappeared for so much less.

'Albert!' I hissed, my heart racing.

But all Albert did was walk over to the tapestry opposite us and touch the picture of the horse pulling a carriage on it. Was it my imagination, or did I hear a *click*, and was the tapestry now rippling beneath his fingers?

'Help me!' I cried.

The tapestry blew out towards us briefly, lifting away from the wall, and revealing something I'd never known about the big house.

# Chapter Nineteen

Albert slipped into the slim alcove behind the tapestry, dragging me with him.

We heard the door to the library groan open, followed by the clip of the Kommandant's shoes stepping out into the hall.

'Halt!'

We didn't need to know a lot of German to understand what he wanted the soldiers to do.

We could hear the clock *tick-tock* and the boots *trip-trap* down the hallway towards us. They stopped right in front of the tapestry. Albert caught his breath.

The Kommandant muttered something to the soldiers, but I couldn't understand a word. I pressed into the back wall of the alcove as if I could melt through it, and discovered it wasn't made of stone as I'd expected. I felt around with my left hand. It was smooth, though parts of it stuck out and dug into my back and legs. I traced shapes, squares that felt like wooden panels. I chanced a look at Albert but he was staring straight ahead.

Suddenly he began to shake. It made the tapestry shake too.

The footsteps were clicking away from us now, but anyone else could pass by. If he didn't stop, we were going to be caught. I squeezed his hand and mouthed for him to keep calm, but it was as if he didn't know I was there.

I let go of Albert's trembling hand and pressed the panels behind me, but the wood was solid.

The boots paused, then moved back towards us along the corridor, getting closer and closer.

Then I felt it. There was a notch, a hole. I pushed two fingers into it and heard a click, then gasped as a whole section of the panelling disappeared behind me. I fell back with it and grabbed for Albert's hand at the last moment, dragging him with me. We toppled onto a hard floor. I heard the boots come to a stop on the other side of the tapestry, just before the panel clicked shut again.

We huddled together. It was so dark I couldn't see him, though I could hear him panting.

'Shhhhh,' I whispered, as loudly as I dared.

Albert shushed.

There was a scuffling sound, as if the tapestry had been pushed aside, then we could hear hands pressing against the wood. My heart thumped in my stomach, my throat and my head, all at the same time. Then there was nothing. Silence. The soldiers had gone.

I dropped Albert's hand.

'Where are we?' I whispered.

He didn't answer. He sounded as if he was trying to remember how to breathe.

I got to my feet and felt around with my hands, reaching out, trying to get a sense of the place. Was it a cupboard? Were we stuck in here? Panic gripped my throat and I stepped towards where I thought the door would be, but I tripped over Albert and fell hard. Dust flew up and I coughed, then panicked the soldiers would hear, but I couldn't stop. Albert thumped me on the back and, after what seemed like for ever, I finally caught my breath. I took a deep gulp of air, expecting the stale taste of dust, but it was fresh and icy cold. I could feel a breeze.

I remembered the way the tapestry had seemed to lift and fall, and yet we'd been in the middle of the house. The breeze must have come from in here, from an exit. That meant there was another way out!

'El?'

'Shhh.'

I was concentrating. If I turned my cheek to the left, I could just feel a tickle of fresh cold air. If I turned my head right – nothing.

I turned my head left again and stood up straight. My knees cracked.

'What is it?' Albert whispered.

'A way out,' I said, 'I think.'

'Oh, that,' he said.

I turned towards his voice.

'What do you mean?'

'Well, I know where the way out is,' he said.

The knot in my stomach twisted. He'd acted like he was a statue and then had been so scared and shaking, he'd nearly got us caught. Now he was saying he knew how to escape all along, as if none of that had happened, and this was just a game.

I narrowed my eyes. They were beginning to adjust to the dark, and I could see a standing, Albert-sized shape now.

'I can show you,' he said, 'if you like.'

'If I like!'

'Shhhhhh,' he said. 'I've got a torch here, somewhere. I keep it for emergencies.'

I watched him scrabble around, then a light beamed straight into my eyes. I twisted away.

'Sorry.'

My eyes saw white, red and purple shapes, then slowly I made out Albert, now sitting on a stack of old cushions piled into one corner. Behind him was a thick wall crusty with cobwebs and some things that looked like the kind of barnacles you find under a boat. I turned in a slow circle. To his left was the back of the panelling. It stretched much further than the door we'd come through, and covered one whole wall. Behind me was another wall, made of old stone, which bent round in a curve towards a thin, pitch-black opening. We were in what felt like a large cupboard. I grinned, because this wasn't an ordinary cupboard – it had a secret passage.

'Where does this lead?' I asked Albert.

'Out,' he mumbled.

'Out where?'

'To the old barn.'

I knew the barn he meant. It was patched with crumbling cream stone and wooden beams, and slanted to the right as if it was sinking into the ground.

'I'll show you,' Albert said, 'but we should hide for now. The soldiers will be looking for you. This is a good place to wait until they've checked the house and grounds.'

'They'll be looking for you too,' I said.

Albert snorted. 'I don't think so. Here.'

Albert threw me a cushion. Threads hung from it as if a cat had half scratched it to death.

The secret passage in the wall was inviting. I just wanted to get away from here, but Albert was probably right. I put the cushion on the floor and sat on it, my arms hugging my knees. I looked across at Albert. Something didn't feel right. Why wouldn't they be searching for him as well? I thought about the names he'd called Maddie and how he'd told me to go away at the door. He was talking and acting like them . . . Perhaps it was worse than I thought. Maybe Albert wasn't being forced to work for the Germans . . . Maybe he *wanted* to? My own best friend? Could that be true?

Albert sat up and rested his head against the crusty wall. 'This is such a mess. I told you not to come.'

He picked up the torch and began to toss it from hand to hand. The light flipped round the room. It made me feel sick.

'Stop it.'

Albert carried on as if he hadn't heard.

'Albert, stop that!'

'I know already,' he said suddenly, 'if that's what you're worried about.'

He pointed the torch at my face.

I shut my eyes and turned away.

'Know what?'

'About Amma. About you. About everything.'

Cold air breathed down my neck from the passageway. I shivered. It was the way he'd said Amma's name, like it was a bad word, which was strange because Albert had always loved Amma.

'What about Amma?' I said.

'Nothing.' He shrugged. 'Except I know she works for the Germans too.'

My eyes couldn't settle on his face – the light from the torch made a shifting outline, creating Albert-shaped shadows.

'She's not the only one,' I said. 'Your mother works for them.'

Albert flinched at that. 'She was forced.' He sounded pained. 'You don't understand what it's like.'

'Because I don't have a mother?' I said, staring back into the light until my eyes watered.

Albert blanched. 'No, no! I meant because we had no choice but to give up our house for them. We have to *live* alongside them, every second of every day.'

'And give them the garden and Maddie's house too then,' I said, staring at the floor.

'It's not Maddie's house,' Albert snapped back. 'It's ours, we own it. We own yours too. It's only an old barn,' he said. 'We could take it away anytime we liked.'

'Just like you did with Maddie's?' I got to my feet. 'Will you have us disappear as well?'

Albert started to speak then shut his mouth. The light moved away from my face to shine up at the ceiling again.

'You're stupid to think you can do anything to change things,' he snarled.

My head snapped up.

'Oh, I know about that too,' he said.

I tried to keep the tremor from my voice. 'Know about what?'

'The Resistance,' he said. 'I know you're with them.'

# Chapter Twenty

I gulped.

How could Albert know about the Resistance? Had he been following me? Had the Kommandant made him spy on the whole town?

The knot in my stomach turned into a stone, hard and round and heavy. My eyes darted to the secret passageway before I forced them back to his. Looking away was a real giveaway, Monsieur X said. It would reveal your intentions. I took a deep breath.

'I don't know what you mean,' I said, trying to keep my voice level.

'Yes, you do,' he said, scrambling to his feet. 'Eloise, it's alright. I know because I'm in it too!'

I kept my face as still as possible. I didn't believe him. If Albert had been shut away in the big house for weeks, how could he be working for the Resistance? Yet how else could he know about me helping them if he *wasn't* in the Resistance?

He held out a dusty-looking, green, glass bottle and flipped open the top. The cork was sticky with sugar. I reached for it and gulped the lemonade down.

He came closer.

'If we're both working for them, we should help each other.' He fiddled with the switch on the torch. 'François said I could help them from the inside, since I'm around the soldiers all the time. That's why I stayed here.'

Albert held the torch between us. He'd said François' name, but what did that mean? Did he know him? Or just know *of* him? Was he really with the Resistance, or was this a trap?

'Mother wanted me to escape from here, but after Father . . .' Albert stared at me. The light from the torch made dark circles under his eyes. 'When they took him, I had to do something to fight back.'

I gasped. Albert's father had been taken too!

For a moment neither of us said anything. Cold air breathed in and out of the secret passage. I put the empty lemonade bottle onto the floor and asked the thing that could make all the difference between us.

'Why did Maddie go?'

Albert didn't answer.

'Did you tell them she was a Gypsy?'

He shook his head, staring only at the floor.

'That's what you called her,' I said. 'That horrible German word for Gypsy, but Maddie was just Maddie. She wasn't dangerous.'

His hand gripped the torch.

'I didn't tell them,' he said.

'I don't believe you – you threw stones at us!' I said.

Albert looked up. 'She was my friend too, El.'

I thought about the last time we were all together. Before everything changed. We'd promised to pick redcurrants for Albert's mother. She'd given us baskets and a picnic to share; a bottle of home-made lemonade – exactly like the one Albert had just given me – boiled eggs, a lump of cheese and the rolls I'd brought from Amma. We picked the berries till our palms were red then ate our lunch by the river. Maddie and I had plunged our scratched hands into the cool water. Albert had jumped in, fully clothed, splashing us both. We'd screamed then laughed.

A smile crept onto my face, but another cold breeze set me shivering.

'You weren't her friend,' I said. 'Not when it mattered.'

Albert pulled at his jumper. I noticed the ends were ragged, as if they'd caught on something. Now that he was close, I noticed that he smelt a little too, as if he'd worn that jumper for days.

'I didn't mean what I said,' he started to say, but when

I snorted he met my eyes and hissed, 'I didn't!'

He stared at the floor, at the ceiling, at the pile of cushions. Anywhere but at me. He sounded sincere, but these were telltale tics that he was lying. My head and heart hurt trying to work out what was true and what wasn't.

'Antoine had said things about Mother, that people were talking about her helping the Germans. But he said he was on my side, and would tell them she didn't have a choice; that she had to help them because of Maddie's family being on our land.' Albert took a breath. 'He said it was the Gypsies' fault the soldiers were in France anyway. It was just words, just a stupid game, at first . . .'

I crossed my arms and met his eyes. Just a game. More like Albert felt he had to act that way to prove the Brodeur family honour. No matter who he hurt.

He returned my glare fiercely, then, all of a sudden, the fight left him. His shoulders drooped.

'You have to believe me.'

I still wasn't sure what I believed.

'We could work for the Resistance together, El,' he said. 'You and me. Like before. Remember?'

The last time we'd played detectives we'd fought over who would play Monsieur X. I felt it should be me because, one, they were my books and I knew him best, and two, I was going to be a detective, but Maddie had whispered an idea to me. We'd let Albert be Monsieur X, then we'd hide and give him the fright of his life.

'He'll hunt us, but he won't find us,' she'd said, 'and meantime, we can have these.'

She'd put her hand into the pocket of her red and green striped summer dress and pulled out a handful of sugared almonds left over from her sister's wedding. I'd grinned and let Albert be detective. He'd smiled so hard Maddie and I had almost felt guilty, but not enough to share our sweets.

The idea that we could work together in the Resistance felt so exciting, like we'd be playing Monsieur X for real this time, but something didn't feel quite right.

'Come on. The patrols will have got bored looking for you by now. I'll show you the way out,' Albert said, taking my hand.

I paused. 'Why don't you think they'll be looking for you too?' I said.

He shrugged. 'I live here,' he said simply. 'I'll be fine. I'll say I didn't see where you went.'

I frowned. That wasn't exactly an answer, though he didn't look nervous any more, just hopeful.

He said he hadn't told the Germans about Maddie, but he'd also called her Gypsy scum and acted like he never wanted to see either of us again. Had he meant it? Maybe it had it all been an act to gain their trust? To be able to stay in the house and learn things he could pass on to the Resistance?

I had to think this through like Monsieur X would. I had to ask the right questions.

'Why did you tell me to get lost?'

Albert blinked. 'You've seen what it's like out there,' he said. 'There are soldiers everywhere. They don't need much of an excuse to pick on locals. I was worried about you.'

'I'm not talking about today,' I said. 'Before, with Maddie. You told us *both* to get lost.'

This time his face reddened. He swallowed.

'You have to believe me, El,' Albert said, 'I never meant to hurt Maddie. It was supposed to be a warning, for both of you. To watch out for people like Antoine. He would have done worse than throw stones if you'd stuck around or fought back.'

I rubbed my nose.

'Look, El, you can trust me. My father was arrested for no good reason.' Albert shook his head. 'I don't even know where they've taken him. I've only got Mother left now. I'm just doing what it takes to keep her safe.'

I shut my eyes and saw my own father's face floating in front of me. I would do anything to get him back.

'Eloise?'

I stared at Albert's outstretched hand.

Maybe he was sorry and maybe he was telling the

truth about being in the Resistance. Maybe his father's name was on the list too. Maybe I could rescue both of them. And our friendship. If he passed my test.

'I'm not leaving,' I said, turning back towards the house. 'Yet.' I took his hand. 'I need something from the library.'

Albert's eyes widened, but before he could speak, I carried on.

'The papers I took? They had Father's name on. It was a list of prisoners being taken away on a train. The Resistance need it so they can work out how to rescue them. Maybe your father's with them.' I crossed my arms. 'We need to get that list to François.'

Albert shook his head double time.

I quailed at the lie I was about to tell my best friend, but I had no choice. I needed that list and I wasn't sure Albert would help. 'This is my first proper assignment,' I said. 'François wants me to steal it, or I can't be part of the Resistance . . . and you and I won't get to work together.'

Albert paled.

'Look, there are so many names on there, Albert. People's mothers, fathers, brothers, sons.'

He looked away.

'Nan said everyone had lost someone,' I said, 'and if we get the list, we can at least get some of those people back. My father, Albert. And maybe yours.'

# Chapter Twenty-One

My words hung between us.

Albert stared at the floor, shuffling from foot to foot. 'What are you going to do?' he said eventually. 'March back in? Ask the Kommandant nicely?'

I flinched. 'I don't know.'

The truth was that when I thought about the Kommandant – his cold smile, his grip on my wrist, the violence in his voice – I wasn't sure whether I could really do this.

'It's not a game, El. Monsieur X makes it look easy, but helping them isn't like that. You have to think, to plan. If you go back in there now you'll be caught . . . and taken away.'

I glared at him, then my jaw dropped. He was wrong – Monsieur X did have the answer! In *The Mystery of the Ghost in the Castle*, he'd proved there was no ghost in the end. The castle was filled with secret passageways and doorways just like this room. The town had even thought the detective was the ghost for a while. Then he'd shown them the castle's secrets.

I took a breath. 'Are there any more passageways or hidden rooms like this one?' I looked around the room. 'Anything that could get us back into the library?'

Albert's mouth twitched, as if he was about to tell me something, then he stared at the floor.

'Nothing useful.' He paused. 'You'd be safer at home,' he said, scuffing a shoe in the dust. 'I want to find the prisoners as much as you, but the Resistance can find another way. You were lucky I was able to help you in the library, El. Next time, I might not be able to save you from the Kommandant.'

I cringed at that, but I couldn't let it stop me. The papers were here. Why should someone else take the risk, and not me when I was right here, right now? I searched for the panelling notch that opened the door. When I found it I turned back to Albert, grinning, and my foot knocked something. A canvas bag toppled over.

'Wait!' Albert called, crossing to me quickly.

I pulled the bag towards me. Something inside it crackled and chinked. Inside I found another two bottles of lemonade, some dry crusted rolls, a wrinkled apple, and bars and bars of chocolate. I gasped.

'Albert, there's so much food here . . .'

I picked up a roll and bit into it. It was still good.

'They're not mine,' Albert said quickly, his eyes darting to the chocolate bars.

I pulled one of them out. It was wrapped in reddish-brown paper with a white word across the front: *Schokolade*.

I turned to Albert, the bar heavy in my hand.

'They didn't give them to me,' he said, his voice squeaking, 'if that's what you're thinking. I stole them.'

I glanced inside the bag. There were at least twenty bars in the bag, maybe more.

'From the kitchen,' Albert carried on. 'There's a door at the back of the pantry. They think it's hidden but I know what they're keeping in there.'

He stared at the floor.

I narrowed my eyes. 'What are they keeping in there?'

He shrugged. 'Secret supplies. Chocolate and things. It's where I got those.' He picked up a bar. 'Have one,' he said, but I shook my head. 'You might as well,' he said, dropping it back into the bag. 'You've been eating them for months already.'

I started towards him then stopped. Amma always had enough chocolate for pastries, though I'd never seen it wrapped like this. I thought about her *pain au chocolat*, the papery soft munch of the pastry, the chocolate creamy and thick inside. Had Albert really stolen the chocolate bars or were they payment from the Germans for his help? Something niggled me. I wasn't sure what to believe.

I swallowed the last of the hard roll. I didn't have time for this now. Only one thing mattered.

'I'm not leaving till I get the list,' I said.

Albert huffed. 'There is something . . .' he said. 'Not a way into the library, but somewhere you could hide there, I think. Father told me about it years ago, but I never found it.'

I shook my head. 'That's no good. I need a way out once I've got the list.'

Albert groaned with frustration. Then he rounded on me. 'Look, there's no way you can do this. If you leave now you can go home and be safe. I'll talk to François. We can try to get your list another time. If you try to get it, you'll ruin everything!'

'I need it, Albert,' I said, trying to keep my voice low. 'They could move the prisoners any time. I can't just go home and wait, pretend everything is normal, because it isn't. People are disappearing from town . . . being sent to terrible prisons.' I swallowed. I hadn't wanted to think about this, but if it was the only thing that would convince him. 'Your father might be sent to one – unless we do something about it.'

Something passed across his face then and he sighed, resigned.

'Alright,' he said. 'I'll get you time in the library, but I can't promise you long.' He came closer. His breath smelt of chocolate. My stomach turned and rumbled at the same time. 'Then you have to go,' he said. 'Promise?'

I nodded, almost fainting with relief.

'Come back here when you're done.' He pointed to the secret passageway. 'It goes down a bit, then along for quite a while. The door at the end is heavy, but if you push it hard enough, you'll get into the barn. You'll have to be quiet along the passageway, quiet as a mouse.' He swallowed. 'There are soldiers everywhere.' He held the torch out to me. 'You can have this.'

I took it. 'What if I don't make it back here?'

Albert looked me straight in the eyes. 'Then you'll be caught,' he said. 'And there'll be nothing I can do.'

I gulped.

For a few seconds we stared at each other.

'Ready?' he asked.

I nodded.

Albert put his ear to the back of the panelling. 'Stay behind the tapestry until the coast is clear,' he said, then looked down at the torch. 'You'll want to save the battery.'

I switched it off, put it on the floor and waited.

Albert opened the panelling and was gone. I slipped out behind him and flattened myself into the alcove.

He was braver than I thought, to help me. I'd been

wrong to doubt him. He *had* to be with the Resistance. My heart was only thudding so loud because I was nervous, not because I was worried he might be about to hand me over to the enemy . . .

# Chapter Twenty-Two

I pressed my back against the panelling. I could hear a knock at the library door, then a groan as it opened. Albert spoke, but I couldn't make out the words.

The Kommandant didn't say anything.

Silence stretched out.

I let out a slow breath, then held it in again as Albert's voice rang loud and clear.

'I promise, Kommandant. I saw her. She went that way. We might still catch her..'

I felt a roar in my head, my muscles tightened as if I was getting ready to run a race. I swallowed the lump in my throat then peered round. Albert was following the Kommandant away from me.

The man in the dark suit went ahead slowly. For a moment it seemed like he wasn't walking, but gliding. His polished shoes didn't click across the wooden floor like the soldiers' boots. Albert turned and caught my eye, twitched his head towards the library, then hurried on.

'I promised, didn't I?' he said again to the Kommandant.

I slipped out from behind the tapestry and, after looking left and right and seeing no one, I raced across the hallway and slid into the library. I shut the door behind me, wincing as it clicked.

The library was just as I'd left it. I darted behind the table and sifted through the wastebasket. But it wasn't there.

I spread out each sheaf of papers from the basket in front of me, running a finger down them, but only one had the red and black cross and none of them said the word *bahn*.

I thought about how the Kommandant had taken the papers from me. Perhaps he'd put them somewhere else now? But there were no papers on his desk at all. I noticed a small cabinet wedged underneath the right hand side of the desk. Maybe the list was in there.

Suddenly there was a clicking noise.

I stood up, my heart beating so loud I could feel it in my mouth. My throat felt tight. The clicking got louder and louder. Boots! Boots on the floor outside!

I looked left and right, then back at the desk. I couldn't hide under it; there wasn't enough room. The clicking was close. I felt prickles all over my back. The clicking reached the door. I was about to race to the wall, press myself against it so I'd be behind the door when it opened, when the clicking passed and faded away.

The soldier had walked on.

I opened my eyes and let out a long breath.

On the desk was a blue glass paperweight with bubbles of air trapped inside and a heavy silver frame with a picture of a pale woman wearing a lot of make-up, her blonde curls pinned under a hat with a net on it – like the one the woman had been wearing in the car. I peered closer and could see a beauty spot above her top lip. It was the same woman. She must be his wife. I thought about Albert's mother and how she'd worn a lot of make-up, once. Now this woman was living in her house and using her tea set.

I lifted up a blotter, flipped through the ream of clean sheets underneath, but there were no papers. I'd have to try the cabinet.

I rattled the top drawer, but it wouldn't open. I tried the second, third and bottom, but they were all still locked. I turned back to the desk. There had to be a key.

I ran my hands across it, lifting everything. I found the small key hiding beneath a stack of blotting paper, and was about to put it into the lock when I heard the door handle turn.

I froze. The handle paused. Voices came from behind

it. The Kommandant and, perhaps, Albert.

I looked at the cabinet, then at the desk, then at the bookcases lining the walls. Albert had said there was somewhere to hide in here, but where? There were two large windows with slivers of daylight peeking between the shutters, but there wasn't time to try to unlock them and escape that way. I looked at the books locked into their glass cases and felt my stomach flip. Why hadn't Albert made his father tell him where the hiding place was?

The door handle started turning again, the door opening slowly inwards, before stopping to the sound of an urgent voice. I stood and ran left then right towards a tower of books, three books thick, by the wall nearest the door. Then I noticed something. Beside me, one of the glass cases was slightly open, a key sticking out of its lock. On the lower shelves the books inside looked odd – shiny and flat. I leant down, and up close I saw they weren't actual books, but pictures of books. On the higher shelves were two real books that looked as if they were about to fall out. I pushed one back in and to my surprise I heard a *click* then a *clunk*, and all of a sudden a small gap appeared lower down. Where the pictures of books had been, there was now a space wide enough for me to crawl into. I threw myself onto the floor and wriggled into the hole.

The library door rattled as I pulled my legs in and turned round. I felt for the fake wall of books and tried to pull it back across, but it wouldn't move, so I pushed open the glass door of the bookcase and grabbed a small pile of books stacked alongside it, dragging them in front of me. I wondered if the stack of books would be high enough to hide behind, but it was too late to do anything more. The Kommandant was in the room.

I heard him shut the library door and cross to his desk. I kept absolutely still.

The crawl space was dark and dusty. The little light that came in from the opening showed dust motes floating around me like stars. I looked up, but it was pitch black. I tried to move back, but felt the wall, cold and firm behind me.

Then I heard Albert. He was here with the Kommandant!

'I don't think so,' he was saying, his voice shaking.

'When we find her,' the Kommandant said, 'we can ask her.'

'I'm sure it's a mistake,' Albert said.

There was silence.

Ask *her*? Were they talking about me? Ask me what? My legs began to shake as I strained to hear more.

'Our agreement only stands,' the Kommandant said, 'if you do exactly as I say.' There was a pause. 'Wait. What is this?' the Kommandant asked.

I scooted onto my side to peep out of the hole at the bottom, but there wasn't enough room to see.

I heard a book thump, then the tap of something small pressed onto the desk.

The air felt heavy as the Kommandant spoke in a low voice, saying words I couldn't catch.

Then I remembered the key. I'd dropped it when I heard the door! He must have found it out of place, on the floor.

'But I've been with you, Kommandant,' I heard Albert say. His words rolled out faster and faster. 'I told you where she'd gone. I told you everything. Please, I've kept my promise. She's just a simple village girl. She wouldn't know anything. She can't even read properly.'

Inside my hiding space my face reddened. Couldn't read, indeed!

The Kommandant spoke again. His voice was still quiet, but Albert's voice was loud and shrill.

'I don't know,' he replied, 'probably food. Everyone wants food. I doubt she'll be back. Likely frightened off.'

He laughed, but it didn't sound like his normal laugh. It was high pitched, like he was trying to breathe properly.

The Kommandant replied, and though I couldn't make out the words, the menace in his voice was unmistakable.

'Yes,' Albert said. 'Yes, I promise. I understand.'

I heard the squeak of leather, then steps coming towards me, and I tried to make myself even smaller. Had he seen me? Had he seen the open bookcase?

'Then our deal is intact,' the Kommandant said.

He was standing right in front of the bookcase. Through the small gap at the bottom I could see his black shoes pointing towards me. They shone with polish. His suit trousers hung perfectly even over each shoe, folded over once, the line down the front as sharp as if it had been drawn with a ruler.

I held my breath. Sweat dripped down my back. My fingernails pressed into my palms. This was it. I'd be caught for sure.

'Yes, Kommandant,' Albert said. 'I'll do it.'

'Good.'

The glass door swung shut and I heard the key turn in the lock, before they headed back out of the library.

I gulped.

He hadn't caught me, but I was locked in!

The walls pressed in close around me. It was boiling hot. I wiped the hair from my face and tried to catch my breath, but the air was as thick as soup.

My stomach rumbled. The dry roll hadn't been enough and I wished I'd taken one of Albert's chocolate bars. I thought about Amma. She'd be so angry when I got home. If I ever made it home.

Thoughts swirled crazily around my head, but one stood out.

Albert had said that he'd do it. *Do what?*

That was the last thing I remembered before my head hit the floor.

# Chapter Twenty-Three

When I opened my eyes it was pitch black and my skin was hot. Had I shut the window? Where was Amma? I blinked and blinked, trying to get my room into focus, but the darkness stayed. Then, with a jolt, I remembered.

I tried to sit up, but my muscles screamed from being crunched into a ball for so long. I lay back down in an awkward curl and tried to loosen my fists, finger by finger, then flexed my toes. My feet prickled with pins and needles, the backs of my calves as hard as stones. I stretched out my shoulders, turned my neck left and right and slowly felt my body come back to life.

I shifted onto my side, turning my head towards the hole at the bottom of the bookcase.

As I peered through the glass door I followed the sliver of moonlight creeping through the shutters and slicing across the Kommandant's desk. Moonlight! I must have passed out. I'd been stuck in here the whole day! Amma would be more worried than angry now. Maybe she'd even come looking for me and the Kommandant would connect her to me. What if he arrested her?

I had to get out of there.

I shuffled onto my knees, stirring up dust. I coughed and coughed, holding my throat with my hands. It felt scratched inside.

I thought of Albert and wondered why he hadn't come looking for me, then I remembered he'd said he didn't know where this hiding place was. He must have thought I'd left. I was on my own.

A rush of fear almost made me black out again, but I concentrated on moving the books in front of me aside, and felt the glass. I was locked in, but I could break out. It was risky and noisy, but I had no choice.

I took a breath of warm air and tried not to choke on it. Then I leant back, pulled my knees up in front of me and pushed both feet forward, hard.

The glass shattered.

I pushed again, kicking out at the shards to make a space wide enough for me to crawl through. Then, using my heels to dig and pull, and my hands to push, I wriggled through the hole.

Glass tinkled and crunched beneath me like some kind of awful music. I rolled onto my front and shards of glass scratched my legs and arms, and then I was through. I stood, listening hard.

Silence.

But I knew I wouldn't have long. Someone had to have heard the noise. I ran to the desk and reached under the blotter, but the key to the cabinet had gone.

I rattled the cabinet drawers just in case, but they were locked tight. I peered into the wastepaper basket, but it was empty.

This was all taking too long. I couldn't bear to leave the list behind, but if I didn't escape now, I'd end up on it!

I ran to the library door and pulled the handle.

It was locked.

I really was trapped now. Good and proper.

I rattled the door handle again just in case, but it didn't help.

Would the Kommandant greet me with his cold smile when he found me here? I thought about Amma, all the trouble this would bring her, and felt like I might faint again.

I squeezed my eyes tight. I wouldn't let that happen. I couldn't lose her and Father!

When I opened them I saw that I was facing the shutters, moonlight still peeping through them. It lit up the desk like a pointing finger and shone across a large wooden board that had been wheeled in front of the bookcases. It reminded me of the blackboards at school, though this one had a large map of France with black and red pins stuck in it.

I blinked.

Moonlight. Shutters. The window!

I ran to the nearest one, hoping it wouldn't be locked too, and pulled the shutters apart. I lifted the latch up, pulled it back, then gently pushed at the glass. It wouldn't budge. I pressed both hands against it and pushed again. There was a squeak then the glass moved out an inch.

I waited, listening.

Nothing.

Then something caught my eye. I saw that symbol again, the black twisty cross on a sheaf of papers stuck to the board. I crept closer and my heart leapt. The word *bahn* was written at the top. I lifted the paper and sure enough the list of names was underneath. I'd found it! I pulled the top page off and the rest fell, floating to the floor. I gathered them up into my arms, but something else caught my attention.

A book lay on the floor just behind one of the boards. I reached for it and pulled it towards me.

It was a Monsieur X book, but without a proper cover. There was no title, but with its crisp pages, it looked new.

Suddenly there was a noise from behind the door.

I shoved the book and the papers under one arm and

pushed at the window with the other. It squeaked wider. Then, with everything in one hand, I quickly heaved myself onto the windowsill.

Behind me the door rattled and a key moved in the lock.

I pulled my legs up and swung myself over the ledge, and was about to jump out when the library door swung wide.

'Eloise?'

I froze – it wasn't the Kommandant's voice. It was a woman's. I turned and saw a shadow in the doorway. I scrunched my eyes to try to see better. It was the woman from the car!

Suddenly there was a shout from somewhere else in the house. 'Eloise?'

The Kommandant!

I flinched. She flinched.

Then behind her I heard the sound of boots clicking on wood.

Soldiers!

My heart was beating fast, my hands were shaking. I had to get out of here! But in that moment, the woman spoke.

'That's mine,' she said softly, closing the door behind her. She crossed the room as I sat frozen. She could yell and wake the house, call for a hundred soldiers at any time. So as she held out her hand, all I could do was pass her the book.

She stared at it.

'I've always thought authors should use names that are important to them.' She looked up at me. 'Don't you?'

My head was a whirl of confusion. She'd found a strange girl in her husband's office, in the middle of the night. I was obviously trying to escape and she wanted to talk about Monsieur X books?

'Eloise?' shouted the Kommandant. He sounded closer now.

I flinched again, looking behind her to the door.

Her head dropped to one side as if she was sizing me up. 'I could tell him I didn't see you,' she said. 'I could say you were gone by the time I unlocked the door.'

I opened my mouth to ask her why she'd want to help me, but there was a noise outside and she interrupted.

'Go!'

I threw myself out of the window, falling the metre or so to the ground, my shoes squelching into mud. The papers flew out of my hands.

Light flooded the library.

I froze. Then, gathering up the papers as best as I could, I ducked behind the Kommandant's hulking car. I thought about my bicycle. I'd left it round the back of the kitchen, evidence I hadn't actually left the house, but to get it would mean passing all those tents and soldiers. No, it was too late for that now.

I checked left, then right. I could see three trucks parked in a row across the grass, but I couldn't see any soldiers.

From the library, I heard glass crinkle and knew they'd found my hiding place. There was a shout, then a rustle above me and I ducked down further as a soldier jumped out of the window. I had to run – now.

I raced across the gravel, using the trucks for cover, the mud sucking at my shoes. Behind me I read more shouting and a door open and slam back on its hinges.

The gravel was easier to run on, but I knew I couldn't take the road back home. The sentry would be waiting at the gate.

A whistle pierced the air, and fear coiled in my stomach.

I skidded across the edge of the gravel, then, hugging the list tight to my middle, I ran into the grass on my left.

It was hard going. The grass had grown wild and reached up to my thighs. I pulled my way through as if I was wading through a thick sea.

I heard crunching behind me, saw torches flickering through the night. The soldiers had reached the road. I ducked down into the grass and worked my way forward as quietly as I could.

My heart thumped in my mouth, my head, everywhere. I forced my legs up and down, up and down, as I pushed through the meadow – then I stopped dead.

The grass!

I turned and saw the neat pathway I'd made. Flattened grass and mud – a trail that would lead the soldiers right to me.

I kicked out in frustration, looking back at the whole house, lit up now, as if everyone was awake.

I looked around, panic pawing at me. It was too late to get back to the road – the soldiers would catch me if I did – but I had to get out of the meadow. I felt panic push at my back. I had to get away, but how? I forced myself to think. What would Monsieur X do? Where could I go?

I thought of Father.

The forest!

I closed my eyes and tried to remember the way.

Another shout came, from the road this time. They must have found my trail. My eyes snapped open and I ran towards the forest, zigzagging a little to try to make my path less obvious.

I got right to edge of the meadow and crossed into the cool dark of the old trees, but it was too late.

I turned to see four soldiers following my trail, and behind them were another four or five, their torches slicing the night with yellow and white stripes.

The ground ahead of me was rough, hard-going. They'd catch up with me in no time.

I'd never make it.

I had to hide.

I turned to the nearest tree, but the first branch was too high up. I ran on and passed three more till I came to one with a branch low enough for me to swing myself up. I shoved the list down the front of my shirt, reached high and pulled myself onto the lower branch, before reaching out for the next. I'd climbed up three more branches when I heard a crack on the forest floor.

The soldiers were here.

I wrapped my arms around the trunk, the list shushing against my chest. I pressed my cheek into the bark and dug my fingers in. The smell of resin reminded me of last summer. Albert, Maddie and I had made a treehouse.

*Crunch.*

Torchlight swung through the tree trunks.

It had been easy. We'd got the idea from *Monsieur X and the Mystery of the Invisible Man*. We'd placed two planks where three of the tree's branches met the trunk. We'd hung sheets and blankets above us.

*Crack-crunch.*

Soldiers shattered pine cones beneath their boots.

We'd had picnics in the tree until it rained.

I gripped the trunk harder.

The rain had meant the end of summer.

Slivers of bark floated to the forest floor.

The rain also meant a new school term. But would any of us be there next year?

I held my breath.

I could hear whispering.

'Warte mal 'ne Minute.'

The soldiers stopped in response, then there was silence.

No one moved.

I peered down and saw three of the soldiers standing right underneath my tree. They were waiting, listening for any sign of me. Then, from a few metres away, another soldier pointed and the other three followed him.

They crunched their way back to the edge of the forest as I let out a shaky breath.

I counted to twenty, thirty, then a hundred. Then I counted again.

The soldiers didn't come back.

I slid down the trunk, but my hands were tired and they let go too soon. I landed with a *whump* on the forest floor and froze, listening.

I could see the lights of the house through the trees. Torches flickering through the woods in the opposite direction. The soldiers were still looking. They hadn't given up

I got to my feet and ran.

# Chapter Twenty-Four

I darted round the tress, running as fast as I could, jumping over dead branches and fallen pine cones. I felt the soldiers on my heels, imagined I could hear their breath and feel the light of their torches slicing across my back.

I clutched the list to my middle to keep it safe and dry, my breath heaving in-out, in-out like a roar in my ears. I ran for what seemed like hours until suddenly, I couldn't feel anything under my feet.

I slid down a bank of grass and mud and landed at the bottom of a ditch with a squelch. I held still and listened.

Nothing.

I rolled onto my knees, my hands sinking into the gloop, then very slowly stood up. I peered over the edge of the ditch. No shouting. No lights. All around me the forest looked dark and empty.

I sank back, resting my head on the bank, but I hadn't escaped. Not yet.

I grabbed handfuls of the long grass at the top, grateful the blades were like straw from the hot sunny days, and pulled myself out the other side of the ditch. I'd ended up circling through the forest and joining the main road. The road home.

I looked back towards Maison de Noyer and saw the lights were still blazing. I quickly slipped my wet shoes off – a trail of muddy footprints had almost caught Monsieur X out in *The Mystery of the Haunted House* – and then I was running as hard as before. I forgot about making no noise – my breath was rasping. I forgot about how hard the road was and how it dug into my feet and hurt like nothing else. I forgot everything. I only wanted to be home. I only wanted to see Amma.

I ran and ran and ran until our little house loomed out of the dark. It was quiet and there were no lights on of course, because of the curfew, but no one was waiting outside either, no Amma coming out with her gun to warn off strangers.

Was she still there?

I was about to run in when a movement out of the corner of my eye made me pause. There was a scratch and a tiny flame appeared to hover in the air.

I froze.

The flame was attached to a cigarette and the cigarette was attached to a soldier standing right outside our home. He shook out the match, sucked on his smoke and sighed.

I took a step back, then another and another. I looked around, but it was pitch black. I couldn't think of anywhere else to go. If I retraced my steps I'd reach the big house in no time and the soldiers would grab me. They were probably still searching the forest too. Home was my only hope.

I bit the edge of my thumbnail and tried to think. Just then the soldier began to cough. He turned away from the road and I took my chance to tiptoe as quietly as I could behind him, then scurry up the path.

I didn't stop till I reached the back door. I glanced behind me, but I couldn't see him. I lifted the latch, but the door was locked. I dropped to my feet, feeling under the bucket we used for kitchen scraps for the chickens. My fingers touched cold metal. Our spare key. I'd just picked it up when the door swung wide.

I pushed myself flat against the back wall of the house, risked a peek inside.

The kitchen was dark. I couldn't see anything. I thought of Maddie's house with the soldiers living there.

Suddenly an arm reached out and pulled me inside. The door closed quickly and quietly behind me, then a light shone into my face. I turned my head away. Were there soldiers inside?

'*Mon chou!*'

Amma!

I blinked through the harsh light.

'Turn the light away, Felix.'

I turned to see who she was talking to. The blurred red, orange and yellow shapes around the table resolved into François, Nan, and Grizzly Grey Beard. Here was proof that Amma knew them, but I was too distracted to care – Grizzly Grey Beard's name was *Felix*? I began to giggle.

The giggle turned into a laugh and then I doubled over, my arms wrapped around my middle. Felix was the name of our goat. He was grey and had a grizzly beard too. It was perfect. I heard the scrape of chairs one after another and then I was being pulled to sit at the table.

'Not yet, Amma,' François said.

I looked up.

The laughter faded from me just as quickly as it started. I began to cough. I rubbed my nose and was surprised to find it was wet. I was crying and hadn't noticed. I went to wipe my eyes and noticed I still had my shoes in my hands. I dropped them.

Amma handed François a tea towel and he brought it towards me gently. He sat next to me in his scratchy jumper, the sleeves slipping down over his hands. I let him mop my eyes and cheeks as I looked round the table. Nan stood at the top where Amma usually sat and Grizzly – no, Felix – sat on my right. They stared. All of a sudden I felt cold. I began to shiver.

'A blanket,' Nan said, and Amma seemed to conjure one up, which François placed round my shoulders.

I pulled it tight round my neck.

There was a sharp, scraping noise behind me and I jumped, but it was only Felix pulling out a chair.

François muttered something at him that sounded cross and Nan glared at him so fiercely I almost felt sorry for grizzly Felix. Amma, fussing at the stove now, turned and placed a steaming cup of brown liquid on the table in front of me. I lifted the cup towards my mouth. As the steam rose and wound its way up my nose, I gagged. The sweetness reminded me of the sickly smell of Albert's breath and the mould in the hiding place behind the tapestry. Suddenly I was back at the house.

I thought of Albert and all those bars he said he'd stolen, how I'd felt being trapped in the library, wondering if I'd ever escape, and the chase through the forest, running so hard because my actual life depended on it.

'*Schokolade*,' I said, then my shaking hands dropped the cup onto the floor where it smashed. The brown chocolate slid in rivers over the flagstones.

I shook myself. I wasn't stuck in the house or caught

by soldiers. I was home. Safe.

At the far back of the kitchen the old stove pumped out warmth towards me. I looked up to see Amma's familiar housecoat, the sleeves of her blouson pushed up her thick arms, her face round and warm. Her cheeks were red from the heat in the room; a thin film of sweat lay across her forehead and her hair was bound up in curlers beneath her headscarf. She wiped her hands on her apron. White flour fell to the floor like soft powdered snow. I stared at the flagstones. The river of chocolate. I thought of the house. The soldier outside!

For a moment the kitchen lurched sideways. My stomach flipped over.

'There's someone, a soldier, outside. I had to –'

'He's gone,' Felix said, his eyes sliding to the shutters and back again.

'They've been walking past all day,' François said. 'We'd come to offer Amma our help finding you. Then the patrol arrived and we couldn't leave.'

I shut my eyes. I'd put them all in such danger.

I felt Amma's hand on my arm.

'*Mon chou*,' she said.

When I opened them again the floor was clean. I let the blanket fall away and felt my chest, pressing a hand to my middle.

'Are you hurt?' Nan asked.

I shook my head and tried to stand.

'Wait,' Amma said, but I yelped. I looked down. My socks were brown and stiff with mud. I bent to take them off and fell backwards. Felix caught me and lowered me back onto the chair. Amma knelt.

'You get on, Amma,' François said.

Amma gave François one of her long looks, but eventually stood, huffed, and shuffled towards the oven.

'Nan, some hot water,' said François, before turning to me. 'Let's take a look at your poor feet.'

They did sting and throb, but I had to show them why.

I reached inside my school shirt and brought out the list. The pages were crumpled and crusted with mud and sweat. Bits of bark and pine fell to the floor. I placed the pages onto the table and tried to smooth them out.

'I got stuck at the house looking for this,' I said. 'I stole it from the Kommandant's office.'

Nan grabbed the handle of the kettle, Felix pulled his chair towards me, François stared at the muddy papers, but I was watching Amma. She straightened up, but she didn't turn around.

'It's a list,' I said, my voice sounding a lot steadier than I felt, 'with Father's name on it.'

There was a beat of silence. Then François spoke.

'You've managed to get what we've been trying to find for weeks,' he said, smiling at me.

Nan placed a bucket of warm water down for my feet and held onto the back of François' chair. Felix leant across me. Together he and François spread the papers out.

'I know the word *bahn* means train,' I added, flexing my feet in the soothing water. 'We learnt that in class.'

François ran a finger down the list. 'There,' he said.

I caught my breath. He was pointing at Father's name.

'And there and there.' He pointed to two more names, then another three, and on the second to last page, another two.

'Oh.' I couldn't help crying out as I read those last names. *Alphonse and Giselle Brodeur.*

Felix looked at me. 'Do you know them?'

I nodded. 'Albert's parents,' I said, glancing up at Amma, 'but only his father's disappeared. I saw his mother. She's cooking for the soldiers at the house. She . . .'

I didn't say that she looked awful, tired and washed out.

François frowned and shared a look with Felix.

'And Albert?'

'He helped me escape. Well, sort of.'

I told them about the tapestry and the secret room behind it and how Albert had lured the Kommandant out of the library so I could get inside. I thought about telling them about the *schokolade*, but I didn't. Something about it made my insides squirm, but I didn't want to get Albert into trouble.

'What happened to Albert?' asked Nan. 'Did they realise he was helping you?'

I felt goosebumps creeping up my legs. 'I didn't see,' I said, 'but he's got the hiding place behind the tapestry if he needs it, and the Kommandant seemed to believe him when he said he didn't know where I was. They talked and Albert said . . .'

I frowned trying to remember exactly what I'd heard when I was hiding in the library, but it had gone. I shook my head.

'I don't know.'

François nodded.

'Why didn't you tell me he was working for you?' I said. 'Albert and I have been friends since we were small. Was it because you didn't trust me yet? Not properly?'

François glanced quickly at Felix. 'We haven't been able to speak to Albert for a while,' he said. 'We weren't sure what had happened to him.' He patted my hand.

I blew out a breath I didn't realise I'd been holding. So Albert had been telling the truth. I was right to trust him.

The clock above the stove ticked the half hour. I looked down at my feet. The water was brown and bits floated across the top.

'There's something else,' I said, staring at the swirling

twigs and leaves. 'I think the Kommandant will know I have the list. And he knows my name. He was there at the church when I hid the tin, and so was Père Tremblay.' I pulled my feet out of the bucket. They made a wet slapping sound on the flagstones. 'The Kommandant caught me in the library, back at the big house. He said something about the tin in the church.' I took a breath. 'He knew all about it.' I bit my lip.

François shared another look with Felix. 'That's how they got Leon,' he said.

Felix nodded.

François looked at me. 'The old man in the house where you first met us all.'

I remembered him, half hidden in the corner, looking so much like his greasy threadbare armchair, and felt sick to my stomach. If I'd been better at hiding the tin, if I'd done something different that day, maybe he wouldn't have been caught.

Nan took the bucket of dirty water away and unwrapped an oilcloth. Inside was a small bottle with a cork stopper, some cotton wool and a few needles. She poured some of the clear liquid from the bottle onto the cotton and dabbed it on my right foot. It stung, and I pulled it back, but she held it firmly. My foot was covered in scratches, red and pink lines criss-crossed all over with a purple bruise curling round my ankle like a hand.

Felix took the papers over to the stove, opened the top right door, the bit where Amma stoked the fire, and, after glancing at François, who tapped his forehead to show he'd memorised them, threw them in.

'Do you know what the list is?' François asked.

I thought I did know but I shook my head just in case. I bit my tongue as Nan started on my left foot. As the liquid hit those scratches it stung like a hundred bees.

'It's a deportation list,' said François softly. 'Do you understand what that is?'

Behind him Amma thunked another tray onto the table. Felix poked a stick into the flames to push all the papers in as Nan dabbed at my toes.

'It's a list of prisoners that are to be put on a special train,' he said, when I didn't answer, looking at Amma as if checking it was alright to tell me. Amma gave a small nod without even looking at him. 'A train that goes all the way north-east, to a place called Natzweiler-Struthof.'

I nodded. I'd read that stamp on the papers.

'It's a prison camp,' he said. 'It's where the Germans send Resistance fighters.'

'If they don't murder them first!' Felix said, slamming the little oven door shut.

François glared at him. I looked down, watching as Nan bound my feet in a long roll of what looked like strips off an old, faded, yellow curtain. The home-made bandages were tight – too tight. My feet felt too big for the bandages, as if they were trying to escape. I winced then looked from Felix to François.

'But surely if he's in a prison camp he'll be safe? And when the war ends, we'll know where to find him.'

François took my hands in his. He glanced at Amma again then looked back at me. 'No one comes back from that camp.'

He stared at the stove as if he could see though the door into the flames and the list that would now be ash. It felt like I'd turned to dust too.

'All the prisoners on the list, including your father, are scheduled to be taken there on one particular train. The list you found mentions the time and date the train leaves here,' François said.

I looked behind him. Amma was standing there, her arms folded. Nan stood beside her, rolling her oilskin back up. Felix had his hands clasped in front of him on the table.

'The train leaves tomorrow.'

# Chapter Twenty-Five

Tomorrow!

The train that would take Father and all the other Resistance fighters away – for ever – was leaving town tomorrow.

I looked at Amma, Nan, François and Felix in turn. They stared back as if waiting for *me* to say something.

I pushed my fringe out of my face. 'So we have all the information we need to rescue them now, don't we?'

François shared a look with Felix. It wasn't a hopeful one.

'You have to!' I yelled at them. I hadn't risked everything for them to do nothing!

François rubbed his eyes.

'It'll be difficult,' Nan said.

'Bah!' Felix said, pushing himself away from the table.

'But not impossible,' Nan finished, glaring at him.

'We'd need more help,' François said, looking at me. 'But we're the only Resistance left here.'

I nodded. I would help. He didn't even need to ask.

There was a thump as Amma banged an old apple crate onto the table. Thin baguettes peeped over the top like stalks of wheat.

'She's done enough.'

'I want to help,' I said. I pushed myself away from the table. 'I can do it, Amma, and they need me.'

Amma looked across at Felix, who began to fill the other crates with baked rolls that had cooled on the dresser.

'This isn't one of your books,' Amma said, wiping her hands on her apron. Her voice went quiet. 'There isn't always a happy ending.'

I looked at Nan, imploring her to stand up for me, but she was helping Felix pack bread, deliberately not looking at Amma or me.

I swallowed. 'I know, Amma,' I said, getting up. I bit back a cry. My feet were swollen and prickled, as though I'd stepped on needles, but I pushed the pain aside. It didn't matter. 'If I can help, I should,' I told her.

'No,' Amma said.

'This isn't fair!' I said looking round at them all. 'None of you were going to help Father. Too difficult to find out where he was, you said.' I pointed to Felix.

'And now we know!'

'I didn't mean that *you* should find out,' François said. 'And how did you hear that anyway? Were you eavesdropping?'

I looked away.

'Amma's right,' he went on. 'You've done well, but that's enough now. The rest of us will just have to manage.'

'And with no bicycle and no baskets, the best thing you can do is stay here and help me prepare for tomorrow's order,' Amma said.

I felt my cheeks grow hot, and sat down heavily. Nan gave me a small smile as they finished packing the crates. It was alright for Nan. She was sixteen and could drive and knew how to do first aid and wore trousers. I felt a twist in my stomach. Why wasn't I sixteen? Nobody would stop me helping if I was.

'You keep your adventures inside a book from now on,' Amma said.

'Perhaps we'll see you in time,' Nan said, getting up and putting her coat on.

I looked up.

'We'll take the delivery to Maison de Noyer in the van,' she added, with a nod to François.

'But they'll recognise you, François!'

He smiled. 'Nan will drop them off. Felix and I have other work to do if we're going to be ready before that train leaves.'

Did that mean they were going to attempt a rescue after all? I felt like screaming with frustration. Why wouldn't they tell me anything? And why couldn't I help? I'd got them the list, hadn't I? And they needed all the help they could get.

Chairs scraped. After double-checking there were no soldiers outside, Felix followed Nan out the back door and helped her load the crates into a small brown van with faded blue lettering on it, half hidden under the willow branches round the side of the house. With a wave she started the engine and the little van chugged down the lane.

Felix watched her and then, with a wave that looked like he was throwing something at us, he set off across the field behind our house.

I felt a hand on my shoulder.

'Don't worry,' François said. He glanced behind me at Amma then hunched down so his head was level with mine. 'We'll find him,' he said. 'You rest your feet and help your Amma.'

'But if she changes her mind . . .' I said.

He gave me a smile, then stood. With a nod to Amma, he turned and followed Felix. I shut the door behind him, leant against it and let out a long sigh.

'Enough of that. Come and help me,' Amma said without turning round. 'And you'll need something in your stomach.' She handed me some bread covered with a scraping of butter and a sprinkle of sugar. I let the crystals dissolve on my tongue and tried not to think about the extra rations we must be getting from the Germans so she could spare me this treat. After I'd finished, I joined her at the other end of the table where she was shaping loaves. I tried to lose myself in the rhythm of baking, like she did, forcing back tears of anger, disappointment and even relief.

It wasn't long before the knock came.

I grinned. The others had decided they couldn't do without me after all!

I flung open the back door, but to my horror it wasn't François standing there. It was a soldier. He was tall and so thin his green uniform seemed to hang off him as if his shoulders were a coat hanger. His hair was cut really close to his head, which made him look bald under his cap, and his hands clutched his belt like he was holding on. I gulped. He wasn't the only soldier. Another older and even taller soldier who filled out his uniform to bursting was bent over examining the tyre tracks in the mud leading out from under the willow tree.

Time seemed to stand still. I felt cold air blow across the back of my neck. They'd come for me. And now they were tracking the others!

Then Amma spoke. 'The delivery is on its way.'

She stood at my back, pulling the edges of the blanket around me so that it covered my muddy clothes.

The young soldier looked at her then at me. He had watery-grey eyes. His face was tanned and he had small wisps of hair across his chin, the beginnings of a beard.

'And you should be getting ready for school, little one,' Amma said, smoothing my hair back with her hand and turning me away from the door.

'Wait,' the soldier said, staring at me. 'We're looking for a child.'

'A child?' Amma said. She pushed me inside, but the soldier put his hand on her arm. She drew herself up and stared at it so hard that the soldier coughed, then removed it. He gave a half look over his shoulder then clutched his gun.

'Someone broke into the Kommandant's house.'

I felt Amma bristle at that. It wasn't his house, it was Albert's parents' house, we all knew that.

'A child? I doubt a child foiled your security, monsieur.'

The soldier looked at the ground and then slightly behind him again.

Amma leant towards him. 'You're Vicq's boy, no?'

The tips of the soldier's ears grew pink as he nodded.

Amma held his gaze for a few long seconds. 'Well, my little one has just woken, as you can see.' She hugged me to her side. 'She is still in her blanket.'

The soldier looked me up and down, his eyes resting on my feet.

'Ah yes,' Amma said, 'we lost our bicycle so she has been walking to school.' She put a hand to her chest. 'Six miles,' she said. 'It is a fair walk, as you know, and with her old shoes, she will get blisters.'

For a moment no one said a word, and I pressed the side of my face with mud still on it into Amma's housecoat and tried to rub it off.

Eventually the soldier gave a small nod to me then to Amma. He opened his mouth to speak, but the other soldier was suddenly right behind him. He clicked his boots together and we all jumped, even the young one.

'Well?' he asked.

The first soldier shook his head to answer.

The second soldier nodded, turned to Amma and looked down his long nose.

'This child *was* at the house yesterday though,' he said. 'She delivered bread and left baskets and a bicycle.'

There was a pause then Amma turned to me, a scowl spreading across her face. Then she fired her words.

'*Lost*, you said. *Lost* the bicycle. Now I hear from this gentleman that you *left* it behind. Well, what do you have to say for yourself?'

My jaw dropped.

Amma turned to the soldiers. 'I don't suppose you

brought our bicycle with you?' She didn't give them time to answer before shouting again. '*Lost! Forgotten* more like.' She put her hands on her hips. 'Always off in a make-believe world. She reads too many books.' She lowered her voice and leant towards the soldiers. 'A girl with no mother needs discipline or she runs wild.' She turned to me. 'Did you go off with your friends instead of bringing it home? Well, you can go and collect it right this minute.' Amma straightened up. 'Wait, better yet, you can walk to school and back today to learn your lesson, then collect it later.'

She looked at the soldiers. 'Lost, indeed. Thank you, gentlemen. I shall deal with this.'

The older one narrowed his eyes, staring at me quite intently, then he clicked his heels again and gave a sharp nod. As they turned and walked away, my heart hammered beneath the blanket. Amma waited till they reached the road before closing the door. Then she leant against it and shut her eyes.

'Amma?'

She didn't answer.

I pulled on the corner of her housecoat, muddy from where I'd wiped my face.

She opened her eyes and looked straight at me.

'Amma, that was incredible. You completely fooled them.'

I felt as light as a puff of Amma's flour. We'd done it!

'We're safe,' I said, grinning with relief.

But Amma brushed my fringe out of my eyes and shook her head.

I understood. We were safe right this minute, but we weren't out of the woods yet.

Amma looked around the kitchen, at the sacks of flour on the table, the pats of butter oozing in the heat; everything waiting to be baked.

'I'll help you,' I said, following her gaze, but something was still worrying me. 'That other soldier, the older one. He kept staring at me, Amma. I'm sure he knew something.'

She looked at me closely and her face fell. 'He must have noticed the mud,' she said, wiping it off my chin.

All of a sudden there was another knock.

We jumped.

Amma spun round and stared at the wood as if she might see though it.

'Hide!' she hissed.

'But they already know I'm here,' I whispered.

'Now!'

*Bang, bang, bang.*

I fled, but barely made it to the bottom of the stairs tottering on my sore feet.

*Bang, bang, bang.*

Amma tightened her headscarf round her curlers, straightened her housecoat then reached for the latch.

# Chapter Twenty-Six

*Bang, bang, bang.*

Amma threw open the door. 'What is the meaning of this?' she said.

But this time it was a friend.

Amma stepped back as he slipped in. I forgot my sore feet and ran, jumping straight into his arms.

'François!'

François gave me a hug then looked at Amma over my head.

'It was close,' she said.

'I saw. A local boy, wasn't it? And a German? We saw them on the road. I hid in case you needed help, but it looked like you handled it.'

Amma sat down at the table and sighed. 'Our own boys,' she said. 'Using them as soldiers.' She looked at François. 'You're all so young to be caught up in this.'

'They'll be back,' François said.

'They'll be back,' Amma agreed. 'Like a dog after a scent. They know something isn't right here.'

I thought about what the soldier had said about the baskets and the bicycle. The Kommandant knew my name, what I'd taken, and that I had something to do with the tin in the church. The woman in the house had seen my face when I'd tried to escape. She'd promised not to tell, but could anyone on their side be trusted?

'You have to go, *mon chou*.'

Go? Go where? I wondered. Did she mean I could join the mission to rescue Father? But Amma's eyes were dull, and realisation slowly crawled across my skin. She meant leave. She meant I had to get away from here. Away from Amma. Away from our home.

The soldiers were chasing a girl they'd seen running from the big house. The Kommandant was already suspicious of me after the church and knew I'd tried to take things from his office. As soon as the soldiers reported back to him, he'd know where to look for me and it would only be a matter of time before someone was scared enough to point them in the direction of Amma's house.

I noticed the dark bruises under Amma's eyes. How could I leave her alone? The baking was only part of it. Even if I wasn't here, the soldiers would still come calling. I knew Amma could handle them, but how long would they put up with her refusing to say anything about me? How long before they decided it was better she was gone too? I turned to tell her my fears, but she reached for me and took my hands.

'One day the war will be over,' she said to me. 'And it might be sooner than you think. The soldiers' days are numbered, but that makes them all the more desperate.'

Her hands felt warm, and I could feel the strength of what she was saying, that one day all this would pass. Father would sit in his chair at the table, Amma would bake only for pleasure, and I would go to and from the big house whenever I liked.

'But until then . . . you must go.'

My heart twisted as the happy thoughts in my head dissolved. She gave me a small smile. I noticed her eyes were grey around the edges with brown smudges in the middle of each one. I'd never noticed that before. Monsieur X said to be a good detective you had to notice all the little things. If I'd missed the true colour of Amma's eyes, what else had I missed?

'*Mon chou?*'

I didn't want to listen and had to force myself to concentrate on what she was saying.

'It is too dangerous for you here now,' she said.

I tried to turn away, but firm hands kept me facing her.

'I should have stopped you.'

Tears sprouted in the corner of her eyes. I'd never ever seen her cry. It pierced my heart.

'I'm sorry, Amma,' I said. 'I only wanted to help.'

Amma let go and I threw myself into her arms. I sank into her soft middle, wrapped my arms around her and sobbed. Her head rested on mine.

'I didn't mean to cause so much trouble,' I said. 'But I had to get the list. I had to know where he was.'

I felt Amma's head nod next to mine then she patted my back.

'Take only what you need,' she said, pulling me away. 'And take it quickly.'

I rubbed my eyes.

'Only what you *need*, yes?'

I ran, as best I could, upstairs to my room.

Inside it looked just the same as before, as if nothing had changed at all, as if I wasn't about to run for my life. My bed was rumpled, and a glass of water sat on the small nightstand along with my books.

I stripped off my dirty shirt, vest and skirt and slipped into a clean lemony-yellow blouse, dark red jumper and deep blue skirt. I pulled a pair of long socks on over the bandages and tried to stuff my feet into plimsolls but they wouldn't fit. I quickly took off the socks, and unrolled the bandages. My feet looked bruised, but not bloody, so on went the socks, a second pair for padding, then the plimsolls. My feet still felt scratched and sore as I grabbed another skirt and some underwear, then ran next door into Father's room.

'*Mon chou?*' called Amma.

I took the small oilcloth bag he'd used for hiking trips and put in my spare clothes. I looked around the room, trying to drink everything in. I'd tell him, describe it to him when he was free so he would know his room was waiting for him when it was safe to come home.

When it was safe for both of us.

I was just about to leave when I saw one of his jumpers, the thick brown one, slouched over the back of his chair. I stuffed it into the bag.

'You must go – now!' Amma said.

I was about to run downstairs when I spun round. There was one last thing I couldn't do without. I ran to my bed, reached underneath the pillow and grabbed the soft, well-thumbed pages of *Monsieur X and the Ghost in the Castle*.

Then I ran down the stairs to the kitchen.

'Take good care of her,' Amma said to François, looking at my bulging feet.

I threw my shoulders back. I wouldn't let her know they were hurting already. She had enough to worry about.

'I'll be back before you know it, Amma,' I said.

I beamed at François but he didn't return my smile. Instead he nodded at Amma, then reached for my bag. I hoisted it onto my back, but he shook his head.

'We have to run,' he said.

I handed it over.

I glanced at Amma, but she'd turned to the table and was pouring flour from a tub into a large, cream mixing bowl. I watched as she tipped out exactly the right amount without weighing it. Flour whumped into the bowl, little particles floating up and out the sides.

'Bye,' I whispered.

Amma nodded, her face hidden, her shoulders tight. I slipped my arms around her, pressing my face into her back, and all of a sudden she turned and hugged me so tight I could hardly breathe. I felt her shoulders and I knew she was crying again, which made my heart clench. Then she squeezed me, let go and turned back to her baking before I could say or do anything else.

François pulled me out of the door then, as if thinking I might change my mind, and we ran across the road and into the woods. The sun was warm, the sky was clear and the air was so still that I knew by lunchtime it would be unbearably hot.

We ran and ran. At first my feet throbbed, then they stung and then I couldn't feel them at all. François took us round the edge of the forest. I knew this route.

This was the way I'd chosen for Father when we played detectives . . . but François couldn't know that, could he?

I counted each time my feet hit the ground to try to keep pace with him – one, two, three, four, one, two, three, four – but it wasn't long before I began to run out of breath. I wanted to stop. I wanted to ask François if we were going where I thought we might be going, but François was fast and I had to run twice as hard as normal not to be left behind.

The sun was blistering. Birds called to each other. Wood pigeons cooed as we raced past, cheering us on. The muddy parts of the ground had dried to crusts that crumpled under our feet. I longed to stop and shrug off my jumper, but I the soldiers were out looking for me. We couldn't waste a second.

We only stopped when we reached the end of a small lane that led to the river. François crouched down. He flapped a hand behind him so I'd know to do the same. I crawled like a crab till I was huddled next to him. We listened.

At first I could only hear the gurgling of the river. The *plink plop* of a fish, more cooing. The pigeons were here too. Then I heard something else. Voices.

I grabbed François' arm. It was as solid as a tree branch. He turned and put a finger to his lips. I nodded.

We shifted closer to the riverbank.

I heard a *tink, tink, tink.*

A boat.

*The* boat!

I was right about where we were going.

I started to rise, but François pulled me back down.

'The boat,' I whispered. 'Are you going to hide me on Father's boat?'

François didn't answer, but took out a crumpled piece of paper from his pocket, scanning it intently.

All of a sudden a shadow fell over us.

'Well, well, well, what do have we here?'

# Chapter Twenty-Seven

The shadow fell dark and cold on us like we'd been dipped into the river. François and I looked up at the same time. He started to pull me behind him as the man looming over us stepped back and threw off the hat and scarf covering his face.

It was Felix.

'That'll teach you,' he said and gave a deep laugh.

Before I could blink, François was on his feet and pushing Felix backwards. Felix had both hands up and was still laughing as François raised a fist. Another voice rang out.

'Stop it, both of you.'

We all turned.

Nan slammed the door of the brown van she'd parked at the end of the lane. She reached out a hand to me.

'Come and help, Eloise.'

I ran over and helped Nan pull an old grey-green tarpaulin over the van, before we followed François and Felix along the bank upriver past the tall reeds and yellow grasses, which parted in the early morning breeze, revealing glimpses of the boat. Rounding the corner, my heart leapt. It *was* Father's boat! I could see the rope tied in the special knot Father had shown me before, and the patch on the side where the boat's name had been ripped off. It was a little weather-beaten, but still in good repair.

François jumped onto the deck and felt around the wooden frame of the cabin for the key.

I grinned at Nan, then ran ahead past her and Felix. I was about to jump onto the boat when the cabin doors flew open from the inside.

Felix reared back.

Behind me I heard a *crick-cruck* of a gun, then another. I glanced back to see Nan and Felix taking aim.

'It's alright, it's me.' Albert's head appeared out of the cabin.

'Stupid child.' Felix barged past me. 'You could've got yourself killed!'

I turned to Nan. She stuffed her small gun down the back of her belt and trousers.

'Come on,' she said, a hand on my shoulder.

But I could barely believe what I was seeing. Albert

was here! I let out a breath. He was safe after all. I'd been worried he'd get into trouble for helping me get into the library, or was stuck hiding in the room behind the tapestry trying to avoid any more trouble.

François and Felix disappeared with Albert into the cabin. I jumped on board and ducked inside after them.

'I knew you were safe,' he said, shooting me a grin.

'Quiet,' Felix hissed, but I gave Albert a smile back.

It had been dark and cramped when it had been just Father and me, but now there were five of us and the boat tipped with every movement.

I squeezed in next to Albert on the wooden seat. His hair stood out in stiff tufts and his jumper looked like it had even more holes in it than before. Nan sat on my other side and pulled the cabin doors shut. Only then did François open a small grille behind him. The sound of the water floated in on a gentle breeze, which was good because it was starting to get really warm and a bit smelly.

François spoke first. 'Why are you here, Albert?'

Albert opened and shut his mouth like he was a fish. 'You told me to meet you here,' he said at last, 'if I had something to tell.'

'You didn't leave a message under the loose brick to tell us to come here,' François said, frowning. 'We have a routine.'

Albert looked down, nodded. 'So why are you all here?'

'The soldiers are looking for the girl who broke into the Kommandant's office,' François said. 'Eloise couldn't stay where everyone could find her.'

'But they can't be looking for El,' Albert said. 'I told them she was stupid, that she couldn't read, that it couldn't be her.'

I thought about the woman who'd helped me, and whether I should tell them about her. She knew I wasn't stupid and that I liked to read . . . but if I did tell them, they'd know I only got away because she helped me. Would they still trust me? She was the enemy after all.

'Bah!' Felix reached into the inside pocket of his grey jacket and pulled out a pipe. 'As if that would be enough to stop them arresting someone they thought was guilty.'

'I did my best,' Albert said. He swallowed. 'Eloise got away, and you got what you wanted, didn't you?'

François looked at me, but I was watching Albert. His face was pale and he'd begun to sweat. I could understand why – it felt as if the air was running out inside the cabin.

'Anyway, I have more news,' Albert said. He swallowed again. 'Eloise told me the list was about prisoners and the station. I overheard the Kommandant talking about it to the soldiers.'

François, Felix and Nan shared an eager look.

'There's a train ready to take the prisoners away. It's going to leave earlier than planned. The same time, but one day earlier,' Albert said.

François shook his head. 'How did you overhear this?'

'I was standing on the other side of the library door when he was talking about what the troops needed to do. I could hear everything, I promise,' Albert said, his eyes darting from face to face.

François looked at me, then at Nan and Felix. Something about what Albert said niggled at my brain.

'They know we know,' François said.

Felix nodded, and Nan sat back, her feet planted firmly on the cabin floor. But something else felt wrong.

'I heard you,' I said, looking at Albert, 'in the library. Talking to the Kommandant while I was hiding in the bookcase.'

Albert frowned. He darted a look at François then back to me.

'I did hear you saying I was just a child and that I couldn't read. But you also said you'd promised something to the Kommandant.'

Albert's eyes grew so wide I could see the white bits around his pupils.

'It was nothing,' he said, swallowing as if he had something stuck in his throat. 'I just said I'd promised to help him find you, that's all.'

His words made sense, but my heart sank. I didn't want to, but I couldn't ignore the evidence. Albert wasn't making eye contact and he was sweating more than the rest of us – everything about him screamed that he was nervous around us. That he wasn't telling us everything.

'It's not safe,' I said, feeling suddenly shivery, even though the cabin was baking hot.

Nan patted her side, where I knew her gun was hidden. 'We'll keep you safe,' she said.

'No, that's not what I mean,' I said, my heart starting to race. I could barely look at Albert. Could I be wrong about him?

I stared at François, Felix, Nan – all steady and looking back at me with concern – and then at Albert, sweaty and pale in the corner.

'I mean . . . I think it might be a trick.'

I darted a look at Albert, thought of all that hidden chocolate. Too much to have stolen without it being noticed . . .

'Albert tried to cover for me, but the Kommandant already knew I was with the Resistance,' I said. 'So the Kommandant might think Albert knows things to do with the Resistance.'

I shook my head trying to put it together as Monsieur X did when he explained everything at the end of every story. I took a deep breath.

'It's like in my books. The Kommandant might think Albert was working with us. With you. So what if he used that? Made sure Albert had the wrong information so that he'd tell you . . . to make you change your plans.'

Albert paled. His skin looked grey. François, Nan and Felix looked at each other uncertainly.

'Are you saying he might have used Albert without him knowing?'

I tried to swallow the lump in my throat. I wished that was true, I really did. But the nervous way Albert was acting meant it couldn't have been by accident. I stared at him and he looked straight back at me, pleading. I couldn't tell them. It was too big. I needed to be sure.

But something else was worrying me. There was another possibility, a much worse one . . . One I remembered happening to Monsieur X.

'Or maybe it is true, but the Kommandant doesn't mind us knowing.'

The others looked confused.

'I mean, he might be counting on Albert to tell you the news straightaway, just so that they could follow him to where he'd meet you.'

For a moment time seemed to stop. Everyone stared at me, then at Albert. There was the *tink, tink, tink* of the boat on the water, and then we all heard it. The shout.

'*Es ist hier!*'

# Chapter Twenty-Eight

The shout came again. Louder this time. Closer.

'*Es ist hier!*'

François scrunched himself round in the small cabin and peered through the grille.

'What are they talking about?' Albert asked, but Felix put a hand over his mouth.

My stomach felt like it had fallen through my feet. It was one thing to worry about it happening, but to actually hear the soldiers around us made my insides turn to liquid.

'They've found the van,' said Francois. 'Not us.'

Albert began to struggle under Felix's arm.

'Oh, let him go,' said Nan.

'The girl's right. We don't know if we can trust him,' growled Felix.

'They might not have followed *him* . . .' said François,

turning to Nan.

'No,' she replied. 'I was careful, and just delivered the bread. In and out. No trouble. Nothing to raise suspicion.'

François was waiting, though, still staring intently at Nan. 'There's something you're not telling us.'

'Alright,' she said, shrugging. 'I might have left them a little present.'

François raised his eyes to the roof of the cabin. 'I thought we said we'd wait till tomorrow.'

Nan leant in. 'Well, if the train is leaving today then it's a perfect distraction. They'll have put more guards at the house now, fewer at the station.'

'What present?' I asked.

Nan looked at me. 'A small . . . device,' she said.

'Explosives,' Felix added gruffly then pointed the end of his unlit pipe at Nan. 'Tell it like it is.'

I looked at Nan, my eyes wide. She was so brave, she made me want to be just as daring, but at the same time I felt sick at the idea of a bomb going off at the big house. Nan shrugged.

'Not where anyone would be hurt,' she said, then grinned, 'though the kitchen might be out of action for a while.'

Albert started shaking.

'Your mother wasn't there,' she reassured him. 'I made sure it was empty.'

Outside we could hear more voices gathering. Then the *crick-cruck* of guns. My breath caught in my throat. Would the soldiers think an abandoned van was all there was to find? My eyes flashed to Albert. Or did they have a reason to expect to find people here too?

All of a sudden Albert lurched for the cabin doors.

'No!' I whispered.

'Grab him!' hissed François.

Felix snatched a fistful of Albert's jumper. Albert's feet kicked out, one caught my side.

Nan grabbed his legs and Felix pinned his arms, one hand round Albert's mouth.

'Traitor!' snarled Felix. 'Why else would you try to escape when they're surrounding us?' Felix's grip tightened. 'Did you make a deal with them?'

Albert's eyes darted wildly. He shook his head at me. 'No! You don't understand!'

More shouts outside. Closer. Then closer still.

They'd heard us!

'We need to get out of here,' Felix said. 'Now!'

François flung open the cabin doors and ran to the aft of the boat. I stayed frozen on my seat and watched as he began to pull at the rope around the rail to release the boat from its moorings, but it wouldn't budge. The knot seemed to be jammed and worse, something on the rail made a loud clunking noise each time he pulled.

'*Da drüben!*'

The soldiers moved towards us.

François looked up then flattened himself to the deck as a *rat-a-tat-tat* spilled across it.

'Get down!' Nan yelled and I ducked in my seat.

Outside I watched François reach up to pull on the line, his face red, his mouth a tight grimace.

*Rat-a-tat-tat. Crack!*

Gunfire showered the boat. Bullets thudded into the wood around us. Felix shoved Albert to the floor and lay over him. Nan pulled out her gun and pointed it between the slats of the grille, ready to fire back.

But it wouldn't be enough. Escape was our only option.

I squinted at the bull rail. The line was tied in a round turn and two half hitches instead of the usual cleat hitch. It made it harder to undo, Father said, but sturdier. François either hadn't seen what type of knot it was or didn't know. Behind me Nan had started firing. Albert was crying out. Felix was struggling to keep him down out of harm's way. I gulped. It was down to me.

I dropped to my knees and began to crawl up through the cabin doorway.

*Crack! Pang! Thunk!*

A bullet hammered into one of the doors above my head, swinging it back on its hinges.

I dropped to the deck, my heart beating wildly.

'Get back!' yelled Felix.

I wriggled my way towards François.

*Rat-a-tat-tat. Crack!*

François looked up and his face fell when he saw it was me. He swept his head to the right, as if to tell me to get back inside, but I shook mine. I pointed to the knot, tried to mime pulling it open.

François frowned at first, then nodded furiously. He held up a steady hand, palm out.

I waited.

*Rat-a-tat-tat.*

*Thunk. Phut. Phut.*

More bullets sank into the side of the boat.

François reached behind him and pulled out a gun. It was short and black though it shone bright in the morning light. He *crunk-cricked* it, then flapped a hand at me as if to say 'Now!'

I scrabbled forward till I caught the rope, reached my hand towards the ring it was knotted to as François jumped up and fired at the soldiers.

I managed to unwind the rope from the first hitch but there was an extra knot in the second.

I pulled and twisted, but the boat was caught on the current and kept pulling the line taut, tightening the hitch again.

I turned to François, and we ducked back down again.

*Rat-a-tat-tat.*

'We have to pull the boat in towards the bank,' I shouted. 'Make the rope slack, then I can undo the last hitch.'

François looked towards the cabin and beyond at the wheel. I followed his gaze, squeezed his arm.

'I know where Father keeps the starter key,' I said. 'And I can steer.'

I was just about to scrabble back to the line when he grabbed my hand.

'Once you've got us loose, fast as you can, Eloise, yes?'

I nodded.

*Phut, phut, phut.*

Bullets rippled across the boat and thunked into the wood panels. Behind me François shot back.

*Bam, bam, bam.*

A quick glance inside the cabin showed me Nan shooting through the grille then ducking back. Felix had opened a port window and was shooting out of that. He had one foot on Albert, who was curled, hands over his head, on the floor.

'Now!' cried François.

He pulled on the rope and the boat swung, bumping into the bank. I reached over, my head low, and frantically unhooked the last hitch, letting go as the rope slithered through my hands.

*Rat-a-tat-tat.*

I crawled fast and low to the cabin and squeezed through the little doors that led up to the helm.

*Bam. Bam. Bam.*

Staying on my knees, I lifted up the seat and felt underneath for the keys.

I couldn't believe it. There was nothing there.

*Phut, phut, phut.*

*Crack!*

I ducked, hands over my head as Nan, Felix and François returned fire. I leant into the storage box under the seat, pulled out a tarpaulin and watched the keys skid across the floor. I grabbed them, stuffed the right one into the ignition and turned it.

The boat coughed like it had a cold. I held the key turned and waited, remembering what Father had said.

*'Patience, Eloise. She'll see you right.'*

The boat coughed once more, and then spluttered. Outside bullets *phut, phut, phutted* into the boat.

I closed my eyes and held the key tight.

All of a sudden the splutter turned into a chug-chugging sound and the boat lurched. I let go, pushed the throttle forwards and grabbed the wheel.

*Rat-a-tat-crash!*

I threw my arms up in front of my face as the glass in the windscreen smashed into a thousand little pieces. My heart beat faster than it ever had, like there was a twelve-horse race inside of my chest. Then I felt the familiar thrumming of the boat under my feet as it began to move.

Bullets pinged off the bits of glass still clinging to the sides.

I gripped the throttle with one hand and held onto the wheel with the other. I couldn't let go and I couldn't hide from the bullets. Our lives depended on it.

I had to hold on.

# Chapter Twenty-Nine

The boat vibrated through my feet.

'Eloise?'

I felt a hand over mine. I looked up. It was François.

'You can let go now.'

I looked around for the soldiers, but there weren't any. The sound of gunfire had gone. I'd been so focused on the boat I hadn't realised. I uncurled from my half crouch and stood up on shaking legs.

'Let go,' François said again gently.

I peeled my hand away, but my palm stayed curled as if I was still clutching the wheel.

Around me the boat was a mess. Slivers of glass littered the deck, winking in the sun, and chunks of boat were missing, leaving gouges of wood and splinters sticking out at odd angles.

I peered over the jagged edge of the aft, but there was

nothing behind us. I watched a tall tree disappear as we went around a bend, the dark grey river churning in our wake. We'd done it. We'd got away.

'Show me what to do,' François said.

I looked at him, but couldn't quite hear what he was saying. My ears were still ringing.

'Eloise . . .' He was speaking slowly now. 'Show me how to steer the boat.'

I nodded.

As I put his hand on the throttle and moved the wheel to keep us straight ahead, Nan and Felix came up behind us.

'Great work, Eloise,' Nan said.

I felt a warm blush across my cheeks. 'It's easy to steer really,' I said.

Nan put an arm around my shoulder. 'It wasn't easy and you did great,' she said. 'Trust me, take a compliment when you get it.'

I nodded, a feeling like a warm flame flickering inside me.

'The soldiers?' I asked. I knew they wouldn't give up.

François glanced back at Felix then at the river. The boat chugged merrily past a meadow filled with wildflowers on one side and tall green reeds on the other. Birds sung and the sun shone. It was as if the last half hour hadn't happened.

'We're going towards the town, yes?' he asked.

I nodded.

'Then they'll be waiting for us at the first bridge we come to,' he said softly.

Felix growled.

'Not if we take the short cut,' I said.

François looked round. 'The short cut?'

I nodded. 'Father showed me. The river splits in two just before the first bridge, Pont de la Paix. The other route is hidden under some willows. You pass by a repair yard, then you join the main river at the next bridge.'

I pushed my fringe out of my eyes. 'There's good fishing that way,' I said, my heart twisting with the memory. 'That's what Father said, anyway.'

François wiped a hand across his face. Nan was shaking her head in relief, grinning too. Felix was nodding.

'Good,' Felix said. 'We can get out before the split. Then we let the boat carry on down the river. They'll find it, but they won't find us.'

'And the prisoners?' asked François.

My breath caught in my throat.

Felix sighed. 'If the train really is leaving today then we have . . .' He looked at his watch. 'Three hours to get to the station and somehow get them out of there. Not enough time to contact anyone further afield for help. We'd have to stop the train ourselves.'

François looked thoughtful. 'Would you have enough explosives to do it?' he asked Nan.

Nan nodded. 'I have some supplies in town,' she said. Then all of a sudden she fell into the side of the boat. François reached for her and she yelled, 'No!' She held her right arm away from her, staring at a small blot of red on her shirtsleeve that was growing larger and larger.

Nan had been hit!

François sat her down.

Nan's face was pale, but she grinned. 'It's nothing. I'm fine.'

François and Felix shared a look.

'Is there a first aid kit here?' Felix asked me.

I leapt back into the cabin. Father had said there was food under the wooden seats. It wasn't for us, he'd said, but perhaps there was something in there I could use.

I lifted up the first seat and shook myself. There wasn't any food. Instead an oblong green metal box filled the space. It had a catch and I was about to lift it when Felix caught my hand.

'No,' he said, shutting the seat top. 'Try the others.'

I gave him a look, but he'd already turned back to Nan.

Inside the next seat box were clothes and boots. I slipped a hand underneath but there was nothing there.

I tried the third and last seat. Here I found the food,

boxes of biscuits, dry bread and packets of things with no names on. Underneath, at the bottom, I found what looked like a sewing kit. It would have to do.

I brought out the kit, grabbed one of the shirts from under the other seat and ducked outside.

'Good enough,' Nan said, seeing the kit. Sweat had broken out across her forehead.

François ripped off her shirtsleeve. Dark red blood pulsed from the top of her arm, oozing towards her hand. I took a breath. The air smelt of rust and salt.

'Steer the boat,' François said. 'Tell us when we get to the split in the river.'

I nodded, jumped up and pulled the wheel a little to the left, keeping the throttle at a steady forward pace. I chanced a quick look behind me.

François had ripped off a piece of the shirt I'd given him and was tying it tight above Nan's wound.

'Is there any . . .?' Nan's voice wavered.

Felix nodded and moved back into the cabin. When he came back he had a bottle of clear liquid. He pulled at it with his teeth, spat out the cork and handed it to François. She gasped as he sloshed some over the wound, and then more over the needle and a small penknife. He doused some of the shirt in the liquid too and offered it to Nan. She nodded and he stuffed it into her mouth.

'Ready?'

Nan shook her head then, after a beat, she nodded.

François took his penknife and dug it into Nan's shoulder.

I looked away.

I smelt salt, rust and the sharp tang of alcohol. Nan cried out and my stomach flipped. I felt sick crawl up my throat and swallowed it back down, trying to concentrate on the river, the wildflowers poking out through the grass and the reeds waving like we were royalty passing by.

I watched a flock of swallows fly overhead, turn, then fly back the way they came, as Nan's legs beat against the floor of the boat then stilled. There was a *plink-plosh* sound as François threw the bullet into the river. Then quiet. I pulled on the throttle to slow the boat and glanced back.

François was biting the cotton off the needle close to Nan's arm. He grabbed a ripped piece of shirt and tied it round like a bandage. Felix had let her go and was rustling in one of the seat boxes for a coat. He threw it over her then went back into the cabin.

François put a hand on Nan's good shoulder.

'Thanks,' she whispered.

Turning back I saw the willow tree just ahead, trailing its branches into the water and I let the boat come to a slow stop. François cocked his head.

'We're here,' I said, 'this is where the river splits.'

They got to their feet, ready to help moor the boat. I looked at them. The three of them. Someone was missing.

'Where's Albert?'

Felix raised his eyebrows. 'The boy?' he said. 'He's long gone.'

# Chapter Thirty

'Gone?'

My stomach fell. I looked left and right. *Where* had Albert gone? And when? I hadn't even noticed when the soldiers stopped firing, and then I'd been distracted with Nan and all the blood . . .

'He must've jumped over the side when they were shooting at us,' Felix said.

I touched the jagged edges of the side of the boat. 'He's not . . . I mean, he wasn't . . .' I couldn't finish the sentence. 'Was he hit?'

Felix threw up his hands. 'He was on the floor the whole time. He was safe enough.' He shrugged his shoulders. 'But then I had to cover our escape. I can't be expected to babysit. He must have taken his chance and run back to his friend, the Kommandant.'

My stomach twisted at his words.

I screwed my eyes tight, trying not to think about Albert throwing stones at Maddie and me, him promising something to the Kommandant. Not Albert, not a traitor, please.

Then I shook my head. They were little things, compared to this – a betrayal that put all our lives in danger. He couldn't. He wouldn't. But then why had he been so nervous on the boat? And why did he jump overboard, into the water?

François ran a hand through his hair. 'Eloise, I'm sorry,' he said. 'I know you were close. But we don't have time for this. We need to get off the river.' He took my hand. 'Set the boat towards town. Can we make sure it follows the current?'

I shook my head. 'But we can jam the throttle to keep her running. It's fairly straight to the Pont de Vieux. She might bump against the banks a little but she'll get there.'

François nodded. I steered the boat up to the left bank, where he and Felix lifted Nan off. François came back on board and I steered us over to the right, where the river split towards Father's short cut. François handed me a spare boot and we stuffed it under the throttle and tied the trailing laces around it tight.

He grinned. 'Ready?'

I nodded.

'Hope you can swim, Eloise.'

I let go of the throttle. It thrummed and pushed at the boot, but stayed jammed. François grabbed my hand. I reached for my bag, looped it over my shoulder. We ran across the deck and jumped straight over the side into the river.

I squealed.

Water crashed around me. I lost François' hand as I sank under. I shook Father's bag off my shoulder and swam back up, breaking through the surface with a gulp of air. François pointed towards the bank half concealed by enormous willows, their branches trailing into the water, and we swam towards it. Felix reached a hand through the branches and pulled us up. I turned and lay on the sweet-smelling grass. I was soaked and my bag was soaked, but the sun was warm and dappled through the willow fronds. I pushed my hair out of my face. If I closed my eyes I could be in the field outside the big house. Maddie and I would be reading her favourite book, *Monsieur X and the Strange Messages*, and Albert would be running around begging us to play chase and everything would be alright.

A shadow fell across me.

'Time to go,' said Felix.

I stood up and squeezed what water I could out of my skirt and jumper, swung my dripping bag over one shoulder, and we set off.

We kept to the bank, the willows hiding us like a wall of green. We passed the boat yard, abandoned but for the skeletons of upturned, broken sailing boats and an old tug boat lying on its side and sinking into the mud.

Felix and François supported Nan, and we ran when we could, my sore feet squelching in my shoes, my hair drying in rats' tails that slapped against my cheeks, my bag leaking river water down my back. François kept stopping to close his eyes for a few seconds – remembering the way, he said – but he'd always start running again before I got a chance to catch my breath. The sun was creeping higher in the sky and my stomach rumbled. I'd begun to drop further and further behind when all three of them stopped.

'Are we here?' I asked, catching up.

I looked around to see we'd come the full length of the short cut. In the distance we could see Father's boat chugging along the river. We watched till it disappeared.

François nodded and we all turned to follow him up the bank and onto the road. He pointed into the distance.

'Madame Levee's house,' Nan said to me, with relief in her voice.

We'd just set off towards it when there was an almighty bang. It sounded like thunder and lightning and a hundred tin cans clashing, all at the same time.

I dropped to the ground and covered my head with my hands.

There was a second bang, smaller than the first, but this time I felt it clatter my bones. A sharp smell of smoke drifted towards us. I looked up coughing and wiped my hair off my face. The others were all staring behind me at the river. From the distance, where Father's boat had just disappeared around a corner, came a long, twisting plume of grey smoke.

# Chapter Thirty-One

'Father's boat!'

Felix held out his hand.

'Better the boat than us,' he said, helping me up before walking on.

François followed him, holding Nan to his side, but I stood staring at the grey smoke as it churned in spirals towards the sky.

They'd blown up Father's boat.

'Eloise!' François shouted.

Reluctantly I peeled my eyes away, but a little hope had pierced my heart. With the boat gone, the soldiers might believe we were dead and stop looking for us. That would give us some breathing room, and maybe the element of surprise. They wouldn't be expecting us at the station.

We limped our way to Madame Levee's. About halfway along the dirt road we turned off and crept down another bank to find ourselves at the opposite end of her street. There was a small park with two iron benches and a gravel *boule* piste, where one scratched silver *boule* had been left behind.

Felix was to go first. Without a pause he strode onto the tree-lined pavement, head up, arms swinging, but about halfway up the street he stopped to lean against one of the trees. There he began to fill his pipe.

I looked at Nan.

'What's he doing?'

'Letting us know to stay put,' she said.

Then we saw why.

Two soldiers were walking towards him, but stopped right outside Madame Levee's front door.

Everything went quiet. I heard the fluttering of a bird's wing, the buzz and hum of insects, my breath ragged.

The soldiers looked up and down the street.

I stopped breathing.

They saw Felix, who nodded, lifted his pipe, then started sucking on it. They stared at him for a few more seconds, then one kicked Madame Levee's door in and the other followed behind. Felix started whistling, as if everything was completely normal and the soldiers meant nothing to him.

I felt my stomach tip over. What were we going to do now? Nan desperately needed somewhere to rest. She couldn't go much further. And we needed to make a plan – fast. The train was leaving in two hours!

All of a sudden there was a noise behind us. Shouting and dogs barking – lots and lots of barking.

A patrol!

'I'm thinking,' François said, as if he'd heard me. Then he put his arm round Nan, as if they were sweethearts. 'Come on. We'll walk straight past. Find somewhere else. It's our only option now.'

I helped hold Nan up. She was deathly white. Her hand felt clammy as it clasped mine.

The three of us walked towards Felix who frowned and shook his head. He whistled again and this time I understood. *Woot. Pip. Woot, woot, woot.* It was morse code – and it meant 'no'!

I glanced at François, but he shrugged his head to the left. The barking was getting louder. Felix darted a look behind us and paled when he saw the dogs. He nodded once.

My stomach was dipping, then rolling. My mouth felt dry and I kept licking my lips. I gripped Nan's hand tight.

We reached Felix and he doffed his cap. Then we passed him, getting closer and closer to the house. We were only two doors away from Madame Levee's when a soldier stepped out. We kept walking. I tried not to stare at the door hanging off its hinges, tried to look normal

– but I could hear Nan's breathing falter. I looked down. She was dripping blood. I risked a glance behind me, saw drops all along the pavement. My heart sank. We'd left them a trail. The dogs would have no problem following our scent. I looked up as the soldier turned towards us and I felt as if all the air was being sucked out of me. Would he see the blood? Would he recognise me?

'Here!' a voice hissed.

At a doorway on our right stood an old woman in a headscarf, a lady so skinny her cardigan looked as if it had been wrapped around her twice. She beckoned to us. 'Do you need me to ask again?' she whispered.

François hesitated for only a second, then dragged us in. Felix slipped through behind us when the soldier was looking the other way – and the door was shut tight. For a second we stood in the woman's hallway. It was wallpapered in green with clusters of pink roses in such detail they looked real. The woman tutted when we didn't move and shooed us all into a back room. Inside it was dark, the shutters closed. Only when we were all in there did she turn on a pink side lamp with a heavy fringe, making its tassels wave.

'I'm Yvonne,' she said, 'Yvonne Rudellat. And I think I just saved your lives.'

François introduced himself while I helped settle Nan into an old green armchair, a faded yellow blanket across one of its arms. Then he looked at Felix, who pulled up a chair to a reddish-brown round table and sat down heavily. Yvonne went to leave the room and both Felix and François jumped, wondering where she was going, but she held up her hand.

'Relax. If I wanted to hand you in, I'd have only to scream. And I don't plan on doing that.'

Felix nodded and sat down, wiping a hand across his face.

When Yvonne came back she carried a tray with a pot of tea, cups and several dry-looking biscuits on a plate. She turned to me and I realised for the first time just how old she was. Her hands were like twigs and her wrists looked like they might snap any minute. Her hair was white where it peeped from under her headscarf, and her face was free of make-up; her tanned skin folded into leathery creases, but her eyes were bright and shining with a fire that seemed to fill her small frame from the inside.

'I know you, of course,' she said, looking at me. 'You're the spitting image of your father.'

My mouth dropped open.

Yvonne looked at François then Felix then at Nan, who'd closed her eyes. Then she smiled at me.

'He's well liked,' she said, 'and your Amma bakes the very best bread.' She took a sip of tea. Her next words carried an undertone. 'For those who can still afford it.'

'It's not her fault,' I said. 'She had to help them. Without that money –'

Yvonne put her teacup down. 'I don't mean any harm, child,' she said softly, 'only that things have got so bad, no one can afford anything but these old things.'

She passed around the plate of biscuits. They looked grey and sort of like oat biscuits, except they were really thin with tiny holes in. I took two, one for me and one for Nan. Felix took one and as he chewed he screwed his face up in disgust, but swallowed it all the same.

François pulled at the threads on his sleeve. Somewhere in the distance we could hear the barking dogs. Beside me Nan's breathing hitched. Felix said we had to wait for the dogs to pass and for the soldiers to leave Madame Levee's, but I was mindful of the grandfather clock ticking quietly in the corner, counting down the seconds until the train left along with Father and the all other prisoners.

I looked at Nan. The red was seeping through the coat now. I rolled the sleeve back and pressed my hands against the soaked bandage.

'It's no good,' François said. 'We won't make it to the train. Not now.' He slapped the table. 'It's hopeless.'

My heart clenched. Did he mean it? We couldn't give up now! Father's life depended on us. I looked at Felix. He usually had a different opinion and I hoped he would this time, but he looked just as defeated.

'Things aren't always as bad as they seem,' Yvonne said, pouring out a second cup of tea for everyone. 'Everyone says it won't be long now. The British are coming.'

'But they will not be here today, madame,' François said and put his head in his hands.

'I don't have much,' Yvonne said, 'but perhaps I can still help.'

François looked up. 'Our friends have been taken.' He nodded at me. 'Eloise's father among them. We don't know where they're being kept or if they're alright, but we do know that we have an hour until a train leaves, carrying them to a camp from which they won't return.' He took a breath, his hand in Nan's. 'We don't have any supplies, and our explosives expert is injured. They've taken almost everyone we've been working with so we've no help, and we're completely surrounded by soldiers who are looking for us.' He shook his head. 'With respect, madame, how can you possibly help?'

Yvonne took a sip of her tea, then she smiled.

# Chapter Thirty-Two

We hung on Yvonne's words.

She put her empty cup and saucer down. 'I have a car,' she said.

François' shoulders drooped, and I couldn't help but feel the same. That was it?

'Thank you,' he said, 'but we're going to need more than that if –'

Yvonne rolled her eyes. 'You can get away, boy, and that's all you can do now.'

Felix nodded. 'She's right,' he said, 'we can't stay here long. They must know we were at Madame Levee's house, and before long they'll start going door to door, questioning the neighbours.'

I thought of the blood trail. They'd find us alright, but it wasn't only that.

François looked at my horrified face. I understood we

had to move on, but to leave town? Leave our one chance of saving Father? And all the other prisoners?

Nan squeezed my hand. 'We'll find him,' she said, 'even if we have to go to the camp and –'

I shook my head. 'No.' I loved her for saying it, but even I knew that could never happen.

'There's nothing we can do, Eloise,' François said. He came over, took both my hands in his and sank to his knees. 'I'm sorry,' he said. 'Stopping the train was our only chance, but with Nan injured and the soldiers everywhere –'

*Bang! Bang! Bang!*

The noise came from Yvonne's front door.

'They're searching the houses,' she said, clearing the cups from the table. 'There's no more time for talking. Go – now. Out the back door, through the garden. There's a gate behind the shed. Turn left and follow the alleyway to the end. Turn left again and you'll see a green Citroën.'

She took a set of keys from her other cardigan pocket and held them out to François, but he was staring at Nan. She looked like she was asleep, her face smooshed into the side of the armchair. Her right arm was swollen, her hand like five fat sausages. Blood had seeped onto Yvonne's armchair.

'You'll have to leave her here,' Yvonne said.

He shook his head. 'Never.'

'She'll slow you down. I can hide her. I'll put her to bed and tell them she's ill. We'll have to hope they won't look too closely.' She glanced at Nan. 'She won't make the journey.'

François stared at Nan, then took the car keys, closing his hand over Yvonne's brittle one.

'Thank you, madame.'

*Bang, bang, bang!*

'Go,' Yvonne said.

With a last look at Nan, François gave the keys to Felix, and we ran out the back door, across an overgrown garden and through the gate behind the shed. We slipped into the alleyway, weeds crawling through the cracks. We crept along, ducking low past Madame Levee's house right to the end of the street. Then Felix stopped, put up his hand.

Two soldiers rounded the corner. One held onto a large black and brown dog with its nose pressed to the ground. We flattened ourselves against the alley wall. I held my breath as they passed.

We waited. I counted to twenty-three, then Felix peered round the corner and this time beckoned for us to follow. We kept to the left-hand side of the road, following the dog at first, then we ran across to the other side.

The green car sat in front of a small garage. A wiry

ginger cat eyed us from the bonnet where it was sunning itself.

I looked behind us. Nothing. No one.

Felix thrust the keys into the lock, opened the other door for François and the door behind for me. Then he jumped in and started the engine, a *vroom* so loud I felt everyone would be able to hear it. The ginger cat leapt off. We heard a shout. More barking.

'Go!' François said.

Felix stamped on the pedals and we whooshed forwards.

'Where are we going?' I asked.

'Tours,' Felix said, 'if there's enough in the tank.' He looked at the gauge on the dashboard. 'We'll have to change cars. The boys at Chinon might have some petrol or another car. We can try them.'

Tours . . . I bit my lip. I knew they would only ignore me if I argued, but it felt so wrong to be heading away from Father, from Amma – from everything I knew, everyone I loved.

François was staring out of the window. I wondered if he was thinking the same, worrying about leaving Nan.

I stared at Felix's face in the rear-view mirror, his mouth set in a grim line, his hands gripping the wheel.

My gaze fell to the window. I saw a sign for the station up ahead on the left. I looked at my watch. The face was cracked, but the hands still ticked round. I felt like screaming. Father was probably there. Right there! I pointed at the sign.

'Please,' I said, a sob working its way up from my throat. 'Please!'

Suddenly François wrenched the wheel from Felix. The car swerved to the left. Felix swore, pushed François away, grabbed the wheel back and straightened the car before we hit the ditch. The brakes screeched as he pulled the car to a stop.

'What the hell do you think you're doing?' he shouted.

François turned to him. 'We've got to try, haven't we?' he yelled. He grabbed Felix's arm. My heart leapt into my mouth. 'They'd do the same for us.'

Felix shook François' hand off. 'What can the three of us do?' he said.

François glanced at me. 'It's not too late until the train's gone, right, Eloise?'

I nodded. 'And we don't know what we can do until we try.'

Felix hit the dashboard. 'This isn't one of your books. We *have* nothing,' he said. 'There'll be soldiers everywhere and they'll be armed.'

'We'll think of something,' François said. 'We'll create a diversion, we'll find a way.'

Nobody moved. I barely breathed as the car idled.

Would Felix help us? Would he agree? I know we didn't have a plan, but if we could just get to the train station, I was sure we'd think of something. Father was there. We had to try everything we could to save him and the others.

The silence seemed to go on and on, as if it might last for ever. Then, without a word, Felix released the brake and pulled the car into the road.

François looked back at me and nodded.

Felix took a left then a right down the long Rue de la Gare towards the station. The buildings grew further apart. I could see the turning. In my head I could hear the trains. We were close. We were going to make it. I imagined Father waiting, knowing we'd come to save him. François would cause a diversion, Felix and I would get him out of the train and . . .

Felix slowed the car to make the turning, but someone was there at the junction. They were waving – right at us.

'Albert!' I yelled.

Felix slammed on the brakes.

I fell hard into the back of his seat, my head banging against the headrest.

The car stalled. Felix turned in his seat, his face crumpled into a scowl, but I pointed at Albert. He was waving at us like he was mad.

'It's really Albert,' I said. 'He's alive.'

'Exactly,' Felix said as he and François shared a look.

'Incredible he managed to evade all those soldiers after being seen with the Resistance, isn't it?'

I didn't know what to say to that.

'So what's he doing here?' Felix asked, opening his door.

Albert was running towards us now.

In a flash, Felix leapt out and grabbed him. François slid over into the driver's seat and started the engine. Felix, his hand round Albert's mouth, picked him up and threw him into the back of the car next to me.

An old man with a basket passed by on the other side of the road, but when I caught his eye he looked away. A woman huddled in a blanket against the wall of a boarded-up shop didn't even look up. I noticed she had bare feet and was hugging something in her arms. I supposed people had seen this, and worse, before.

Felix slammed the back door, then got into the front. 'Go!'

François drove off, swerving around a man and his dog as they stepped out to cross.

'Where have you been?' I yelled at Albert. 'Why did you leave us?'

Albert looked down at his lap. 'El, I need to tell you something.' He glanced at Felix and François in the front. 'I need to tell you all something, but you have to turn the car around, right now.'

'We can't,' I said, 'we've got to –'

François interrupted me. 'Where did you go, Albert?'

Albert flashed a look at him, then at me. 'I'm sorry,' he said, looking at my watch. 'It's nearly five. I know where you're going. That's why I'm here. I have to stop you.'

'You admit it!' Felix said, bending round. 'You're working with them!'

My hand went to my mouth. He had really betrayed us!

'No!' Albert shouted. 'Look, you can't go to the station,' he said, as if his words were being forced out his throat. 'It's full of soldiers.'

'We know,' François said. 'Soldiers loading prisoners onto the train for the prison camp.'

'No, you don't know!' Albert was really yelling now. I'd never seen him like this. Crazed. Almost wild. 'You don't know anything!'

The sign for the station got larger until it filled the small windscreen.

'Don't stop here, please don't stop the car,' he cried.

Albert pulled at the back of François' seat, then his shoulder. The car swerved. Felix tried to grab his hands, but Albert was screaming.

'It's a trap. There's no train!'

Felix and François looked at each other.

Albert beat his hands against the back of the seat.

'I lied to you!'

Time seemed to slow down. It felt as if we'd all stopped breathing. Then François revved the engine and the car *vroomed* forward with a lurch past the turning to the station.

Albert sank into his seat.

I looked behind me. The station was already a spec in the distance. I dug my nails into the seat, let out a cry. What was happening? Was there really no train?

'El, I'm sorry.'

I looked at Albert. He had a red and purple mark under his left eye, a small jagged cut in the middle of it. His knees were dirty and brown, and yellow bruises splattered up and down his knees. And some part of me was glad that he was hurt.

'Why?' I said, my voice wobbling. 'Why would you betray us?' I felt tears coming and that made me more angry. I wanted to hit him. I wanted to throw gravel at him and call him names. How could he have done this?

He shook his head. 'I know you hate me, El, and I'm sorry. I'm sorry!' he said.

I pushed my hair out of my face, tried to think.

'If there's no train then where's Father?' I took a breath.

Albert swallowed. 'You need to understand . . . They took *my* father, El,' he said, looking at me, then down at his hands. 'When they took over the house, I made a deal. I said I knew some people in the Resistance . . .'

He glanced at François and Felix up front. François was staring at the road ahead but Felix caught my eye in the rear-view mirror. 'I lied about that too,' Albert said. 'I hadn't joined them then, not properly. I knew who they were, though, so I tried to help out when they let me. I wanted to be like Monsieur X, you know?' He looked up and I stared at him as if I was seeing him for the first time. So much of him seemed familiar, but he didn't look or sound like the boy I knew. 'They were going to take Mother too, but they agreed to let her stay on as cook and housekeeper if I told them things. About the Resistance. About the town. And the people.'

Felix turned in his seat. 'You led them to the boat, boy. That was more than information, that was nearly our lives! They shot Nan! How do you justify that?'

'I didn't have a choice!' Albert said. His shoes began to beat against the seat as if he had a tic, as if he couldn't stop it, or he wanted to kick something badly. 'I had to give them something after *you* turned up at the house!' He looked at me. 'I told the Kommandant you were stupid and you didn't know anything, but he said I was lying, because you took papers with your father's name on them. He knew your father's name, Eloise!'

I shut my eyes. Yes, I'd told him that at the church. He would've known Albert was lying.

Albert carried on, sighing. 'So I had to tell him what

I knew – that you and the Resistance were planning to stop the train.'

I swallowed a bitter taste in my mouth. I'd told him about that when we'd hidden in the secret room so it was my fault the Kommandant knew. And all because I'd trusted the boy I'd thought was my friend.

'He came up with a plan for me to tell you the train departure day had changed, so they could capture you.' Albert blew out a breath. 'He didn't know you were still right there under his nose in the library! Or that you'd escape his soldiers in the woods!' He grinned at me. 'I mean, El what you did should be in a Monsieur X book of its own.'

Albert reached for my hand, but I threw it off. 'Monsieur X would never betray his friends.'

'Why didn't you tell us about the trap on the boat?' asked François.

Albert rubbed his eyes with his sleeve as if he was trying to erase something. 'When he told me his plan, the Kommandant said I'd lied to him about you already, El, so I needed reminding where my loyalties lay.' He swallowed. 'Mother's gone now, and he said I'd be going with her unless I did exactly what he said.'

Nan said she hadn't seen her when she'd made the morning deliveries. It sounded like Albert was telling the truth, about this at least.

He looked up at me, his eyes flashing. 'But I didn't know they were going to follow me to you!' Albert let out a sob.

I thought about what he was saying. 'I suppose the Kommandant knew his plan to trap us at the station *might* work, but following you would *definitely* lead him to us . . .'

I glanced at Felix in the mirror, who nodded his head.

'I didn't mean to betray you. I didn't mean to lie,' Albert sobbed. 'I wanted to help, I wanted to be a part of the Resistance, to help people and stop the soldiers. And now I've lost both my parents, helped the enemy, and put you all in danger.'

'But why did you run away from us on the boat?' asked Felix.

Albert gulped. 'I . . . I was scared. Scared to stay with you in case I was shot, and scared to go back to the house in case the Kommandant was there. I ran and ran and then all I could think of to do was wait here, near the station, in case you believed what they made me tell you.'

Albert sobbed in huge gulps and hiccups that filled the car. I felt torn. I hated seeing him so hurt, but I couldn't comfort him, not after what he'd done. He'd betrayed us. Even if he felt he had no choice.

But there was something good in what he'd said, something that warmed my heart.

The train leaving today was a lie. So, according to the deportation list I stole, that meant we had a whole extra day to rescue the prisoners. To save Father. That gave us time to find explosives and time to plan.

François was clearly thinking the same thing. 'So the train didn't leave today?' he asked, slowing the car.

Felix looked at him. 'I know what you're thinking,' he said to François, shaking his head, 'but it's still going to be tough, even with an extra day . . .'

But Albert looked stricken. 'The Kommandant was actually happy you took that list, Eloise. They were always updating them and he was smiling that weird smile when he told me he knew what you'd stolen. He . . .' Albert struggled with his words. 'He said it was an old list,' he mumbled. He gave a quick glance to me then looked at Felix. 'The train to the camp left days ago.'

A silence fell, so heavy it seemed to fill the car.

The train had gone.

Father had gone.

For good.

# Chapter Thirty-Three

Albert's words echoed round and round my head. After everything that had happened, everything we'd risked, the train had gone and Father with it.

It was a few seconds before I noticed François was revving the car. It stuttered, hopping forwards, then screeched as it tried to go faster.

Albert had his head in his hands. He was mumbling something.

Felix turned in his seat. 'Say that again.'

Albert looked up. 'The train left days ago,' he said. 'But . . .' He peered at me, then looked back at François and took a deep breath. 'They kept some people in cells,' Albert said, 'under the house. There's a cellar. I never knew it was there, but it runs under almost the whole of the house. They kept their supplies in there.' He reached for his pocket then gulped. 'And some prisoners.'

He looked at me again. 'I'm sorry,' he said.

I frowned.

'El . . . I saw your father there.'

I sucked in a breath. I tried to say something, but no words came out. Instead, I turned away. François had wound down his window to let in some air, but the breeze seemed to choke me. Something stirred in my stomach and all of a sudden my words rushed back.

'You saw Father?'

'I'm sorry, I couldn't say anything. The Kommandant –'

'You knew I was looking for him. You knew I was worried sick. Amma too. You knew and he was there, in your house, all this time.' I shook my head as if I could clear the buzzing noise filling it from the inside.

'But –'

'But nothing, Albert! You don't betray your friends,' I said. 'No matter what.'

He rolled his eyes. 'Monsieur X is all very well,' he shouted, grabbing my arm, 'but what if the Kommandant told you he'd make *your* mother disappear if you didn't do exactly what he said? What if it was *your* mother *and* your father he said wouldn't ever come back?'

'It *is* my father!' I shouted. 'It's *everyone's* father, or mother, or brother, or sister, or uncle.' I conjured up Maddie's pale face, her thick brown hair parted in two, a trickle of blood running from the cut above her eye. 'Or best friend.'

I narrowed my eyes. 'Is it your fault they took Maddie away? You never gave me a proper answer before, and it's time you told the truth. About everything. Did you tell them about her? Did you?'

Albert kicked the back of François' seat then yelled. 'I didn't have to! They knew her family were Gypsies! And by the time the Kommandant arrived, Maddie and her family were already gone. I don't know if they took them or they left or what happened.'

He took heaving gulps of air. 'I didn't have a choice. You think I did, but I didn't.' He looked down at his hands. 'I was trying to help,' he said, quietly. 'I only did what I thought was best, even if you think it was wrong. I wanted to get Father back and save Mother, and now *my* life's at stake too, El. When the soldiers opened fire on the boat, they must've known I was there too, don't you see? I realised when I was running away that the Kommandant was never going to trust me, that I didn't matter to him at all, and that no one would be safe, whatever I did for him, whatever he promised. So I came to find you and now everything's a mess and . . .'

He gnawed his thumb.

His words rattled me. They made a sort of sense in my head, but my heart wasn't ready to think much of Albert.

'Father can't be . . .' I couldn't say it. If I said the word, it would somehow be true. I tried to slow my breathing, wiping away angry tears, and looked at François. 'Isn't there anything we can do?'

'I thought you might say that,' he said, with a heavy sigh. 'But I don't see what. They'll be at the camp by now. We can't attack there, it would be suicide.'

Albert shook his head. 'And you can't trust anything the Kommandant says.' He shrugged. 'He said those papers weren't up to date, El. What if the train went somewhere else?'

'You could be the one lying,' Felix said.

Albert shook his head like mad. 'It's the truth,' he said. 'I'm not lying about this. I don't owe them anything. Not now. If I go back, they'll just put me on a train.'

'No,' I said slowly. 'He's telling the truth.' I shot him a look. 'Finally. I can hear it in his voice.' The gears were clicking in my head. Albert was telling the truth, but the Kommandant was full of lies. Monsieur X said that sometimes you had to listen to what was behind the words being spoken to find the real truth.

'The prisoners . . .' I said, turning to Albert. 'You said some were in the cells, under the house?'

Albert nodded. 'They marched them off a lorry straight to the cellar. I tried to go back later, but it was always guarded.'

I looked at Felix. His eyes had narrowed.

'We can't trust what the Kommandant has said, unless we put the pieces together ourselves.' I leant forward. 'What if they didn't put them *all* on the train?' I said. 'What if they didn't put *any* of them on the train?'

Albert shook his head, but Felix rubbed his beard.

'A bluff?' he said.

'Maybe,' I said. 'Perhaps the Kommandant knew he couldn't really trust Albert after the library. Perhaps what he said about the train already leaving was a lie to put us off a rescue . . .'

Albert started to speak, but I interrupted.

'I know you think I just want Father to be alive,' I said, 'and I do, but we have to check every possibility – there are other people missing too. What if your mother's there?'

Albert paled. 'Nan set off a bomb in the kitchen,' he said. 'That's where the entrance is to the cellars.'

Panic flared inside me. 'All the more reason to go and check for prisoners then! François – we need to get to the house!'

'We don't have as much petrol as I thought,' he said, pressing his foot on the accelerator. The little car spluttered and jumped forward, but we didn't gain any speed.

'We're not going to make it that far and still have

enough petrol to get out again,' Felix said.

'We need another car,' I said, but we'd been lucky with Yvonne. No one else in town would dare help us now. I racked my brain trying to think who did have a car and where they kept it.

Suddenly Albert gave a shout. 'There! Turn left, now!'

The veins stood out on his forearms as François gripped the wheel and swerved the car off the road. It bumped along a rutted lane not much more than an overgrown path. Albert and I were lifted off the seats, slamming down hard each time the car hit another rut. The path led around the edge of the forest, the trees shading us from the main road.

'Keep straight ahead,' Albert said. 'Then right.'

We turned onto a faint path. Up ahead a large wooden building squatted in the far corner of an overgrown meadow. Where were going?

'Take a left here,' Albert said.

'Here?' François said, frowning.

Albert nodded. 'You can hide the car in the woods.'

The car snapped twigs and bumped over lumpy, muddy furrows. Low hanging branches scratched the roof and the green car *tink-tink-tinked*. Then it gave a cough, and stopped dead.

'Not here,' Albert said, 'we should go further in.'

François shook his head. 'No more petrol.'

Albert flung the back door open. 'What are you waiting for then? Come on, I know where there's a car!'

With a quick look at each other and a shrug, we leapt out after him. Albert raced towards a wooden building his father used to keep his tools in, scythes and axes and all the things we were forbidden from ever going near. What was he up to? I watched as he skidded round the side then disappeared through a door. Felix ran through after him, then a moment later popped his head back out and roared with laughter.

'What is it? What's wrong?' François said.

We hurried to the doorway.

When I peered in, it was pitch black. Slowly I made out something sleek and shining and glossy. I realised what I was looking at just as Felix answered.

'The boy's only gone and got us the Kommandant's car!'

# Chapter Thirty-Four

The Kommandant's car!

Albert patted the car and bowed.

François ran his hands through his hair. 'Are you serious?'

I peered through the dark windows to the soft seats inside.

'It's the only one I could think of,' Albert said. 'Besides, it's Father's barn, so I'd say we own whatever's in it.' He put his hand into his left pocket. 'Oh, and I forgot to tell you.' He pulled out a set of keys. 'I was so angry with the Kommandant earlier that I stole these.'

He unlocked the driver's door, opened it, leant in and pulled out a cap. 'I think it suits me,' he said, popping it onto his head.

Felix snatched the cap from him. He smoothed down his own hair and squished the cap on top. Then he took the keys from Albert. 'It's certainly one way to get around without being stopped. But not with children on show. In the boot. Now.'

He unlocked it, and Albert and I climbed inside.

'Wait,' I said, 'we *are* going back to the house, aren't we?' I stared at François.

François was about to answer when Felix slammed the boot shut. Then everything was muffled, as if we were underwater. I heard a door bang shut, a soft purr and gentle buzz as the car began to move. Then the car stopped, there was another thud – as François got in, perhaps – and we bumped along the road.

I willed my eyes to adjust to the darkness.

'We'll check the house,' I said, to myself. 'We have to. François will persuade him, I know it.'

I felt Albert shift next to me, but he stayed silent.

'How did you even know the car was here?' I asked.

'They took over all the barns except the one you live in,' Albert said. 'I checked when they first got here, after the Kommandant clipped my ear for touching his precious baby.' He snorted. 'He moved the car here after that. Serves him right if it's ours now,' he said.

It was hot inside the boot. Soon enough sweat poured down my back and began to pool under my arms and knees. I wasn't sure how I felt about being this close to Albert. Hearing about his lies, that he'd known where

Father was, had made me feel sick – made me wonder if I could ever be friends with him again. But he'd come clean and he'd found us the car. I sighed. Would I ever be able to forgive him?

All of a sudden we lurched to a stop. There was a shout from outside. Then another shout. The sound of boots on the road and rumbling.

'Soldiers?' I asked.

'Shhhhh!' Albert said, but surely no one would dare look in the boot of the Kommandant's car?

One of the car doors clicked open, then shut so violently it shook the car. My heart started racing. We were caught and any moment the boot would open and that would be it. I'd never find out where Father really was, and Amma would never know what happened to me.

Albert took my hands in his. It felt normal and comforting and at the same time all sorts of wrong too. I tried to pull away, but he held them tight.

'Tell me you understand, El, please?' Albert whispered. 'I'm not asking you to forget,' he said, 'or even forgive me, but if we get caught . . .' He let that thought hang for a moment, his breath hitching. 'Well, I just want to know that we're still friends. I'll say sorry for ever. I'll do whatever I can to make things right. You're my best friend. I am sorry, El.'

I sighed, and gave his hand a squeeze. 'Albert, I . . .'
I started to say, but the car moved off again. What was
happening out there? I hadn't heard any voices or screams
or anything . . .

The car ran smoothly, as if the road was brand new. I
couldn't picture where we were. Then there was a lurch
and the car sped up. We purred along, then the brakes
squealed. Albert and I were flung against the back of the
boot as the car came to a sudden stop.

'We'll run,' I whispered to Albert.

'But we don't know what's happened or who's driving,'
he said.

'It doesn't matter,' I said. 'As soon as they open the
boot, just run.'

He gripped my hand. 'I won't leave you, El. Not this
time, I promise.'

'This time it's a plan,' I said. 'Look, it's like *Monsieur
X and the Ghost in the Castle*. They shoot at him and the
ghost, but they can't follow both and so one gets away.'

Albert didn't answer.

'If we run, we have a chance,' I said.

The engine switched off. Doors slammed. Feet
pounded.

Silence.

I felt my muscles tense, waiting.

There was a rumble – another engine. A truck

approaching. Boots stamping on the road. Getting closer. Stopping.

I took a deep breath. The boot swung open. Sunlight flew in. On impulse, I flung my arm against the light, then realised I'd missed my chance to run. I got to my feet and, as the spots in front of my eyes cleared, I saw a soldier.

He was blond, with sticky-up short hair, like the brush we used to clean the dishes. When he turned round I saw his skin was bright pink and looked stretched, as if he wasn't used to being in the sunshine. He was older than François, but not by much. For a moment we stared at each other, then he raised his gun and pointed it at us.

'Run!' I shouted.

Albert was halfway out of the boot when he grabbed my hand and pulled me with him.

'Halt!' shouted the guard.

I ducked, cringing against the bullets that were surely headed our way, but Albert yanked my hand, forcing me to keep up.

I heard a *crick, cruck* and risked a glance back. The soldier was bent over his gun. His hand was shaking. He looked up, his eyes wide. Then slowly, as if he wasn't even aware he was doing it, he let his trembling hand drop. I gasped. He couldn't do it! He couldn't shoot us! I turned back to Albert and we ran as fast as we could into the trees at the side of the road.

We didn't stop till we were deep into the forest. Albert finally let go of my hand and I fell to the ground, trying to catch my breath and not be sick. I could hear Albert wheezing too. I looked up. He was staring back the way we'd run.

'Nothing,' he said before I'd even asked.

'Did you see François and Felix?' I said.

Albert shook his head.

I looked around, trying to get a sense of where we were. The forest stretched from our town of Amboise to Monteaux. Parts of it bordered Albert's family's land. I glimpsed the mountains through the gaps in the trees. It would take a while, but I knew that if we ran towards them we'd get to the big house. We could check for prisoners, maybe even set them free! I turned to Albert.

'No, El,' he said.

'You haven't heard the rest of my plan,' I said.

He shook his head. 'I don't need to. You want to go to the house, to where there's even more soldiers when we've only just escaped from some! We got lucky, but the soldiers at the house will be on their guard after you got away. And what about François and Felix? Shouldn't we be looking for them?'

I felt a pain in my chest. 'You heard the noise,' I said. 'The other engine, the boots stamping closer and closer.'

Albert's brow furrowed.

'What if they've been taken?' I explained. 'What if we're the only ones left who can help?'

Albert looked towards his home, a few miles away through the trees. I wondered what he was thinking. He'd promised in the boot of the car to help, but now, when it came to it, would he run and hide instead?

'The little barn,' I said. 'You told me that's where your secret passage leads to, yes?'

He nodded.

'So we could use it to sneak into your house, check the cellars and find out if there are any prisoners still there.'

Albert bit his lip.

'I know what you're going to say,' I said, 'but what if it's not too late? What if there's even a tiny chance he's still alive?' I sniffed back any tears that threatened to spill. 'It's worth trying, Albert!'

When he still didn't speak, I realised what he wasn't saying.

'You're not going to come,' I whispered, 'are you?'

Albert shook his head. 'I'm sorry, El,' he said. 'I can't.' He began to pick at his nails. 'The Kommandant meant what he said. I ran off so they know I've betrayed them and if they catch me now they'll send me to a camp.'

'But, Albert,' I said, my voice getting higher, 'your mother could be in the cellar. You said you'd help and you're just giving up. You're giving up on me and your family and my family and –'

'No, El, I'm just . . .' Albert stared at the floor. He took a couple of deep breaths before facing me. 'I'm scared,' he said. 'I'm sorry, but that's the truth.'

I didn't say anything. I knew what it felt like to be scared, to be afraid that you might get shot or be sent away or lose all your family. But I had to check the cellars. Father was worth all my fears. He was worth my taking the chance. Otherwise, what was the point? We might as well let the Kommandant and all his soldiers do whatever they wanted.

'You can go and warn Amma then, tell her about Felix and François being missing,' I said eventually, crossing my arms. 'I can do this myself.'

Albert took a step away, then another and another. I watched him walk off with a heavy feeling that settled in my stomach and felt as if it was dragging me to the floor. He really was going. After he promised he wouldn't abandon me again. I know I'd told him to go, but I hadn't meant it.

I turned away and began walking through the forest, lead-footed and heartsick, when I heard something behind me, someone running. My heart began to pound as I looked back, but it was Albert, his face alight, his legs pumping like pistons.

'I'm coming with you.'

I felt something in me lift. He'd changed his mind!

'It's like you said, El,' Albert said, as we sprinted through the trees, our steps surer with purpose now. 'What if we're the only ones left who can help?' He took my hand. 'Besides, I promised, didn't I?'

It wasn't long till we reached the main road. We shared a look. It would be faster if we walked along it, though there was a big risk we'd be spotted. Sure enough, we'd only walked for a few minutes when we heard rumbling and a large brown truck appeared over the horizon. We threw ourselves into the hedgerow, hoping it would be thick enough to shield us from the soldiers' eyes.

We waited. And waited. I counted to sixty as the trucks passed by. I'd never seen so many all together. And they were heading away from the house.

After the last truck disappeared, Albert's hand tugged mine, back towards the forest, and I nodded. The road wasn't safe. With all those trucks on the move, something was going on and my stomach churned knowing we didn't have a clue what it was. Albert knew the regular comings and goings of the soldiers at the house so I'd thought we could sneak in. But things were clearly changing. We could be walking towards anything. Maybe the bomb had revealed the secret passage from the kitchen to the cellar. Maybe they'd discovered the room behind the tapestry, our only way in and out . . .

Our feet crunched across the forest floor, but that was the only sound. Under the trees it was as quiet as a library, and that made my thoughts seem too loud.

I had Albert with me. That would help, wouldn't it? But did that mean I was safer or that there were two of us to worry about?

I swallowed.

Monsieur X believed in plans. He said careful planning was essential for the successful detective, but then he also said that you had to trust your instincts.

Well, that was all we could do now.

# Chapter Thirty-Five

As we ran through the forest, my head filled with thoughts of how my daring rescue mission would go. The prisoners would all be in the cellar and we'd set them free. If Father wasn't there, then we'd find out what was really going on with the train and stop it before it got to the camp. Father and I would be reunited at last and everyone would come home to their families.

I imagined him walking through our doorway, the feel of his scratchy chin against my cheek, his arms hugging me all the way round as I buried my head in his neck.

'*Come under my wing, ma rose.*'

I swallowed a sob and caught my breath. We'd reached the edge of the woods and I stared out from the safety of the trees. We were here.

The old barn lay between the front door of the big house and the orchard full of blackened trees. We never played in the barn, partly because it was falling apart, but mostly because it was so near the graveyard. I shivered. The trees clustered around it were spindly, old and half dead, the graves poking up from the ground like broken teeth. We'd have to pass through them to get to the barn, but, if we were careful, the trees would hide us from the trucks and tents around the house.

I crouched down, beckoning Albert to follow as I crept through the grass, so tall here that it was waving over our heads. I hoped the movement wouldn't give us away.

'My ancestors,' Albert had said to Maddie and me once, looking at the few mouldy stones left. 'Mum said something terrible happened and they lost a whole wing of the house. They watch over us, she says, but I think she only tells me that to stop me running about upstairs.'

I couldn't help it. I grinned at the memory of when life was so normal.

I was scared and I was tired and I was so very hungry, but remembering things like that made me feel as if Maddie was still here with us. Maybe it was alright to think this was like a game of Monsieur X, if it helped. *Monsieur X and the Great Prisoner Rescue*!

Suddenly there was a slam.

Then another.

And another.

Doors, but I couldn't tell where.

I dropped to the ground and lay on my front, my breathing hard and fast, my heart beating triple time. With my cheek pressed into the grass I saw a little round stone. I grabbed it tight and waited.

When I didn't hear anything more, I lifted my head, checked Albert was still with me and crawled around the largest headstone.

The barn sat straight ahead, but to its right, across the grass, was a strange sight.

I'd never seen so many soldiers. There must always have been this many, in their tents or in the town, but now it seemed as if every German soldier in France was swarming around the house. Half the tents had disappeared and they were taking down more. Some were piling weapons and equipment into crates, others lugging heavy boxes onto trucks. The doors to the house gaped open, and soldiers were scurrying in and out like ants with smaller boxes, suitcases and crates.

Were they leaving? I couldn't help but smile. Then my heart lurched. If they were leaving, they wouldn't leave the prisoners behind . . . We had to move – fast! But were they busy enough not to notice if we raced across the meadow to the barn?

I looked at Albert; his face was as pale as Amma's flour, but he nodded. He knew what we had to do. There was no option but to run.

I grabbed his hand and we leapt from behind the gravestone, running as hard as we could, knowing our lives depended on it.

And we almost made it.

Almost.

Bullets found us. *Rat-a-tat-tat*. Something thunked into the barn wall right by my shoulder then pinged to the ground at my feet. We ducked behind the side wall, and I knelt and picked it up. It was boiling hot and burnt my palm.

'*Das Mädchen!*'

Someone must have recognised me – they were shooting at us!

Panicked, I turned to Albert.

'Go, El,' he said. 'Get inside the barn.' He risked a look back. 'I'll draw them away for as long as I can.'

'No, wait!' I called, but he was already running.

The soldiers saw him and pointed their guns away from me and towards him. I slid along the wall until I reached the barn door, pulled back the bolt, and slipped inside.

Silence.

The bullet was throbbing in my hand. I opened my palm and let the misshapen lump of metal fall into my pocket. My hand shook, but I pulled the door behind me quickly and quietly, pushing my eye up to a crack. I couldn't see anyone following, but I couldn't see Albert either. I wanted to wait for him – I needed to know he was alright – but if he was hurt or had run away then it was up to me to get the prisoners.

I forced myself to turn my back on the door, and move deeper into the barn.

Inside it was dark – only tiny slivers of light crept in through the cracks, lighting up the dust so that it sparkled. I smelt a strange burnt scent. I sniffed my stinging, shaking hand, but it wasn't that. This was rich and sweet. I could see something in front of me. I reached out and touched a little stone. There must have been a hundred of them, lying in a rack as if waiting to be counted.

I was trying to work out what they were when I saw something bulky out of the corner of my eye.

'Look for a machine,' Albert had said, as we'd walked along the road, 'old and rusted and stuck in the wall. It will look like an oven. They used to roast walnuts in it, I think. Anyway, pull it away and behind it there's a passageway.'

I sniffed again. Walnuts. That's what the little stones were.

Pushing thick cobwebs and broken pieces of metal and wood out of the way, I faced the machine. It was exactly as he'd said, rusted with a handle on the right side, its large shadow looming across the wall. I grabbed the handle and bits flaked off and spiralled to the ground. I hissed in pain. I'd used the hand that had picked up the bullet without thinking. But I'd need both hands to try to move this thing, so I gritted my teeth and pulled again, as hard as I could. The whole thing screeched as if I was hurting it, but didn't move an inch. There was no way I could pull it away from the wall.

Suddenly the barn door rattled and the bolt slid back. I sucked in a breath. The soldiers must have heard me!

I looked around for options, but the barn door and the passageway were my only ways out. I could hide, but the barn wasn't big – it wouldn't be long before they found me. I grabbed the handle again, pulled then pushed, but it was no good – it barely moved. The bolt on the main door squealed and an arc of light crept towards me.

I turned back to the machine and with the extra light I could now see a thin gap behind it, maybe wide enough for me to slip through. I heard shouting and scrambled around the machine, squeezing myself into the hole. I scraped the palms of my hands as I forced myself through as dust, rust and bits of web clinging to my clothes.

The gap spat me out into a tunnel.

It was even darker than the barn. The floor shifted as if it was sprinkled with sand and the walls felt like thick blocks of stone, cold and rough. If I held out my arms I could touch each side with my fingertips.

A breeze whistled towards me, lifting the hair at the back of my neck and making me shiver.

Then I heard a groan – something heavy and metallic. The soldiers must have seen where I'd gone, and were moving the machine away from the wall. They were coming!

I ran. My feet slid across the sand and the cold air guided me forwards until at last I reached the small room Albert had been hiding in.

The sack full of chocolate sat slumped in the corner. My stomach rumbled, but there was no time for that. I crept to the panelled door and pulled it open, stopping only to listen.

Nothing.

I slipped out, pulling the door shut and waited behind the tapestry.

Still nothing.

Taking a deep breath, I peered out, looking left and right. Albert had said the secret entrance to the cellar was through the kitchen, which was on my left. I started towards it, but the kitchen door began to open so I scrabbled back, ducked across the hallway and tucked myself behind the grandfather clock. One set of boots stomped past. Then another set stomped their way down the great staircase. I glanced at the kitchen. The door was ajar now, but what if there were more soldiers inside?

What if the Kommandant was in there? The footsteps reached the bottom of the stairs and began heading towards me. Then they stopped. I heard a thump. I peered round and saw a soldier. He was bent over a box he'd obviously dropped. This was it. This was my chance! I dashed across the hall, slipped through the kitchen door and held my breath.

But the kitchen was empty. And not just of people.

Cupboards were hanging open, pots and pans missing from the shelves. Crates were piled on the floor, some damaged, all of them empty. But the worst part was where the sink and the giant double oven had been. Now there was just a hole in the wall. A giant crater from floor to ceiling, a gaping space with half a windowpane sticking jaggedly out of one side and the pretty flowered curtains blowing gently in the breeze.

Nan's explosives.

I shivered.

Suddenly I heard coughing behind me – the soldier must be heading this way – and raced into the pantry. I spun round staring at the jars, half empty, some smashed, my feet crunching over old dried beans and glass. Then I noticed something strange. The little bits of glass were moving, as if the floor was slightly sloped. I watched as they rolled beneath a large wooden shelf stacked with tablecloths and napkins. A dead end. Then I heard it. A *plink-plink* sound, as if the little bits of glass were falling down a well. I'd found it – the secret door to the cellars!

I heard another thump and jumped half out of my skin. Was it the soldier? Careful not to let my feet crunch across the mess on the floor I peered round the pantry into the kitchen. The box had been dumped on the table. The soldier had gone. I turned back to the shelf, fumbling along it for a switch or catch or anything to reveal the secret door.

Then, to my horror, the whole wall of shelves began to move all by itself. It pushed out towards me, sweeping glass and dried beans aside.

It was too late to hide. I took a breath and hoped I'd be brave. I wanted Father and Amma to be proud of me, whoever was behind it, whatever happened next.

# Chapter Thirty-Six

The shelf stopped moving, and the pale, blond woman with the beauty spot peered round.

She started as she saw me. Then with a quick glance over the top of my head she grabbed my arm . . .

*Crunch, crunch, crunch.* Someone was coming.

. . . and pulled me behind the shelf door, shutting it after her.

It was pitch black. My heart was beating so loud it was echoing. The cellar smelt of damp, cold stone and something else – like those hot days in the classroom when we weren't allowed to open the windows – but a thousand times worse.

A torch clicked on and swung round until there was a *clink* and a dim light began to glow above.

I stared at the woman. Her shoes were red and shiny with rounded toes. She wore stockings and a suit in two parts that was a slightly darker kind of red and made a V of her top half. She had on red lipstick, and with her blond hair set in glossy waves, she looked exactly like the photograph that had been sitting on the desk in the library.

'*Ich hätte nicht gedacht, dass du zurückkommen würdest,*' she said.

I frowned. I didn't know what that meant.

'I didn't think you'd come back,' she said, switching to French, and pocketing something so quickly I felt sure she didn't want me to see it.

Her voice was quiet and low. Her accent wasn't German, but not completely French either. It was half and half. A sound like velvet, like whispering.

'But it seems as if we are destined to meet in unusual places.'

There was a pattern along the bottom of her jacket. Two lines that dipped and swirled round the folds, like train tracks over a mountain. I thought of a train *click-clacking*. I thought of Father and all the other prisoners. Were they here? If so, where? I looked around, but the bulb was so dim all I could see behind the woman were uneven stone walls, and a gaping hole with steps leading into darkness.

'*Niemand.* There's no one down there,' she said, following my gaze.

Could I trust her? I had to see for myself. I took a step towards the stairs when she spoke again.

'I know what you stole from the library.'

I froze, my eyes drawn back to her. I thought she'd be angry, but something like pride burnt in hers.

'He told me.' She reached out and took my hands.

This close I could see how perfect her lipstick was, like a painted bow the colour of cherries. She smelt of a shop my father had taken me into once; sweet and savoury, like almonds wrapped up in scented paper, like Christmas. I tried to shake away the memory, but felt frozen. She was unlike anyone I'd ever met. I wanted to trust her, but she was a puzzle I couldn't work out and a part of me was so scared, I wasn't sure I was even breathing any more. Why was she in the cellar? If I told her why I was here would she help me again or would she call for the Kommandant?

Suddenly there was a crunching noise from behind the pantry door. The soldier!

'Eloise,' the woman whispered, drawing me towards the far wall and the steps that led down. 'It's alright, I won't let anything happen to you.'

I shook my head, confused. 'Who told you my name? Was it the Kommandant?'

She smiled then. The corners of her eyes made tiny creases. I could see the powder on her face, white, like flour. She threw back her head. Her curls didn't move an inch. 'He didn't need to. I'd know you anywhere.'

I felt as if the floor was tipping, as if I was on the edge of something. .

She smoothed my fringe off my forehead, looping it back with her fingers to make it curl like hers.

I closed my eyes. Perfume snaked up my nostrils. I felt a hundred things at once. I felt as if I was little again, tucked up in bed, at home. I felt as if I could hear nursery rhymes. I felt soft and warm and safe.

My legs jolted. I pulled myself away. The woman's face fell too, but she quickly painted her smile back on.

'You know this secret, don't you?'

I shook my head.

'They lied to you.'

'No.'

Her smile slipped.

'Eloise . . .'

'Don't say my name,' I said. I felt my stomach lurch then rumble.

She smiled. 'I can get you something. Some hot chocolate? Some bread? There must be a few things left. You look starving, so thin. What has Amma been doing? Her job is to feed you up.'

I frowned. 'How do you . . .?'

She leant against the wall, crossing one leg over the other. One red shoe pointed towards me. 'You're exactly

how I imagined,' she said. 'How could I not know you?'
She smiled. 'Oh, Eloise, haven't you worked it out yet?'

She leant forward.

'I'm your mother.'

# Chapter Thirty-Seven

My jaw dropped.

I stared at her red shoe, followed the shine that glinted along its side. There was a small smudge of dirt near the toe that hadn't been polished away.

'Eloise?' She stood. Her red heels clipped together. The noise reminded me of the Kommandant. I thought of the silver framed picture on his desk.

I gasped. 'The Kommandant! You're his wife.'

Her eyes widened just a little. Her mouth thinned into a strange smile. 'Something like that.' Her words sounded brittle.

'But how? I mean, you were married to Father, but then . . .' I frowned. 'You can't be my mother. My mother died when I was born. Amma wouldn't lie.'

'Wouldn't she?' The woman felt in a small pocket at the front of her jacket and pulled out a gold lighter and a packet of cigarettes. She lit one. Her hand shook. 'People do what they have to,' she said.

'Well, Father wouldn't lie,' I said quietly.

She drew on her cigarette and blew smoke out of the side of her mouth. It hovered in the air. 'I'm sure that she . . .' She inhaled again. '. . . and your father . . .' She blew out the smoke. '. . . thought it best not to mention me.' The smoke swirled around her head, hiding her face.

*Father!* I didn't have time to think about this when I needed to find Father.

'Do you know where he is?' I said. 'The list, the papers I stole, they weren't the right ones. Your Kommandant double-crossed us. I need to know where Father's gone.'

The woman smoothed an invisible stray hair on her head with one hand and held the cigarette out in her other.

'Or is he here?' I said, turning towards the stairs. 'I know there were prisoners in here. Was Father with them? Are they still there?'

She flicked her cigarette. 'There were prisoners in the cellars,' she said. 'But not any more. Everyone here is leaving. Haven't you noticed?'

'But why?' I asked.

'Thanks to you and your friends we no longer have a working kitchen,' she said. Her voice lowered. 'And the Kommandant's job is almost done. There's only a handful of Resistance left now.'

I glanced at her. Was that a threat? Did she mean to get rid of me? It seemed as if there was much more to them leaving than she was saying. Was this all a trick? Was she just trying to confuse me – delay me? Were soldiers coming to get me right this minute? But then if it was all a lie, how did she know so much about me?

'Do you know about the train with the prisoners?' I asked quickly. 'The list I took said that the train was leaving tomorrow, but I heard it might have left already. I need to know the truth.'

She looked at me coolly, but didn't speak.

I took a step towards her. 'And if you don't know, the Kommandant does . . . You could find out, if you really care.'

She leant back, stubbing out her cigarette.

I swallowed. 'If you don't, you might as well have sent Father to his death.'

She flinched but I kept my gaze steady.

'Just like him,' she said, 'so sure of yourself, so sure of everything.' She pushed herself away from the wall. 'It wasn't my idea to come here,' she said. 'I might not have been able to raise you, but I wanted to make sure you were happy.'

My heart jolted. Was that why the dark car had really come to our house? To check on me?

She came closer. 'And when I saw you in the library with that book in your hand, it was a sign.' She smiled.

'I knew then you'd received the books I sent. It was only a matter of time before we would meet and when I explained who I was, I knew you'd understand.'

'I don't know you,' I whispered. 'I don't know anything about you.' I felt something thick lodge in my throat. 'I don't even know if what you're saying is real. I mean, if you're my mother, then where have you been? Why did you go? What books did you send? How –'

Suddenly there was a shout.

'Eloise!'

It was the Kommandant! But the strange thing was that we both jumped.

She gave me a twisted smile. 'You were named after me,' she said.

I felt the floor tip again.

'Eloise, where are you? We must leave!'

She looked at the door. Then, when we heard him stomp out of the pantry she focused on me.

'So many questions. So little time,' she said. 'If you can't believe my words, believe my actions – come with me,' she said.

I glanced at the door.

'Not out there,' she said. 'Come home with me.' She grabbed my hands. 'To Germany.' Her face broke out in the biggest smile. 'I'll make it up to you, tell you where I've been.'

'Eloise!'

I jumped.

'Oh, don't worry about him. We can get you out of this tired country. The war will be over soon and I can give you so much! No more rations, no more half days at school or worrying about money.' She smoothed my hair off my forehead then cupped my face in her hands.

My stomach rumbled at the thought of living without rations. 'But the Kommandant knows I'm with the Resistance,' I told her.

'He *was* coming after you,' she said, 'for the theft and for that little tin in the church, but I . . .' She glanced away. 'I redirected him.' She sneered. 'No one will miss that annoying Père Tremblay and it meant you were innocent.' I tried to move, but her hands pressed tight. 'Tremblay was playing both sides, anyway, and the Kommandant was keener to have someone he could imprison as a member of the Resistance than to have his superiors discover it was a schoolgirl eluding him.' She let go and stood. 'I will tell you everything you want to know,' she said, 'once we are home.' She smiled. 'And there will be as many books as you can read, I promise.'

I thought about never being hungry. I thought about whole libraries of books. Her perfume filled my head, making me dizzy.

'What about Amma and Father?' I said.

She pulled me closer so that her mouth was next to my ear.

'You're a caring girl, I can see that. If you come with me,' she whispered, 'I'll get him released from wherever he is.'

I gulped. 'You can do that?'

She shrugged as if to say it would be easy.

Her thumbs rubbed the side of my face, the edges of her nails against my cheeks. I felt a hundred things, all jumbled up together, but there was one thought that rose to the top. The most important one. I had to save Father. Whatever it took.

I nodded.

'You'll come with me?' Her eyes shone, but her words sounded greedy.

I nodded again.

'Eloise?'

My name again, but in a different voice. Not the Kommandant. Not the strange woman calling herself my mother. One that lifted my heart.

She let go of me so fast I staggered backwards. We both turned to the cellar door as it opened wide.

'Amma!' I cried.

She stood in the pantry staring at my mother. Their eyes locked. Amma's face looked drained, but stony too.

'*My* Eloise,' Amma said.

'Eloise!' shouted the Kommandant. He sounded close.

'If I heard you from the kitchen, he will find you soon enough,' Amma said to the woman, her voice hard.

I hesitated, turning to my mother. She was staring at Amma, an expression on her face I couldn't quite read, but it was as if she was closing herself up.

'Go,' she said to me. 'We need to finish here and leave.'

'But if you're leaving, I have to go with you!' She couldn't leave, not without me, not if it meant Father was going to be released. I was the closest I'd been to getting him back home, even if my heart shrivelled at the thought that I wouldn't be here with him.

She dragged her eyes away from Amma to me.

'Go with Amma for now. I'll come for you.'

'But –'

'Go!'

I flinched. Her voice was sharp. I slipped into the pantry and out into the kitchen. I glanced back to see she was staring at me.

'So determined, so like him,' she said, and smiled. 'But you have my hair.'

The door to the kitchen creaked open.

'Go!'

# Chapter Thirty-Eight

Amma took my hand and we ran out the hole in the kitchen wall and into the garden. We raced around to the front of the house where Amma stopped and squeezed me tight, which surprised me, then pushed me away, which felt more normal. Then she held me by the shoulders.

'You're not hurt, nothing broken?'

I shook my head, looking back at the house. I felt a pull towards it, and another towards Amma. I couldn't believe she was here for me. I wanted to tell her everything, but she bustled me away down the drive.

Behind us we heard the front door pulled and latched shut, window shutters drawn.

'Amma . . .'

'Not here.'

We passed the little box at the end where the soldier had been sitting. It was empty. We turned onto the main road that led past our house and only then did she speak.

'They're safe, *mon chou*.'

For a moment I wasn't sure who she meant. All thoughts of anyone else, except Father and the woman claiming to be my mother, had been forgotten.

I stopped.

It was a few paces before Amma realised I wasn't following.

'Nan is fine too,' she said. 'Your friend is looking after her.'

That was good to know, but she didn't understand. That wasn't what was on my mind.

'Is this why you never call me by my name?' I asked her.

Amma's face crumpled.

'You and Father, you never call me Eloise,' I explained. 'Is it because it's her name too?'

Amma glanced behind me, then took a breath. 'Not here.'

But I couldn't take one more step. There were things I needed to know. 'She said she's my mother.'

Amma met my gaze then slowly nodded.

I felt a sob in my throat and swallowed it down. I had a hundred questions, but something else jumped out before I could ask them. 'Then I have to go back. She says if I go with her, she'll find out where Father is and get him released.'

Amma winced, as if she was in pain.

'I have to. I mean, I need to . . .' Tears splashed down my cheeks. My voice shrank till it was so small even I could barely hear it. 'Why did you tell me she was dead?'

Amma took a step towards me then stopped. She opened her mouth, shut it again then shook her head and sighed. 'It is complicated. She is not a woman to trust.'

'She's my mother!'

Amma nodded.

'You lied to me!'

Amma reached for me. I wanted so much to sink into her arms, to go home with her, but everything had changed. I wasn't sure I wanted to be near her right now. I needed answers, but not only from her. I'd often longed for a mother, but she wasn't how I'd imagined. I wasn't even sure I could trust her. Did she mean what she said? Would she set Father free? Or was everyone lying to me? And did I have a choice? If there was even a chance my mother could do what she said, I had to trust her.

Sobs hiccuped through my whole body. I felt torn apart.

'We thought it was best,' Amma said, so low it was like whispering. 'You were so young. Not even a year.' She looked over my head. Took a breath. 'And she left him.' She looked down. 'And you.'

Her hands clasped together as if she was holding

dough, gently shaping it, careful.

'*Mon chou*, I want to glaze this for you and make it sweet, but the truth is not like that. This story is not one that can be honeyed.'

I hiccuped.

'Her head was turned. She left with an older man. She went to Germany.' She shook herself. 'We wanted to avoid you pain. And scandal, yes. Then the war arrived and . . .' She smiled at me. '. . . and you were happy. And I promised your father I would look after you.'

I took a juddering breath.

'She hurt you once,' Amma said. 'Don't let her hurt you again.'

'But she says she knows where he is!' I shouted.

Amma flinched. 'Do you really think *she* would tell you the truth?'

I stared at my feet. My shoes were scuffed so much they were more scratches than leather. What would it be like to have new shoes, perhaps red shoes like my mother? I didn't think she'd lied to me, unlike everyone else in my life.

'You don't know her, *mon chou*.' Amma closed her eyes for a moment. 'At home I have two Resistance fighters and one very worried boy. The soldiers chased him and fired at him. He barely got away, and Felix had to restrain him from coming back and getting you. François has not stopped pacing. He forced Felix to abandon the Kommandant's car with you and Albert in the boot to lure away a truck full of interested soldiers. He has worn the floor with his worry.'

She gave me a small, sad smile. 'The war will end, *mon chou*, and soon. The soldiers have left the big house, running home, so they say. They are not looking for you any more. You can come home. We will wait it out and then we can all make a plan, yes? Together.'

I could picture them sitting at the kitchen table. Felix with his pipe. François fretting in his frayed jumper. Albert pacing back and forth. I wanted nothing more than to join them. I shook my head. No, there was one thing I wanted more.

'She says if I leave with her, she'll get him released. Send him home.'

Amma looked at me with pity. 'She is a woman who will say whatever you want to hear. She manipulates feelings. You can never be certain she will follow through on her promises.' She held out a hand. 'Come home, Eloise,' she said.

I looked up, shocked that she'd used my name.

'It's a pretty name. I will use it, if you prefer.'

'I'm not a baby,' I said.

'I know,' she said. '*Mon chou* is just a nickname, a special name, one we give to those we love.'

I thought of Father calling me his rose. Remembering that made everything hurt. I thought of the woman. I couldn't quite think of her as my mother. My real mother was dead, or I'd thought she was. I wiped my eyes. I couldn't call her 'Mother', but I had to go with her, start a life with her because I couldn't lose the only chance Father had to survive. She might be lying, but what if she wasn't? It was all too much. I stood in the sun and couldn't force my feet forwards or backwards.

'Eloise?'

I looked up. François had appeared on the road behind Amma.

'You shouldn't be out here, either of you,' he said.

'She's my mother,' I told him and to my horror a whole wave of sobbing escaped.

With a confused look at Amma, he walked towards me.

'Come home. Whatever's going on, we'll find a way to sort it out. Felix is already looking into all the possible places your father and our friends could be. The Allies won't be long now. They'll free France and when they get here we can ask for their help.

'Come, now,' he said. François took my hand and gently pulled me along the road, Amma following as fast as she could. It seemed only moments later that we slipped through the back door into the kitchen. I breathed in the familiar baking smells and took in the ticking clock, the smoothly swept stone floors and the fire in the grate.

'El!'

Albert pounded down the stairs, and threw his arms around me. 'You're okay! I knew you would be!'

'Humph!' muttered Felix, from the kitchen table. 'I'm sure the path you've worn in the rug would have a different story to tell . . .'

François shut the back door as Albert led me to the table and jabbered about what had happened to him, as if it was straight out of a Monsieur X book. Amma began to busy herself. She slipped her patterned housecoat on and took the lid off a jar of flour. A puff of white escaped and hovered over the table. It felt odd that everything should continue as normal when my whole life had been turned upside down and inside out. I'd discovered a mother and that she probably wasn't to be trusted. The soldiers were leaving and I had no idea where Father was or even if he was still alive, but I did have a chance to save him. I sighed. Could I really leave all this behind? I pictured him sat in the kitchen, reading the newspaper. He'd be here and he'd be safe, but I'd never see him again.

Suddenly jars rattled along the pantry shelves. Above the oven, pans clinked together.

Then we heard footsteps.

They stopped outside the door.

Amma froze, her hands gripping a tray.

François stood up, a hand reaching for his gun.

Then there was a knock. Several knocks.

*Knock, knock, bang, knock. Knock, bang, knock. Knock, knock. Knock. Bang, knock. Bang, knock, knock.*

François turned to Amma then to me. He frowned and shook his head. Amma glanced at me, an eyebrow raised.

I frowned, then I got it. 'It's Morse code,' I whispered. 'It spells out "friend"!'

I knew then. I knew it would be her. She'd come for me, just like she'd said she would. She was to be trusted, after all. She would get Father released!

I ran and lifted the latch. As I opened the door François pressed himself against the wall behind it. Albert sidled next to him.

Bright sunlight poured in as if it was a completely ordinary day. I felt my heart lift and balanced on my tiptoes, as if I might fly any moment.

'Eloise,' I heard Amma say from behind me.

'Hello, Mother,' the woman replied.

# Chapter Thirty-Nine

I sucked in a breath. I couldn't believe it! I'd been so focused on whether or not this woman was my mother that I hadn't stopped to think about how she knew Amma. I'd always thought Father was Amma's son. I never thought it odd that he called her Amma too. It was just how things were.

'You will not take her,' Amma said in a low voice.

A corner of my mother's left eye twitched then she threw her shoulders back, looked around and smiled. She was wearing a coat that nipped in her tiny waist and had a fur trim around the hem that swirled in the breeze even though she stood perfectly still. Her hat was like a plate on its side with netting around it and I couldn't see how it didn't slip off her head.

'Eloise is very grown up,' she said loudly. 'I'd say she can make her own choices.'

Amma slammed the tray in her hands onto the table. The pastries jumped.

'Asking her to choose you over her father. For the life of her father! That's no choice! But that's just what you want, isn't it?'

The woman swayed a little on her heels as if Amma's words had physically hit her. She turned to me and waited. A hundred things ran through my head. I was curious about her, of course, and I did sometimes wonder what it would be like to have a mother, but the truth was that my life here was happy, or it was till Father had been taken. It all came back to Father. I had to save him. And if that meant going with her . . .

'You swear,' I said to her. 'You swear you'll get him released if I come with you.'

My mother smiled and straightened up, touching her hair as if checking the dinner-plate hat was still there. 'Of course.'

'Can I get my things?'

'No time,' she said, looking to her right. 'We must leave at once. We can buy whatever you need.'

I peered out of the door and saw a truck at the end of the garden, its engine rumbling.

My mother followed my gaze. 'Yes, I would have preferred the car too, but it was stolen. I don't suppose you know where it is, do you?' she asked.

I shook my head fast then wondered if I'd shaken it too quickly and now looked guilty.

Amma reached a hand out to me. I felt something tug at my heart.

'Eloise,' she said, 'you don't have to do this.'

I wasn't sure which of us she was talking to.

My mother held out a hand to me too.

'There's just one thing,' she said, glancing at the truck then back at me. 'He says he can forget your involvement in recent . . . events, but he knows you know where the last of the Resistance fighters are.'

My heart shrivelled.

'You can come with us, of course, and I'll find your Father and get him released, but you must give them up.'

My mouth dropped open. I looked round at Amma, who'd picked her tray up and was gripping it like she might throw it this time. Behind the door I felt François stiffen.

'It's such a small thing,' she said. 'People you barely even know.'

I stared at her, my heart clenching.

'And your father will be a free man.'

I bit my lip; let my top teeth dig in till it really hurt.

'And we'll go to a new home, together.'

Tears smarted behind my eyes. 'I . . . I . . .' I could barely form thoughts, let alone words.

My left hand was curled round the back of the door. I felt François' hand there and linked my fingers with his. I felt raw. I glanced at Albert. The look in his eyes showed me he understood. This must have been how he'd felt when he was asked to betray us. This was the hardest choice in the world, but there was only one decision I could make. I couldn't betray my friends. I wouldn't. Ever.

'You should leave,' I said quietly, my hands shaking.

My mother's lips twitched. 'Come now, Eloise,' she said, her eyebrows lifting and falling. 'We only need a location, but he insists, you see.'

Her eyes darted to the lorry and back. She opened her mouth to speak, but no words came out and I noticed something. Something she covered with make-up and stiff curls, dinner-plate hats and fur-trimmed coats. I saw how tired she was and something else, something I recognised easily because I felt it all the time. She was scared.

Behind the door François uncurled his hand from mine, as if he was leaving me to make this decision by myself. I felt hollow, as if there was nothing inside of me at all.

My mother held out her hand. 'Eloise, I am your *Mutter*.' She shook herself. 'Your mother.'

I looked at the ground. I felt as if I were filled with dirt and twigs and scratched like my shoes. Something gnawed at the edge of my brain too. I was missing something, but I couldn't figure it out.

'Just tell me where they are, and we can go.'

I thought of Father and then of Amma and François and Nan and even grumpy old Felix, who'd stopped being quite so grumpy lately. I thought of Albert and how he'd been tricked, but then he'd been sorry and helped us.

After what seemed like hours, I looked up and shook my head.

There was a shout from the truck.

'Well, then, it is goodbye,' my mother said, her jaw tight, her hand clenched, but shaking too.

I stared at her red toes, drops of blood in the dirt and held my breath, as if that would help stop the words rushing from my mouth, words that would betray everyone if only I could get Father back.

Silence.

Then I watched as the red drops *click-clacked* away.

There was a rumble in the clouds above, then the patter of raindrops on the dry, cracked earth. The rain had come at last. Things were changing. Could I just let this happen? Could I just let her leave?

'Eloise!' Amma shouted.

'Eloise, no!' François said.

But I was already running to the road. The truck was pulling away.

'Wait, wait!' I called.

It stopped.

I stopped.

The back door opened, but no one got out.

I stood and stared as the raindrops pelted down, plastering my hair to my face and sticking my clothes to my skin. I couldn't give her what she wanted, but she was my mother. I couldn't just let her go. Not like this.

I took a breath, threw my shoulders back, pushed my hair off my face, then tried to move towards the door, but I couldn't take one step.

All of a sudden a little brown dog leapt out of the back of the truck. He was a fluffy box with legs, a teddy bear with soft brown eyes and tufty ears. He ran right up to me, his bark a tiny squeak as he scrabbled at my socks.

I knelt to pet him then I heard the *click, click, click* of her shoes.

'Bad dog, bad dog.'

I looked up.

She stood in the rain, letting it pull at her hat as she stared down at me.

'I am sorry,' she said loudly. 'He's a menace!'

'Eloise!' the Kommandant shouted from inside the truck. 'There's no time for this.'

Her shoulders twitched, but she gave me a big smile as she lifted her dog into her arms. 'I'm just fetching the little scamp,' she said over her shoulder in a sing-song voice, before turning back to me.

'I . . .' I took a deep breath. 'I just wanted to say . . . I think maybe I understand.' My eyes flicked to the truck. 'A bit.'

Something like a smile flickered over her lips. She leant closer to me. 'He was watching me too closely before. Here.'

She reached into her coat and held out a book. It had string around its middle and a few sheaves of paper were stuffed into the back, but I recognised it instantly. It was the book I'd found in the library! The Monsieur X book.

'A new one,' she said. 'Not yet published.'

I reached for it with trembling hands. The raindrops hit the paper with a *plit, plit, plit* noise.

'A mystery,' she said, 'with a train journey to northern France for Monsieur X, via a local stop.'

I looked at her, my eyes wide.

'We should never betray our friends,' she said and gave me a small, sad smile. 'Though I had to ask.' She drew closer. 'I couldn't be more proud,' she whispered.

'Eloise!' The Kommandant's voice split the air. 'Leave the dratted dog or I leave without you.'

She hugged the dog tight, then stood. 'I was always good at mysteries,' she said, 'and we all deserve a second chance.'

Then she turned away and climbed into the shelter of the truck. The door slammed and the truck sped away, its rumble fading slowly into the distance. The rain fell in large drops, sliding down my back and filling my shoes. I was hugging the book tight to my chest so it was a few moments before I looked at the first page. A title had been handwritten across it.

*Monsieur X and the Runaway Train*
*E. L. Mutter*

E. L. Mutter? El? Eloise? Could it be?

My jaw dropped.

The books. The Monsieur X books! Every Monsieur X book was written by E.L. Mutter. E. L. for Eloise – and Mutter for mother! A secret pen name for a secret mother? I'd thought Amma was ordering them, but it was my own mother who'd sent them. I looked at the wet package in my hands. She'd written this one too. About a train. In northern France.

I gasped. Father's train! Could it be?

Tears streamed down my face as I yelled into the rain.

'Thank you, thank you, thank you!'

'Eloise, are you alright?'

Amma stood by the hedge. Behind her I saw François peering round the back door, Felix behind him and

Albert staring from a window.

I held the manuscript up in the air. 'I think I've got the answers – about the train!'

No one moved or said a word.

'The books,' I said, trying to explain. 'My mother wrote all the Monsieur X books.'

Amma's hands twitched and I realised that she'd known all along, another thing she'd kept from me. I felt a familiar stir of anger, but those feelings would have to wait.

'She's written a new one,' I said, holding it up. 'I think it's a clue!' I hugged the book tight. 'We can find them!'

# Chapter Forty

I ran back inside and the others followed.

'All of them?' Albert asked, racing down the stairs, his eyes wide.

'I hope so, Albert,' I said. 'I really hope so.'

Felix nodded to a chair so I sat, placing the sodden book on the table and opening it to the first page.

My finger followed the lines as I attempted to speed read, but my hand kept shaking and I couldn't concentrate properly. If I was right, if something about the train was in this book, my mother had done the right thing after all. She was on our side . . . on my side.

'What does it say, El?' Albert said, hovering at my shoulder. His hands twitched as if he wanted to turn the pages.

'It says nothing!' Felix grumped, further along the table. 'As if we can trust the word of a traitor to France.'

I stood up, my chair scraping along the floor.

'She's not a traitor,' I said. 'She's helping me find Father. Why else would she give me this?' I brandished the book at him. 'The clue will be in here, I know it.'

'Well, we'll just wait while you have a cup of hot milk and read it before bed, shall we?' Felix threw his hands up and began pacing round the kitchen.

I stared back at the book. Monsieur X was an excellent detective, but he did like to tie up all the loose ends right before he made his catch. I turned to the last page, but to my horror the book wasn't finished. It ended halfway through a sentence. Panicked, I flicked back through the pages.

'El?'

'Shh, Albert,' I said. I'd seen something. 'There.'

I flattened the spine and spread the book open on the kitchen table. There was a map. It wasn't one of Monsieur X's finest sketches – I wondered if my mother had drawn it in a hurry. I shook myself. It still felt strange calling her that. The map showed the whole of France on one page with a line stretching from our town up to one in Northern France and then off the page towards an arrow, which pointed to the words 'NS'. I gulped. Natzweiler-Struthof?

In a box inset on the bottom right was a smaller diagram. It showed the section of the railway between our local train station and the next one along – labelled A for Amboise and M for Monteaux – with the river following alongside. And right at the bottom of the page were the words *Time and tide wait for no man*, handwritten in ink.

I rubbed at the words, and the ink smudged.

'The train,' I said, 'I think there's still a chance.'

I looked at François then at Amma and Albert, who was rocking back and forth as if he was about to burst if we didn't do something soon. Then I turned to Felix. He was the one I had to convince.

'I think the train's being held here,' I said, pointing at a small dot next to Amboise station. 'But it's what she's written that's convinced me,' I said. 'The same quote appears in another Monsieur X book; he says it because he thinks he's going to miss . . .' I paused. '. . . a train.' I took a deep breath. 'I'd have to read the other book to check, but I think she's telling us that the train hasn't left.'

François grabbed the book and showed it to Felix, who tugged at his beard.

'Surely it's worth a try,' I said. 'If I'm right we can rescue the prisoners.'

'Or walk straight into another trap, where the soldiers catch the very last members of the Resistance in one fell swoop,' Felix said. 'Perhaps this is where all the trucks have gone.'

I bit my top lip. I hadn't thought of that. They'd tried

to trap us once. Was this just another ploy? I thought of
what Amma had said about not trusting my mother. But
she'd seemed so sincere in giving me this clue. She'd saved
me at the library, and again with the tin and convincing
the Kommandant I was completely innocent. Could we
really let the only lead we had on Father pass us by?

Amma dropped a tray onto the flagstones, the clang
telling us she thought this was a terrible idea.

François and Felix looked at each other.

'We're one down without Nan,' Felix said, 'and we've
no weapons . . .'

'We've got Nan's *presents* though,' François said.

I glanced at Albert and he nodded. We both understood
François meant home-made explosives.

It felt hot and still in the kitchen, as if the whole room
was holding its breath. Then Felix broke the silence.

'Pah.'

I could have hugged him.

François nodded to Amma and she disappeared into
the pantry. When she came back seconds later, she was
carrying a wicker basket with a linen towel thrown over
the top.

'I'll carry it,' I said, but François had taken it from her
before I could even blink.

I stared at the book, at the little map, and noticed
something odd at the bottom right of the page. I flicked

back one page, then flicked forward two more to be sure. The page numbers were wrong. The ones before the map said 104 and 105, and the ones after said 108 and 109 so the map pages should have read 106 and 107. But they didn't. They said 2230 and 1406.

Everyone was bustling around the kitchen. I heard the back door open and shut, François murmuring to Amma and Albert tapping me on the shoulder, saying, 'El?'

I shrugged Albert's hand off, realizing what the numbers meant.

'Wait! I'm right. The train's there, but it won't be for long. Look.'

I showed them the page numbers and how they weren't in the proper order.

'It's because they aren't page numbers. See?'

I rubbed at one and a bit of ink came off, leaving half my fingerprint on the paper.

'She must have written these in somehow, like the quote and the title on the front page. She's made them look like page numbers, except they're not.'

I looked up, but nobody seemed to understand.

'Don't you see?' I said.

The back door opened. Felix returned carrying our rusting watering can, which now smelt strongly of petrol.

'Eloise has found something,' François said.

Felix muttered something that sounded like, 'Eloise is

always finding something,' but he put the can down and peered over François' shoulder.

'This one says 2230 and this one 1406,' I explained, but when I was met with blank stares I gasped. '2230? It has to mean half past ten at night.' I smoothed the edge of the page with my finger. 'At first I thought 1406 was six minutes after two, but that didn't really feel right, not coming after 22.30, and then I got it. It's a date. The fourteenth of June?' When nobody spoke, I shook my head with exasperation. 'That's today, tonight!'

Everyone looked at me. The fumes from the petrol in the watering can crept up my nose and settled heavily in the back of my throat as I waited for my words to sink in. There was a pause, then Felix nodded, swept up the can and was out of the door in seconds. François followed with his basket and was about to close the door behind him.

'Wait!' I cried out.

He turned.

'What about us?' I said, glancing at Albert.

François shook his head.

'But –'

'I know,' he said, 'but it really is too dangerous. This one's for us, Eloise.'

He looked at Amma. 'Over the back fence, across the stream and round to the forest. That right?' he asked.

Amma nodded.

'We'll do our best,' François said, then with a quick glance down the road, he ran after Felix.

My shoulders slumped. Amma closed the door, latched it, then walked back to the table. She picked up the tray she'd dropped earlier, gave it a wipe and began to sprinkle water over it. She was baking more bread even though the soldiers had left the big house. I was about to say something when I realised. She was keeping herself busy.

'Come on, Albert,' I said, beckoning him to follow me upstairs, despite the surprised look on his face.

'It's for the best, *mon chou*,' Amma said without looking up.

'I know, Amma,' I said, my eyes downcast, my feet heavy on the stairs, but as soon as we reached my room I whirled round.

'Right, we've got twenty minutes.'

'What do you mean?' Albert asked, his brow furrowed.

'I've got a plan,' I said, grinning.

# Chapter Forty-One

'They're going to the train station in Amboise,' I said, 'so the petrol must be for Yvonne's Citroën.'

'The car we abandoned?' Albert said.

'Yes.' I grinned. 'They've gone through the forest, but I know an even quicker short cut, Maddie showed me once. We can get there in half the time. Then we just have to break into the boot and hide. They're *not* going to leave us out,' I said. 'Plus there's only two of them. If we go as well, we'll double the chance of success!'

I gave Albert five seconds, but he only needed three. He knew the shortcut too. He beamed right back and nodded.

'I'll get us into the boot,' he said. 'Let's go!'

We pulled up the window and tiptoed out onto the flat bit of roof over the kitchen, shimmying down the drainpipe all the way to the gravel. There we paused to listen. Nothing. Not even a bird or a cricket.

We ducked beneath the windows, then we ran.

Racing alongside the road, just inside the treeline, all the way to the forest where we'd left Yvonne's car, we only slowed when we saw it. There was no one else around.

With a nod to each other we ran to the car. Albert reached into his pocket. Several things fell out: a piece of crumpled chocolate wrapper, a small jack and a short, very thin wire. He shoved everything back in but the wire, which he wiggled in the lock. A few seconds later, the boot popped open.

I looked at him in surprise and he shrugged.

'Monsieur X has taught me a few things too,' he said.

After a quick glance around us we jumped in and Albert pulled the boot door over us till it clicked. We were in.

Only a minute later we heard and felt the doors being wrenched back, the petrol *glug-glugging* into the tank, then the whole car rocking left and right before the doors slammed shut. The car gave its tickly cough and we were off.

It bumped and hacked its way along, then settled down to a rhythmic hum. Albert grabbed my hand in the dark.

'We will get back, won't we, El?' Albert asked.

But before I could answer, the car stopped. The boot

swung open and François and Felix were staring in and they both looked absolutely furious. 'Told you I heard something,' grumbled Felix.

I opened my mouth to tell them it had been my plan and therefore all my fault, but François spun round and ducked down. Felix pulled the car boot over us, but didn't quite shut it. We could hear them breathing, but we couldn't see anything.

Then the boot swung open again.

'Thought I saw something. Out,' François whispered.

He pulled me out and Albert crawled after me, and my heart started thudding harder when I saw where we were. They'd parked in the wasteland opposite Amboise train station. We were hidden by thin trees and a rickety old fence with boards missing and barbed wire loosely looped over the top. Huge lights shone so brightly through the boards that we couldn't see anything on the other side.

I turned to François, ready to explain why we were there, but he raised his hand.

'I don't want to hear it,' he said. 'We've only got minutes!'

'Less than that,' Felix muttered, pointing ahead.

We looked and to my horror the lights began to shift. We heard a long squeal and my throat tightened as I realised what I was seeing. The train was leaving. Now!

'Stay here,' Felix said, running towards a hole in the fence. Without a word, François gathered up the basket he'd taken from Amma and caught up with him.

I looked at Albert for a second before he nodded back and we ran after them, squeezing ourselves through the fence. In front of us lay deserted platforms and old tracks half buried under grass, but as Felix crossed these I could see the squat, wooden station building ahead, and behind that, the top of the train, every window covered with planks.

The squeal of the train turned into a high-pitched scream as it began to *thunk-thunk* forward. I was trying to keep them in my sights when François suddenly ducked right, away from Felix, the train and the station. Where was he going? I panicked. Had he given up? I watched the train. Should I follow? I felt a stitch in my side and racked my brain trying to decide what to do. Then I remembered Monsieur X. He always said to go with your gut feeling. I jolted, realising Monsieur X's advice really came from my mother. I took a breath. I knew François. I trusted him. I ran after him.

Away from the station and the lights it was harder to see and I stumbled along in the dark leaping over the old tracks and bits of abandoned line. I was breathing hard. I'd lost Albert and was wondering if I'd ever catch François when I ran right into him.

He grabbed me by my neck, turning me round so he was holding me in a sort of headlock.

'It's me, it's me, it's me!' I said. I wasn't sure he heard because his hand was over my mouth, but he let me go.

'What do you think you're doing, Eloise?' he said, reaching into the basket. He caught me staring and said, 'Stay back.'

I stepped away and watched as he took out what had to be explosives. He pressed a small lump of what looked like clay with wires hanging out of it onto a piece of track.

'François?'

'Shhh,' he said, 'I've got minutes to get this in place before the train loops round here.'

I felt sick. 'But this won't kill anyone?' I watched his hands as they twisted two pieces of wire together.

'It's big enough to derail it, that's all,' he said. 'And the train shouldn't have built up enough speed to do much damage. Nobody should get hurt. Now hold this.'

He held out something square with wires hanging out of it.

*Cruck-crick.*

*Rat-a-tat-a-tat.*

The sounds came out of nowhere. François' body jumped as if he'd been kicked, then he slumped across the track.

I dropped to the gravel, shock fizzing through me. The wiry package rolled out of my hand.

'François?' I whispered.

*Cruck-crick.*

The soldiers were somewhere close, but I couldn't see them in the murky dark.

I pressed my body into the ground beside him, willing myself invisible. If they didn't check François they wouldn't find me, but if I moved, I'd be an easy target. I didn't know what to do. Was François even alive?

Footsteps crunched on the gravel beside the tracks. They were coming. I had to get out of here, but how? I turned my head slowly so I was facing François and nearly screamed. He was staring right at me.

He blinked, put a finger to his lips.

I nodded fast.

He shifted and winced. The crunching footsteps stopped.

I held my breath.

There was another *crunk-crick*, then François leapt up with a roar and launched himself forwards. There was a yelp, a groan, a thump and another *crunk-crick*.

The moon slid out from behind the clouds. François was lying awkwardly, not moving at all. Standing above him, with one heavy boot pressed into his back, was a soldier, who slowly turned his gun towards me.

# Chapter Forty-Two

'No,' I said, shaking my head, my eyes darting from François' body to the soldier's gun. 'No, no, no.'

The soldier tightened his finger on the trigger. Everything slowed down. I think I whispered 'No' again, then I heard a click and closed my eyes.

*Bang!*

I dropped to my knees, my hands splaying out to stop me falling. I gasped, waiting for the pain, waiting for emptiness, my heart beating a hundred times a second. But nothing came. I felt my chest, my head, my arms, my legs. Nothing.

I looked up.

François lay as still as before, but the soldier was lying next to him. I could see his heavy black boots, an arm outstretched towards me and a hand curled like a claw around his gun.

There was another click.

A few metres away behind the dead soldier a shadowy figure stood in a cap and long coat, the collar turned up around the ears. I froze and waited for him to make a move. The figure lifted a hand and I flinched, but all they did was put their gun into their pocket, then smooth their hair back behind an ear, tucking it underneath the cap. A movement that felt achingly familiar.

My jaw dropped.

Was it her?

I got to my feet, squinting through the gun smoke and patchy moonlight. It *was* her! My mother. Her hair was tucked into a low bun under the woollen cap and she was wearing a man's coat, trousers and heavy boots, but there was something in the way she stood as well as that gesture. I'd know her anywhere now. It was my mother and she'd saved my life again.

Something in my heart leapt and I took a step towards her, then another step, but she shook her head and turned away.

My head felt dizzy and my heart felt sick. She'd saved my life, but why was she turning away? And what was she doing here when it seemed like she'd left with the Kommandant?

There was a groan behind me.

'Eloise?'

I spun round.

'Eloise, help me.'

François!

I glanced back to my mother but she'd disappeared.

I ran to François, coughing and spluttering on the grey smoke now thickening the air. It hung so heavy that I tripped over him, landing hard. I knelt by his side, trying to turn him over, but I couldn't lift him. He was a dead weight.

'Eloise, we have to finish the job. Quickly!' He tightened his hand on mine, but then it fell loose.

We heard squealing and a *chug-chug-chug*.

The train.

François shut his eyes and let go of me. 'I can't do this alone,' he said.

I reached for his arm and, taking a deep breath, heaved him onto his front.

We stared at the piece of track, at the small lump still sitting there, which could change everything.

'I can help,' I said. 'Tell me what to do.'

François reached into his coat pocket and pulled out a small toolkit. He handed it to me and pointed to the track.

The train was louder now.

'Wire cutters.'

With shaking hands I picked them out.

'Good. Now the detonator – a bullet.'

I could see the train.

'Do you have the wires?' he asked.

I scrabbled on the ground till I found the wires I'd dropped and handed them to him.

The vibration of the train rattled my bones as François leant over the lump of explosive, fiddling with all the bits and pieces, but he kept dropping bits to clutch his side, blood seeping through his fingers.

I swallowed. 'François, you need to get off the track – now!'

'Just one more second . . .'

'There's no more time – it's here!' I yelled as the train screamed round the corner, its light blinding. I stepped back and watched helpless as François fiddled with the bullet, the wires and the lump of plastic. The lights on the train lit us like a spotlight. As it bore down François dropped something and leant right over the track to retrieve it.

The train was seconds away. I screamed, reached for his jacket as he finally threw himself backwards. He twisted, grabbed me by the collar and pushed me back as the train whooshed past. My head slammed against the ground, but we were safe.

There wasn't a moment to rest, though. François was shouting. I could barely hear as the train rumbled past, trundling over the bomb-laden track. Something glinted in the light and I realised it was wire unloading from a spool held between his hands. We hunkered down behind two large pieces of old track as the train thundered past. François wound the end of the wire around what looked like a watch before turning to me.

'Get ready to duck,' he said. 'Then run.'

He pressed something and the whole world lit up orange and white. I tried to duck down, but everything seemed to slow, then speed up.

François threw himself towards me. The train screeched and shrieked as its wheels left the rails. Hot air whumped over us, and gravel and mud and bits of flaming wood sprayed us in the face. I screamed – I could feel it leave my throat but couldn't hear it. My mouth and nose were full of dust. My ears were ringing and something on my left hand hurt. I looked down.

My hand was burning!

I shook it, then rubbed it back and forth in the dirt. My hand was grey, throbbing, and I couldn't feel it properly. But that was the last thing I was thinking about. Around me the whole station looked like a giant bonfire. Odd shapes stuck out along the track. One carriage lay on its side and two others had twisted and buckled and now rested across the grass and gravel. A lump beside me gradually resolved into François. I shook him. Nothing. I shook him again and tried to turn him over. Underneath he was clean and pale – he hadn't been caught in the blast. His eyelids flickered. He was alive!

Then, I heard it. The *rat-a-tat-tat* of gunfire.

François immediately got to his knees, coughing and spluttering.

'El!' someone shouted.

I spun round and saw Albert running towards us.

'We've found him!' he said.

Father? Father!

'El, he's in the third carriage.' Albert was out of breath and spitting out as many words as he could. 'Can you believe we did it? Felix is trying to get people off the train. There are some soldiers left, but there's a lot more of us than there are of them now. They're fighting their way out! It's chaos, El – we've got to help!'

François was still coughing. I leant down to help him up. Albert took his other arm and together we took his weight.

'What happened to François?' Albert asked.

I turned back to tell him, but that's when I saw Felix further along the track. He was walking towards us with someone by his side. I grabbed François so tightly he yelled out.

'Sorry,' I said. Everything went quiet. I couldn't breathe. I felt something begin to roar, then I let Albert support François and was running as fast as I could, leaping through the dust and debris, my heart beating triple time as I ran straight towards the man next to Felix.

'Father!'

# Chapter Forty-Three

The man walking beside Felix stumbled as he took a step towards me. Felix grabbed his arm and he righted himself. He mouthed something, but I couldn't hear and then I crashed into him, wrapping my arms around him and squeezing tight.

'Father,' I sobbed.

He felt different. My arms went round him easily, as if he was half his normal size and all I could smell was burning wood and ash and dirt and vomit and old clothes and damp, but I didn't let go.

He kissed the top of my head.

Then Felix was shouting and Albert was shouting and someone fired and there were guns going off *rat-a-tat-tat*. I felt someone try to tear me away, but I clung on to Father, felt his bones, his body shaking. What had they done to him? He flinched and all of a sudden I wondered if I was hurting him. I let go and he stumbled into me, and then Felix was there. He put Father's arm around his shoulder. Father's head slumped. What was happening? Was he alright? Had someone shot him? I panicked and grabbed at Felix who swatted me away like a fly.

I screamed and reached for Father, but I was pulled back and hoisted onto someone's back.

'No, no, no, no! Father? Father!'

I struggled and felt whoever had me turn and fire their gun into the grey smoke behind us. All around little explosions in orange and white pierced the night sky.

'Let me go, let me go!'

I twisted round. I couldn't see anyone. All I could see was Felix hoisting my father behind him like a sack of potatoes.

'Father!' I yelled.

'Eloise!'

My head snapped down towards the voice.

'François? But you're hurt,' I said.

'Exactly,' he said, and I could hear the grimace in his voice. 'So if you'd be so kind as to stop struggling and help me then I think we can make it out of here.'

'But what about Father?'

'He'll be alright.'

'And the others on the train?'

'A lot of them are Resistance,' answered Felix. 'They'll

help the others escape and get to a safe place.'

Gunfire roared somewhere to our left. François let me down, spun round, fired then ducked. Then we ran and hid behind a long siding, François wincing, and holding his thigh.

'We need to get everyone to safety,' he said. 'But where?'

Albert had the answer. 'Maison de Noyer.'

'The big house?' I said. 'But . . .'

Then I realised. It was the perfect hiding place. The Kommandant and his soldiers had left; it was big enough for all of us, and the house was good at keeping secrets.

Felix nodded.

Albert nodded back. 'I'll tell the others.' And he was off, darting back to the train.

François groaned. 'It had to be somewhere that far, eh?' He looked at Father then at me. 'We won't make it to the car. There are too many soldiers. We can try to find another, though I don't suppose you can drive?'

I shook my head. It was dark behind the siding but the flames nearby were hot and bright. François was trying to wind something around the upper part of his thigh, but it was soaked through with blood already. We were going to have to walk. Would he make it? Would Father?

'He'll get there,' François said, one hand against my cheek. 'We all will.'

There was a *crunk-crick* close by. François pushed me away.

'Run! Now!' he shouted.

'And don't stop,' Father shouted, locking his eyes to mine.

Pure fear moved my feet. I ran along behind the siding, raced between two old carriages then slid under the last and across the track, all in the dark. I reached the other side and scrambled up a bank and over a fence and then I was running through wet grass – my breath rasping – when I turned round and realised François wasn't with me. None of them were.

I gasped as I looked back.

The station was glowing orange, like an enormous firefly stuck in a jar. Grey smoke hovered above. The train looked like a child's toy, abandoned and broken on the moonlit tracks. People were streaming from the station, escaping onto the road and into fields. Father, François, Felix and Albert would be among them somewhere.

I knew the way back to our village, Father had made sure of it. Everyone was going to Maison de Noyer. I'd find them there. I felt a small glow inside me.

Father would be there. He was with some of the bravest people I knew. I had to trust them. Everything was going to be fixed. We'd saved them all. We'd meet up at Maison de Noyer and everything would be just like it was before the soldiers arrived.

Almost.

I thought of my mother and felt a sting. She wouldn't be there. I might never see her again.

A boom shook the ground beneath my feet. Right where the train had derailed a speck of orange had mushroomed into flames and more twisting grey cloud. The whole station was on fire. Had everyone got out in time? I gulped back tears and worry and nausea. What was it they'd said? *Run. Don't stop.*

With the glow from the station on my left, I fixed the route back to the house in my sight. Then I ran. On ragged feet and ragged hope, I ran all the way.

# Chapter Forty-Four

## One week later

I sat on an old wooden chair I'd pulled next to Father's bed. He was in a single cot pushed against the wall in a room on the first floor of the big house. On a small bedside table sat one of my Monsieur X books and a shallow bowl of greyish soup that had gone cold. Amma had insisted I wasn't to wake him, not to worry that he would only be able to eat very little at first, that I wasn't to fuss or talk too loudly, and that actually it would just be better if I waited somewhere else. I refused to leave him. He'd been asleep for three days and I had so many questions.

I'd only left his room when a tall, burly, brown-bearded bear of a man had come in. Amma had said he was the doctor and needed to examine Father. When he'd come out again, almost an hour later, I'd stopped him in the corridor.

'Is Father alright?'

The brown-bear man paused, narrowed his eyes, then gave me a small nod.

'In time,' he said. 'In time.'

Then he'd gone to see some of the other patients and I'd trailed him. Nearly every room on the first floor was being used. It was usually quiet, though I could hear the occasional groan and sometimes sobs. They were a mixed bunch – a few Resistance people, some of them really skinny like Father, some with broken bones, and some who just stared into space. Felix had got nearly everyone off the train, but not all of them made it back to the house. I couldn't stop thinking that more prisoners would been rescued if I'd stayed to help instead of running away. Though Nan disagreed.

She'd come to see me in Father's room.

'How's François today?' I'd asked her.

She beamed and nodded. 'He'll be walking again soon,' she said.

I opened my mouth to speak, but she interrupted me.

'You did the right thing, by the way,' she said, her hand moving to the clean bandages on her arm. 'You were incredibly brave. François told you to run and you did.'

'But –'

'No buts, remember?' she said. 'Take the compliment.'

I nodded.

A frown passed over her face. 'Have you seen Albert?' she asked.

I shook my head.

We'd found Albert's mother. She'd been locked in a room on the top floor. Perhaps my mother hadn't known. In the Monsieur X books, he had definite answers in the end, but when it came to my mother I didn't, and I still wasn't sure what to believe.

Albert's mother was one of the ones who'd stopped talking. Albert sat with her most days. His father hadn't been on the train. We didn't know where he was.

Nan gave a nod, eased the door open, slid through and shut it again with the tiniest click. I leant over to pick up my book then jumped. Father was looking at me.

I reached for him but stopped. I didn't want to hurt him. Amma had said to be careful.

'My clever girl,' he said, his voice like sandpaper.

I forgot everything Amma said. Father opened his arms and I snuggled into them, sobbing into the rough blanket, his beard scratching the top of my head.

'Come under my wing, *ma rose*,' he croaked.

It was a while before I stopped crying. Father's breath was quiet and even. The light outside was darker. The afternoon sun had been replaced by twilight creeping through the cracks in the shutters.

'Is it over now?' I whispered. 'Will the Germans come back?'

There was no answer. I wondered if he was asleep. I was about to inch off the bed, when I felt him shake his head.

'I think . . .' He paused. ' I think we're safe, Eloise,' he said.

'Will *she* come back?' I asked. 'Mother, I mean.' My voice sounded small and very far away.

Father sighed.

And everything that had been bubbling away in me for days began to pour out as I told him what she'd done, what she'd said.

'Was she a double agent?' I asked. 'She saved my life again and again, and Felix says that someone set off other explosions in the station that night to help cover our escape. It must have been her. She helped us, but then she ran away.'

I felt a stinging in my throat, but couldn't stop.

'I know she wrote all the Monsieur X books, and she was the one sending them to me, and that you and Amma knew all along. You told me she was dead and now she's gone and I don't know if she's good or bad or what to think or what to feel.'

I sat up and wiped the tears that were streaming down my face again. Father stared at the shutters as if he could see through them. He reached for my hand and clasped it to him.

'Her father's name was Xiomar,' he said. 'It means being good in a fight or a battle or something.' He paused. 'He was a detective.'

I gasped. 'Monsieur X!'

My father nodded. 'He used to tell her all sorts of stories and now she's sharing them with you and all the other children who read them.'

I stared at the book on his bedside table.

'I don't think we'll ever really know which side she was on, *mon chou*,' he said. He followed my gaze. 'And I'm not sure anyone can be truly good or bad. Most of us are a mix of both.'

'How can you say that after everything? After what the soldiers did to you?'

He gave me a small smile. 'I'm not sure I believe in good or evil.' He paused. 'But I do know that the best people fight for the ones they love.' His eyes clouded over and he was gone again, staring at something or someone I couldn't see.

There was a knock at the door. After a few seconds, Albert peered round. 'El?'

With a glance at Father, I slipped off the bed. When I reached the doorway Albert took my hand.

'They've found Maddie!' he said.

I grabbed his arms. 'Where? How?'

'On a list. Her name and her mother's and grandmother's. They're in Germany, in a camp.'

I felt as if the floor had suddenly disappeared. A camp?

'Felix's friend, the doctor, says you can get letters to them through the Red Cross. Felix says that when the Allies get here they'll free the camps. And they should be here soon, he says! El, it's Maddie! We found her!'

I tried to smile, but I felt sick. Her name was on a list, but was she still alive? And if she was, would she still be alive by the time the Allies got to the camps?

Albert gave me a little shake. 'I know what you're thinking,' he said, 'but this is good news. Maddie and her family will be alright.'

He sounded so certain I began to believe him. He looked so much older. He was thin and tired like we all were, but there was something else in his eyes. As if they were darker, as if he'd seen things he shouldn't have. I realised then that he needed this. He needed to believe that Maddie was alright, even if we both knew that she might not be. I took his hand, and tried to make my smile more sincere.

There was a cough.

'Albert is right,' Father said as we turned to him. 'We should exercise some hope. After all, none of us on the train expected to be rescued.'

I glanced at Albert. He was looking at his feet and I knew he was thinking about how he betrayed us. I gripped his hand. That was the past.

'Why don't you both go and get some fresh air? Chase Amma round the kitchen or even help her with the cooking.'

'Indeed, there are a lot of us to cook for,' Amma said, appearing at the door, hands on hips. 'They left Maddie's home in a mess,' Amma said as she squeezed into the room. 'And a lot of their belongings are gone. Perhaps you can find some things in the house here to replace them.'

I looked at Father.

He nodded. 'Hope, *mon chou*,' he said. 'There is no end to how much hope we can have.'

He turned, wincing, and put out a hand. I raced forward but Amma got there before me.

'Shoo,' she said. 'You've been in here long enough.'

'Quite right,' Father said. 'And I think I could manage a bit of that soup now.'

Dismissed, Albert and I shuffled into the corridor. Father's door clicked shut behind us. For a second we just looked at each other, then Albert spoke.

'There are rooms on the third floor,' he said. 'I've checked most of them and they're empty, but the one right at the end is locked. Maybe there's something in there?' He smiled. 'Let's make the barn nice for them again. To welcome them home.'

He delved into his pocket and brought out a thin wire just like the one he'd used to pick the car boot lock. I grinned as he held out his hand.

'Hope, El,' he said.

And I thought about how planning to rescue Father had given me hope, helped me face the Kommandant, the soldiers with guns and the times when I was so scared I could hardly breathe. If I had hope through all that, maybe I could carry it with me now. Maybe hope would help all of us look to the future.

'Hope,' I said, taking his hand. Then we raced up to the third floor.

# Acknowledgements

I began writing this book when my son was three months old. They say it takes a village to raise a child . . . this book wouldn't have been possible without my village . . .

I'm incredibly lucky, of course, to have the perfect agent in Bryony Woods, who loved *Eloise Undercover* from the very start and has always encouraged and guided me through the publishing world. Thanks to Ella Kahn & Elinor Cooper at DKW for their support too.

A big thanks to my mum, Marie, for all the toddler sitting, hot meals and home-made cake. So many thanks to my dad, Bob, for being an expert on all things WW2 and for answering thousands of questions – any mistakes in the book are mine.

Thanks to my sister, Rachael, for the mammoth toddler reading sessions, the lovely lunches and the breakfast pow-wows.

The greatest, heartfelt thanks to my editor, Melissa Hyder, who just gets it, gets me, gets my writing, and makes editing easier than I thought it would be.

Thank you to all at Catnip and Bounce, especially Georgina Hanratty, who came up with the title, Louise Corcoran, Sarah Wright, Valentina Vacchelli and Robert Snuggs.

Thanks to Sandrine Gasnier for checking my French translation (again!) and to Maren Thom for checking my German.

I'm thrilled to have the incredible Jessica Courtney-Tickle and Will Steele illustrate another book for me.

Big thanks to Aiden Chapman for the baking course at Bread Ahead. It really was one of my better ideas to have a proper baker in this book. I can't wait to take another course.

So many thanks to my BookBound family – the best group of writers I know. Special thanks for all the support and for generally being amazing to Sheila Averbuch, Vivienne Dacosta and Sara Grant. Extra special thanks to Harry Ball-Weber for my author photograph, my haircut and those endless cups of Earl Grey tea.

Thanks also to super cheerleaders and friends extraordinaire, Ali Cook, Andrew Hally, Laura James and Kate Terence.

I really must thank all the wonderful librarians,

book bloggers, teachers and readers out there. You are superstars.

Last, but definitely not least, thank you to my son, Freddie. Here's to a lifetime of adventures and lots of books.

Sarah Baker, London, 2017

Maison de Noyer holds many secrets . . .

# Through the Mirror Door

Since the accident, Angela has been alone.
When she is invited on holiday with her cousins,
it is her chance to be part of a family again if she
promises to behave herself. But secrets lie in the walls
of the crumbling French holiday home and the
forbidden rooms draw Angela in.
Soon night-time footsteps, flickering candlelight and
shadows in windows lead her to a boy who needs her
help. To save him Angela must discover the truth about
what happened in the house all those years ago . . . and
face the terrible secret of her own past.